Demon Haunted

Grimluk, Demon Hunter vol 2

Ashe Armstrong

Cover Art by Bob Kehl
Edited by Tim Marquitz, Dominion Editorials
Interior Design by Ashe Armstrong

First Edition, October 2016

ISBN: 0996340939
ISBN-13: 978-0996340939

DEDICATION

To my star, and to my friends and the readers I've gained. I love you all.

And, arrogant as it might look, to me: I can do this.

CONTENTS

ACKNOWLEDGMENTS

A very special thanks to the following folks: Tim Marquitz for being so willing to work with me on paying for editing. You are a very rad friend. Krista Ball for basically dumping everything she's learned about this business in my lap whenever I asked (and sometimes when I didn't). Pretty much all of the authors I've come to know for being supportive and kindred spirits. Bob Kehl for being such an awesome artist and once again giving me one hell of a cover. Thanks to Vern and Lexi for giving their specific POVs. To all my original backers for *A Demon in the Desert* for writing such honest reviews. I feel like this book is much stronger and I owe some of that to you. And to the backers for this book. You're all amazing.

Chapter 1

It was nearly dawn when the orc stirred. Quiet sobs brought him out of his slumber, blinking awake in the deep darkness leading to the sun's rise. With a grunt, he sat up and looked towards the source of the sound. The last traces of the campfire flickered weakly. Still, it offered some small touch of illumination against the pale coat that shook as its owner choked back a sob that would have woken their companion if he hadn't already risen.

Grimluk frowned, fuzzy brows creasing in worry. He reached over and placed one large, green-skinned hand on a shaking leg, giving it a start before it relaxed. Slowly, a face turned to look at him, dark hair falling across it to hide one eye, a flicker of dying firelight reflecting off a tear as it rolled down a delicate chin.

"Gwen," the orc said, "you're crying again." She nodded. "Do you want to talk about it, little one?"

The child turned her head away for a moment before pushing the coat from herself and the fire. She rose on her hands and knees and crawled towards him, sniffling, and crawled into his lap to lean against him.

"I miss Momma and Daddy," she whispered as new tears streaked down her cheeks.

Grimluk sighed. "I know." He ran a hand through her hair that almost swallowed her head. "It's okay, little one. Cry as much as you need to."

She shook with more sobs as he held her, rocking gently as the sun began to rise, its dim light spilling into the sky with a gentle push. A little while later, he felt her grow still, her breath evening out as sleep claimed her once more. For a time, he sat there, quietly rocking the little girl.

They'd been traveling for a little over a month, heading east from the Borderlands and into the province of New Gilead. Their destination was Hunter's Hollow, the semi-hidden base of operations for most of New Gilead's demon hunters. Not quite a town but not quite a fort, it merged both into one for utility and comfort.

Gwen had been born in the Wastelands, the ruined and cursed lands of central Ornesea. More specifically, in the mining town of Greenreach Bluffs. Grimluk had adopted her as his sister prior to leaving the town, doing his best to keep the promise he'd made to her, at the time, very undead parents. He thought about how easy it was to protect her from thieves or even trolls. It was much, much harder to protect a child from the pain that came from such a traumatic event. He wished there was some way to make it easier. For now, that meant letting her sleep while he wrestled with the reality of not being prepared for any of this. A measure of guilt swirled in the back of his mind.

To prepare her for the journey, Grimluk began to tutor Gwen in certain aspects of living as a demon hunter and life outside of her protected village. Her first lesson, before they'd even set out, involved a small blood magic spell that offered protection from losing one's way. A spell both important in his line of work and one of the most immediate means of safety he could think of. He'd hated having to show it to her so soon. The spell hurt, requiring the user's own freely given blood. She'd born the ritual though and guaranteed she couldn't get lost as they traveled so long as she had a location or person in mind. After that, he'd taught her about the leshy, deep forest spirits that sometimes came near the roads to lead travelers astray. They also loved to abduct wayward children. She could avoid the former, at least.

The first few days out from the town of Border Rest, she'd been curious, even talkative. Gwen hadn't ever seen anything outside of Greenreach Bluffs, as it sat in the back end of a long, dry lake bed surrounded by sheer cliffs. The farther they got from the only home she'd ever known, the more sullen she'd grown. Fits of tears would take her suddenly and she would wake Grimluk as she called out in her sleep from nightmares. Other nights, Gwen would crawl over and curl up, clinging tightly to him.

This morning, he decided to lay her down and break camp, smothering the campfire in dirt and gathering their things. He strapped a plain, brown leather gun belt to his waist, the matching holster laying against his right hip. The revolver within was massive, with a grip of reddish sandalwood.

He slid into a long, black coat, the tails of which were covered in the patina of a nomad. A soft tinkling sound coming from around his neck from the lead slug necklace he wore. A wide-brimmed, black hat, wrapped by a leather band holding thirteen canine teeth, cast his face in shadow. An elk-skin bag went over his head to hang at his side, waterskins dangling from its strap.

Grimluk tucked Gwen's coat over the bag and, with everything gathered, he knelt down and scooped the girl up in one arm, looping her hat's drawstring over her head. She stirred for a moment, wrapping her arms around his neck but settled back to sleep without another sound. Hunter and ward set off, making for the road once more.

As the sun crept higher, shining through the blue-green canopy of leaves covering that section of road, Gwen's body shivered. "I will walk for her, Hunter." The voice was Gwen's but not.

"Let her body rest, Spirit." Grimluk's throat rumbled for a moment. "And I thought we agreed you wouldn't come out any more." The girl leaned away from his shoulder, eyes like polished onyx regarding him silently. Those eyes were unsettling. He imagined that's how some folks felt looking at him. Orc eyes had large irises to begin with, and his were more of a charcoal color. Though, in the shadow of his hat they might as well have been black.

"You said to avoid speaking through the girl while around others. As I can see and sense, we are quite alone right now. Besides, I would speak with you about Gwen."

Grimluk ran his tongue across one of his tusks in thought before stopping and setting the little girl down. "Speak. Quickly." As they continued, the Spirit clasped its hands behind its back, walking as if it were in the body of an elder. Grimluk wondered for a moment how old the Spirit actually was. Likely several centuries at the very least.

"I know you are quite aware of Gwen's state of mind. As aware as you can be living beyond her mind," it began. "At the least, she finds comfort with you."

"But she's not doing well," Grimluk finished.

"No. And it will only get worse before it can get better."

Grimluk took in a deep breath and let it out slowly. Maybe he should begin the lessons again. Something simpler than basic demonology and how to properly hold a knife. "Spirit?"

"Yes, Hunter?"

He frowned. It was still just as disconcerting to speak to the thing inhabiting Gwen's body as it had been the first time back in Greenreach Bluffs. "Would it help if I started new lessons? Nothing about demons or monsters. And definitely no more blood magic. Maybe teach her the campfire spell and which plants are safe to eat so she can help me gather food?"

The Spirit seemed to think about the question for a moment. It was hard to read, even with Gwen's face. "Perhaps. I would offer assistance with this but she prefers to keep me from speaking. I believe that she blames me somewhat for her parents' deaths."

Grimluk snorted. “You can hardly blame her.”

“I have told you, the demon Priskus’s presence restrained me,” the Spirit said dejectedly. “It influenced me, used me to spread its fear. I did what I could, directed you as much as I was able. But I could not stop what was meant to happen in that town.”

Grimluk sneered at that. “So you've said. I can believe you were hindered but I don't rightly believe for a second any of that was meant to happen.”

Gwen's face looked up at him, the black eyes studying him for a moment. “Would you say... No, never mind it.” The Spirit looked ahead again. “Yes, I think it might help if you taught her something. Perhaps teach her of our location.”

Grimluk's throat rumbled in thought. That would be a helpful lesson indeed. They were traveling through the Sapphire Plains. The right hillside, when you could find one, offered beautiful views of the surrounding lands. “I reckon there are a few things I could show her here on the Plains. I think there’s a herd of buffalo that roam nearby this time of the year. Beautiful creatures.” He grinned to himself. “And damn good eatin’.”

“Very well, Hunter. I suppose I should recede once more. I would appreciate if you did not tell her I spoke while she slept.”

“If she asks,” he replied as he bent down to pick Gwen’s body back up, “I will *not* lie to her.”

“Very well, I understand,” the Spirit said with a sigh as it laid Gwen's head back where it had been. The little body shivered and returned to its natural state. Gwen sighed in her sleep.

A heavy breeze caught Gwen's hat, jostling it against the cord that held it around her neck. Brown locks whirled in the wind for a moment before it died away. Grimluk, cradling her still-sleeping form, dropped to his butt with a grunt. The hill was fairly tall, somewhat of a marker of the end of the forest for some ways, guiding travelers headed into the Sapphire Plains. The top of the hill was mostly level, curving gently to the land below.

Grimluk looked out across the miles of pale-green grass that seemed to stretch forever. He smiled. The sun was high now, nearing noon, the bright mid-day light filling the Plains with a deep heat cut in soft moments by the wind. Wisps of clouds floated low, casting soft shadows here and there. He rubbed Gwen's back lightly and whispered her name. She stirred, groaning for a moment, but buried her head in his shoulder.

"Wake up, little one," he said with an obvious grin. "I have something to show you."

"What is it? Where are we?" she asked, yawning as she leaned back and rubbed the crust from her eyes.

"We're in the Sapphire Plains. Have you ever seen a buffalo?"

"Bufflow? What's that?" She looked up at him, delicate brows scrunched with thought.

"See for yourself," he said, still smiling at her. He turned her around without much effort.

Gwen gasped.

The lake bed Greenreach Bluffs sat in was nothing but hard pan that stretched out for ages. It had grass and a few trees inside the town's borders, thanks to the touch of an alchemist, but nothing like this. The journey so far had passed through forests but now the sky and horizon were clear. All along the rolling carpet of grass, thousands of furry creatures with great, dark humps grazed and snorted.

Gwen climbed to her feet, another stiff gust catching her hat, dangling by its cord. "Bufflow?" She looked back at him to confirm.

Grimluk nodded, pleased at her excitement.

She looked out again, taking it all in. "Bufflow!" There was so much new to take in. "They're so big! Like you!"

"There are some that are even bigger than me," Grimluk said.

"Nuh uh!"

"It's true. Especially the cows."

"But those aren't cows."

Grimluk let out a laugh, "That's right, cows are a different animal but the buffalo that give birth to babies are called cows, too."

"That's weird," she replied with a child's confidence.

"I guess it might be." He shook his head, the grin still in place.

As they watched the herd, a clear calmness washed over Gwen that had been absent for some time. Grimluk let out a sigh, glad for the momentary respite from worry. Even in the hot sun, the view was still gorgeous and worth the heat. He laughed to himself as a thought hit him.

"What?" Gwen asked, still staring out at the herd.

"Sometimes I forget how nice it is to just sit and enjoy the world. I spend so much time focused on jobs." Gwen looked at him and gave a big smile. He smiled back.

"What's a sapphire?" she asked after a moment.

"It's a type of jewel. A crystal. They're usually blue."

"Oh." Her face scrunched up as she looked back out across the Plains. She frowned. "I don't see any blue. Why is it called the Sapphire Plains?"

"Don't rightly know. Maybe the explorer who named it couldn't see colors right so the grass looked blue. Maybe their name was Sapphire. Maybe it was a misunderstood word from one of the tribes in the region. Reckon you could look it up one day."

Satisfied, she finally sat down in the grass to continue her buffalo watching. A heavy cloud rolled overhead, covering the hill and a large swath of land in shadow. Another swift breeze rolled down the hill, tossing Gwen's hair across her face. Grimluk took out a roll of paper from his bag that held a pile of venison jerky. He pulled a few pieces out and offered some of the meat to her.

"We still have some ways to go yet, little one. Reckon it's time to give you some new lessons. No more about demons and no more spells except for one. This one won't hurt."

“What lessons?” She looked at him cautiously, clearly a touch uneasy about lessons.

“First, I’ll teach you the campfire spell, the way I learned it. Then, I’ll teach you how to track animals for hunting and about what plants are and are not safe to eat.”

“No more blood magic?” she asked.

“No more blood magic. Just you helping us get to Hunter’s Hollow and,” he reached into his bag again and produced a small, folding knife, offering it to her, “how to use a knife.”

She nodded and took it gingerly, looking it over as she chewed on her jerky. After a moment, she slipped it into her coat pocket and went back to watching the herd as it began to move away from them, heading towards the north at a lazy pace. Many hours down the plains’ road, now growing over from disuse, Grimluk found a low line of trees to make camp against.

Gwen’s first job was to find rocks to create a small pit with. It took her an hour to find enough good-sized stones but she returned with the last one just as twilight folded over them. While she’d done that, Grimluk had gathered up kindling and enough wood to make a small fire, enough to teach her the little spell. With everything ready, he sat down with her.

“The first thing you need to know, even for spells like this, is to focus your willpower. Do you know what willpower is?”

“No.”

“It’s control and focus. You could say your will is your desire. In this case, your desire, your will, would be creating sparks to start the campfire. Your willpower would be your focus and control of that desire. Do you understand?"

Gwen looked at the small pile of materials. "I think so."

Grimluk nodded. "Now, spells, all spells, big or small or weak or powerful, require strong willpower, not just for the purpose of the spell but also to gather the magical energy needed for it."

"Will it be hard?"

"It might be. I'll show it to you." Grimluk held his hand up. "Spark-a-dark, what's my desire? To lay, to stay, bless this camp with fire."

With the word *fire*, a small shower of sparks blinked out from his fingertips into the air, pushing the growing darkness away for the briefest moment. Gwen looked on, mouth slightly agape.

"Would you like to try it now?" the hunter asked. She nodded her affirmation solemnly. "Hold your hand out towards the kindling there and focus on your fingertips. Picture sparks coming away from them, maybe even a touch of flame. You might have the affinity for it. All I can do is sparks. Can you see it in your mind?"

Gwen scrunched her eyes shut and focused, her hand out and ready. "Sparks," she muttered to herself. "Sparks like Grimluk." She took a deep breath and finally answered. "I see it."

"Hold that thought. Willpower. Control and focus. Now say the spell."

Gwen swallowed and began. "Sparky-dark, what's my desire? To lay, to stay, bless this camp with fire."

A strong shower of sparks, backed by a tiny flame, erupted from her fingertips, pushing away the dark. Fire came immediately, licking away at the kindling and building itself up into the rest of the wood.

"I did it!" Gwen shouted.

A gruff laugh escaped his throat as Grimluk beamed at the girl with pride. "Wonderful job, little one. It took me a few days of trying before I could even make a few pitiful sparks. Reckon you've got quite the aptitude for the magical arts."

For the next few days, Grimluk showed Gwen how to spot plants that were safe to eat and even how to snare a rabbit, though she hadn't the heart to eat her first successful catch. She told Grimluk she wanted to let that one go and that they could eat the next one.

When it came to tracking, she took to it fairly easily. Despite trouble telling some tracks apart, an aspect of the skill that would take years to hone for anyone, Gwen's eyes were sharp and seemed to focus in on the signs of an animal's passing. On occasion, she would get a little too excited about finding those signs and end up flitting between them before remembering they were looking for food. Grimluk, ever patient, would just smile and calmly redirect her with a gentle reminder. The lessons seemed to serve the other side of their purpose. Gwen's mood seemed to improve quite a bit, though the night was still difficult for her. The nightmares seemed to lessen.

As the sun began to sink one evening, casting their shadows far out in front of them, they passed a road sign, faded and scarred from lack of upkeep. Or maybe the one who'd planted it had simply forgotten about it. "Should be a town soon. Not the nicest place but better than Border Rest, least as far as I remember. Passed through it once. Mostly just farmers and a few cattle ranches. Don't remember the name," Grimluk said with a nod.

Gwen said nothing. She looked distracted, fidgeting with the buttons on her coat while she looked around nervously.

"What is it, little one?"

"I don't know. I think I hear something but…" She seemed to strain her ears for whatever it was. "I guess it's nothing."

Grimluk frowned and listened as well. All he could hear was their footsteps and the buzz of cicadas. Nothing out of the ordinary. "I don't hear anything either. Reckon we could stop for the night unless you feel up to trying to make it to the town."

She seemed to give it some thought and shrugged, continuing to fidget with her buttons. They walked on, the evening redness trailing behind them. As the pair continued on, Gwen slowed a few times, looking around in vain for whatever kept pricking her ears. Grimluk still heard nothing but slowed each time, waiting for her to catch up. Then she stopped altogether, trailing behind, bringing him to a halt as well.

"Are you okay?" he asked as he turned towards her. She stood stock still, shivering, eyes wide and fingers clenched at the hem of her coat. He took a step forward just as the temperature fell away in a rush, revealing their breath in steamy puffs.

"It's so mad," Gwen whispered. Her voice was high and breathy, practically a squeak.

A cold scream split the evening air as she spoke. Something unseen slammed down a few yards behind Grimluk, followed by another scream, just as cold but now filled with fury. He spun towards the impact, gun drawn, hammer cocked, eyes searching for whatever it was as the sun sank and cast the world into night.

"Hunter, behind—" the dual-voice of the Spirit started to shout before something silenced it.

Grimluk whirled, twirling the gun around in his hand as he did to use the butt as a club. He swung but met nothing but chill air. Gwen fell back as the thing pushed her away, loosing another furious howl. The hunter grunted a moment later. Something had climbed his back. It was heavy. Impossibly heavy.

CHAPTER 2

The thing on Grimluk's back growled and shifted, nearly toppling him over. He stood still, doing his best to breathe quietly, unsure of what was happening. The thing rocked forward, pushing on him.

"*Hooooooooooome,*" a voice moaned into Grimluk's ear.

Something viscous ran down the chest of his coat. He felt a tendril of whatever it was roll down the back of his neck as well, sending a shiver through him. Ectoplasm. The thing riding his back was a spirit of some kind, wailing and repeating its command. For lack of any other thought, he started forward again. Clouds rolled in overhead, a stiff gust of wind pushing them on and hitting Grimluk hard in the face.

"Gwen, you with me, little one?" He turned and caught sight of her as she got to her feet but the thing hissed at him. He growled but kept his pace slow. Gwen sniffled as she caught up, giving him a wide birth. It was too dark to tell if she'd been hurt but he sighed all the same.

"What is it?" she asked. "It's so angry, why is it so angry?"

"Just keep going," Grimluk replied. "It's a spirit of some kind. Don't worry, little one, we'll be okay."

"It looks like a monster."

"You can see it?"

"Yeah, a little bit. I can see it more now cause it's glowing like the moon through my window at home." She sighed. "I don't like it."

"I know. I don't much like it either." Grimluk couldn't see it but he felt some of the thing's shape. It was bigger than him but stayed in place with no effort. The fingers that dug into his shoulders were mismatched, the lengths and widths all askew. It sat crooked and shifting as it dripped ectoplasm all the while. He wanted it off but he was lacking salt. Salt wouldn't destroy spirits but it could disrupt them. And it certainly packed a big enough punch they'd at least back off momentarily. The thing was interacting with him so he doubted waving his gun through it would disrupt it. Or that it would even let him get his arm up to try.

They walked on, thunder rumbling lightly in the distance. Grimluk looked at Gwen. He hoped the spirit didn't have a twin at hand. He doubted her tiny body could handle the strain, if for no other reason than the sheer size of it. As his eyes adjusted to the dark, he noticed her stealing glances every so often. Whether curiosity or fear, the glances ended with her snapping her head forward. He could feel the thing leaning over toward her, maybe curious itself. Several times, she started to step over and take the hunter's hand only to remember the glowing thing and pull back away, hugging herself instead. The wind howled around them, stiff and carrying the scent of rain.

"It's dripping something on you," Gwen offered. It was a nervous observation clearly meant to break the awful silence.

"Ectoplasm."

"What's echoplas?"

"Ecto-plasm. It's what makes up ghosts and spirits. Some demons, too. Usually manifests when they interact with the material world." He sighed through his nose. There went his goal to avoid any new lessons on the supernatural. On top of that, he could feel more ectoplasm rolling down his back in slick waves. The tails of his coat dripped, leaving a trail of the stuff behind him like a slug. The thing squeezed his shoulders with its massive hands. Hands he could see now, glowing in his peripheral vision.

And the damned thing was getting heavier.

Grimluk grunted and stopped where he was, taking a step back the way they'd come. It was a gamble, a test. One the spirit tried to make him regret. It roared, causing Gwen to shriek, and pushed down on him with a sudden force that caught the hunter by surprise, pushing him to one knee. With a grunt, he rose again and took a step forward. The spirit relaxed a little again.

"Hoooooooooome..." The voice rumbled along with another roll of thunder.

Grimluk continued the trek, keeping his pace

slow and deliberate while he worked out what to do about his predicament. Gwen walked along, hugging herself, worry keeping her face tight with a heavy frown that was clear each time she glanced up at the thing. He wondered if she could even help herself. It wasn't that unusual for someone's attention to be drawn by curiosity and fear. He'd seen it plenty. Done it plenty as an apprentice, studying the malformed shapes of what would become his prey.

"Shut up!" Gwen shouted suddenly. "I'm not gonna leave Grimluk!"

"Little one?"

"It's the Spirit…the one in me. It wants me to run away and leave you! But I won't!"

The spirit currently riding Grimluk's back leaned over towards Gwen again. It let out a breath or a hiss that sent a very visible shiver through the girl.

"Don't look, little one." He wasn't sure what else to say.

She risked a glance at it anyways. Whatever it was doing made her gasp and stumble. She looked away, opting instead to quicken her pace enough to stay ahead of Grimluk. His throat rumbled in worry. He stopped mid-step, just long enough to catch the spirit's attention again and redirect its focus. It started to scream again, shifting its weight to push him forward once more, but he continued on as insubstantial fingers dug into his shoulders, twisting and sharp. The thing growled low at him and hissed its familiar demand in his ear once again.

Grimluk growled back, his patience running thin. "I don't even know where your home is! I can't help you if you won't speak more than a word."

A fat glob of ectoplasm rolled down the hunter's sleeve as the thing went quiet. Long moments passed before it let out a sob, its face twisting in anger. "*Home,*" it barked yet again, its voice growing with an intensity that shook its monstrous form. "*Home! Home home home home home! Hoooooome!*" Its already considerable weight increased again, bringing a loud grunt from Grimluk and slowing his steps.

Gwen looked on as the spirit shook and rocked back and forth on Grimluk's back. He let her know he was okay but something was different now. Instead of fidgeting and looking away, Gwen was staring full on at the spirit. She seemed to catch its attention as the thing lightened its burden some. She took a step towards them and it grew lighter still and relaxed its grip. One misshapen foot touched the ground again, then another. The loss of weight made him sigh. He darted away from the now still spirit to stand next to his adopted sister. His gun slipped back out of its holster, the barrel pointing directly at the thing's face. He got a good look at it now, features all warped and monstrous.

"Little one?" he asked tentatively.

"Hm?" Her voice was dreamy, far off. She swayed slightly as the wind blew in again.

"What are you doing?"

"I think I figured it out," she said, a little less

dreamy this time. "It's another kid, like me. Aren't you?" Its mouth split open in horrific approximation of a smile.

Grimluk realized that the spirit was growing smaller as they stared at each other. His mind had been on protection, and, even with his eye gazing down the sights of the barrel at the glowing shape, it took Gwen's declaration to make him see the situation anew. It was shrinking, growing less monstrous by the second.

"*I just wanna go home. Please take me home. Please*," it begged. "*Please...*" A little human boy stood before them, still pale and glowing and mostly transparent. Instead of anger, the ghost's face exuded sadness. Gwen stepped closer to it.

"I'm Gwen. Um…do you remember who you are? Are you a ghost?"

The boy-spirit looked between the two of them. It stared down the barrel of the revolver for a long moment, a struggle washing over its face. Grimluk lowered the weapon. A sharp flash of lightning illuminated the fresh dark of the night, thunder following it with a loud crash that startled the ghost-child and Gwen equally. The ghost let out a momentary sob and hid its face.

"I'm…my name is Owen. I'm lost."

"Okay, we'll help you. It's okay. Grimluk is a demon hunter."

"Demons?" it asked. *"I think a demon got me lost. I don't remember. I just want to go home. Where's Mama and Papa?"* The spirit's voice threatened to turn into a scream, its body likewise threatening to become gruesome once more. The boy's ghostly

shoulders shook as it took in false-breaths, sharp and panicked.

"It's okay," Grimluk started, attempting to diffuse the situation. "I can help you. Just take a deep breath. Calm yourself." The irony of his comment stuck in his mind but the boy was drawing breath still, however unneeded it was. "Just deep, calm breaths."

"Yeah," Gwen followed, offering it a smile. "Deep breaths. I have to do that sometimes."

The boy stood quietly, its moonlight glow rising and falling gently as it tried to calm itself. *"I miss Mama and Papa."*

"It's okay," Gwen said softly. "We'll find them. Grimluk said there was a town down the road. That's where we're going. If we keep going, maybe you'll see something you know." She offered a smile to the ghost, who just nodded in reply.

Grimluk nodded and finally holstered his gun. "On to town then. Hopefully the storm doesn't hit before we can get out of it." He led on, Gwen and Owen following behind. Part of him was still on edge, waiting for the ghost to lose itself again and climb one of their backs. The ectoplasm had mostly stopped dripping but he could still feel what had rolled down his shirt, sticky and cold. Part of his shirt was matted to his back because of it. More thunder rumbled overhead. If they actually made it to the town before the rain hit, it'd be a gods-damned miracle.

The last of the walk to town was quiet. Occasionally, Owen would start to get agitated but Gwen, always soft, always reassuring, would calm the spirit and they'd be left with the wind and the thunder once again. That was until they were close enough to see the town's entrance. The closer they got, the more agitated Owen seemed to grow. Still, Gwen managed to keep it reasonably calm. Grimluk frowned, worried it'd have another outburst once they got around more people. He figured the easiest thing to do would be to let the pair sit aside while he spoke to whoever he could find.

"I remember!" the ghost-boy suddenly shouted. *"I remember where home is!"*

The hunter turned just in time to see the ghost bolt into the field to his right. He sighed and scooped Gwen up in one arm. Easier just to carry her as he gave chase. It occurred to him that Owen could have died a hundred years prior, running to something long since fallen. "Might as well keep my eyes on the kid," he thought, hoping maybe the opportunity to help it pass over would arise. Lightning illuminated the sky just long enough that he saw a house some ways ahead. The ghost-boy wasn't much farther ahead but instead of slowing down near the house, the pale form drove itself straight through the front door, leaving a rough outline of ectoplasm where it'd made contact. Grimluk set Gwen down as they neared.

Someone in the house bellowed.

"Great," he said.

"Uh oh," Gwen followed.

Before he could give the door a few gentle

thuds with his fist, it whipped open, spilling orange light into the yard, and someone barreled out into Grimluk's chest. He caught and steadied them. It was a man, human by the looks of it, brown hair and average build, his face a mask of shock from the ghost child. Owen followed up behind him.

"Papa!"

The man let out a yelp at the child, and then noticed he was clinging to an orc. He sobered up at the sight of Grimluk's tusks and furrowed brow. "Did you send this thing into my house?"

A sigh passed over those same tusks as the rain finally began to fall, a few fat drops at first before beginning in earnest. "No. Let's go in and I'll explain," he said over the storm.

The man inched around the ghost-boy and back inside the house and motioned for Grimluk to follow. The hunter ushered Gwen inside and pulled the door closed. The house was big enough for a few people to live comfortable, with a simple, one room design. In one of the back corners was a stove and a countertop. The other held a bed on a thin, wrought-iron frame. A fireplace split the room down the center, a wooden rocking chair still shaking in front of it, shadows wobbling across the room. The man collapsed onto the bed, elbows on his knees, hands raking over his face. Owen hovered around him, smiling.

"If you're gonna kill me, you should know I'm a deputy over in Perfection. Sheriff'll get a posse after ya. Don't even wanna know why a big ol' orc has a little girl with him."

"Is that what they're callin' the place now? Couldn't remember the name. Wasn't sure it even had one when I passed through years ago," Grimluk said, removing his hat. He gave his scalp an idle scratch, nails running over the strip of short black hair running down the center of his skull. "In any case, I'm not gonna kill you and the kid's family. Adopted. Was headed to town and got… distracted by this other one."

"Most folks don't tend to travel on foot out here. Especially after dark. You sure you ain't bearin' no ill?"

"Most folks aren't prepared. So no, no ill will. I'm Grimluk, this is Gwen."

The man pulled his hands away from his face and gave a start. Owen was looking up at him, leaning one ghostly hand against his knee. "Jed Duncan," he said, swiftly moving away from the smiling spirit. "And what in the world is *that*?"

A frown spread across Owen's face as Jed moved away. *"Papa?"* it whispered.

"No…" Jed shook his head as he backed away, staring hard at the pale face. The face that was skewed by shadows and a soft glow.

"Little one, I think our new friend is getting upset again," Grimluk observed.

"It's okay, Owen," Gwen said, walking calmly toward him. "It's okay, we'll talk to Mr. Duncan."

"Owen?" Jed repeated. He wobbled and might have fallen but Grimluk stepped in and put a hand on the man's shoulder. He slipped to one knee instead of toppling over. "My boy?"

"Papa!" the spirit shouted again and rushed

over to try and hug the man. It didn't quite work and he passed through Jed.

The shock of the ectoplasm barely seemed to register with the man. Jed stood, wobbling again, and then found his way to his chair by the fireplace. "Tell me everything." The ghost joined him, settling next to the chair and curling up. Gwen did the same, pushing her hat back to let it hang by its cord. Grimluk nodded and recounted the evening's events, with Gwen chiming in occasionally with her own bits of the story. Jed sat quietly, eyes locked onto the crackling fire, taking the whole story in silently.

After a long silence, Jed responded. "Six months back, my son vanished," he began slowly, as if each word took effort. "We spent a month tryin' to track him all over. We never—" He stopped and looked over at the specter. "We never found his body. Or any sign of him to boot. After the funeral, my wife, Betsy, took ill. Local witch couldn't figure any real cause but we all reckoned it was the pain. Gods, it hurt us. She passed earlier in the summer and now here you are, bringin' me my boy's ghost. My boy. Oh, my boy."

Grimluk sighed through his nose, hands folded across his chest.

Jed let out a tense little laugh and turned toward the hunter. "Don't s'pose you got my wife hidden in your coat, too?" He gave another laugh, more awkward this time, like it might turn to tears. "No, no. Of course not. That would be absurd, yeah? Couldn't help but ask. Dear gods."

Gwen frowned. "Why'd you stay then, Mr. Duncan?"

"Blind hope. Maybe I'd find my boy or the person who took him. Maybe I'd keep it from happening to anyone else. Least that's what I tell myself." Jed had taken to staring at the spirit again, whose face was now turned up in sadness.

"Mama," it moaned.

"I know," Jed said weakly, trying to lay a hand on the ghost's shoulder. It passed through but he held it all the same. "Reckon you folks can stay here for the night. Little Miss can take my bed. Don't figure I'll get much sleep."

"Papa…can I see Mama's grave?"

"Tomorrow," Jed said in a creaking whisper.

By dawn the storm had withered into scattered, gray clouds. The ground was plenty damp but by noon things would dry into a sticky haze. Jed Duncan led his guests and the thing that was once his son out and around the house. Half a mile behind it sat a lone tree. Jed pointed them in its direction and marched silently, Owen walking next to him. The ghost was much more translucent in the sun. Gwen watched it, a melancholic interest hanging about her eyes. She took Grimluk's hand as they followed.

Grimluk's throat rumbled in thought. He wondered just how this would all play out. He wondered how Jed would hold up showing the boy ghost its own grave. Mostly, he wondered what was about to happen.

The tree was old and towered over them, strong branches providing shade from the sun.

Two hand-worked stakes poked out of the ground in the shade of those branches, smooth and unfinished. Two more lengths of wood were nailed to the top of the stakes, a name carved on each. Owen looked at the graves, trembling.

"So sad," Gwen muttered, her own lip trembling.

Owen stepped forward. *"Mama."*

Jed choked back a sob, doing his best to remain steely but tears still rolled down his cheeks.

Owen looked to its own grave. *"Papa…is that for me?"*

"Yeah."

"I think I have to go in it. I can feel it."

A long breath poured out of Jed's mouth as he tried to maintain composure. "Yeah, I know it. Your mama's probably waitin' on ya."

The ghost of Owen Duncan turned and held its arms up for a hug. Jed knelt down and attempted to oblige the embrace. Ectoplasm clung to his shirt and cheek. The spirit pulled away and smiled.

"I love you, Papa."

"I love you, too."

"Bye bye."

Owen moved away to stand over the grave. It faded away, no flash or noise or anything to signify its passing. Cicadas echoed across the field, seemingly filling the space the ghost-child had left. For a long while, Jed Duncan stood silently over the graves of his wife and son. Grimluk and Gwen stood quietly, paying their respects at the impromptu funeral. A part of the hunter was relieved the boy had moved on.

At some point, Jed turned to head back the way they'd come. "I'll show ya to town," he said quietly, wiping his face with a handkerchief.

The little house hadn't been too far off the road when the ghost-boy had dashed away. Back on the road, the town of Perfection itself wasn't much farther. A shack of some kind sat on the right as they approached, facing down an intersection where the road that brought them to Perfection split off into the town at a T. Outside the little shack sat a dwarf in a rocking chair with a shield badge pinned to his vest. He and Jed exchanged nods as the three of them turned into town.

Perfection's main street cut a pretty straight path, surrounded by various buildings on either side. A handful of tall lanterns stood in front of the buildings, each one polished to a high shine. Grimluk wondered if horses were allowed into town at all given how clean the road was. The whole place looked like it was scrubbed down and repainted each night. The road ended in front of a long and white two-story building that overlooked the town. A few rolling hills dotted the rim of the town along with groves of trees.

As they passed, a few of the locals gave them funny looks. Gwen took Grimluk's hand as he laughed to himself. What a sight they must be. An orc and a little human girl was a strange sight even in the Wastelands. Jed led them up to what was obviously a hotel. It stood tall, two stories and painted modestly. A long sign sat above the porch that read "Happy Harpy Hotel." He turned to face Grimluk, gesturing with an arm towards the building.

"Reckon you'll want to get set up with a room. Rosie can take care of ya. Tell her I sent ya. I gotta get up to the courthouse. Got a hangin' today."

Grimluk nodded. "Thank you. Before you go, I have somethin' I'd like to bring up."

"What's that?"

"I don't mean to upset you any more but the whole thing with your son's ghost has been botherin' me."

Jed let out a bitter laugh. "Bothers me, too. Why?"

"There's somethin' about it, reminds me of somethin' I read when I was still an apprentice hunter. I can't remember exactly what it was but you can be sure it dealt with demons. And Owen said he thought a demon got him lost."

Jed's brow furrowed deeply. He suddenly looked a decade older than he was. "Demons? I figured you for a hunter of some sort but demons?"

"I really can't recall properly, as I said, but given Owen's comment, it seems connected. You're a deputy, have you had any reports of strangeness? Nightmares? Maybe other missing people or animals?"

Jed stopped to mull the question over. "Not that I can recall. Occasionally we still get some of the previous residents swingin' through, from back when the town was mostly a stop for thieves and smugglers but that's about it."

Grimluk nodded. "Maybe I'm just jumpy then. Appreciate the walk in and the shelter last night."

"Reckon it's only right given your help, however unintentional." Jed offered his hand.

Grimluk gave it a friendly squeeze.

"You watch after him, Little Miss," Jed said to Gwen. "Figure he tends to get into trouble."

Gwen laughed and nodded very seriously.

"Oh, before I walk off and forget, we got a strict policy about weapons in town. I'll need any weapons you have. They'll be kept safe up in the courthouse until you're ready to head out."

Grimluk frowned. "Understood. Can't say it's the first time I passed through a town with such a law." He undid his gun belt and handed it over. A huge, sheathed knife dangled from a loop on the back.

Jed buckled it back and hooked his arm through, letting it dangle on his shoulder. "Appreciate the lack of a fuss."

"My job's to kill demons, not make a peacekeeper's job harder." Grimluk paused for a moment. "At least if I can help it."

"Duncan!" a voice bellowed from down the street.

Jed sighed and turned to the voice. "Sheriff Stockburn?"

The voice belonged to a halfling decked out in an outfit similar to Jed's. His hair was a short, muddy brown going gray at the temples. A brass shield-badge dangled on his vest with the word

Sheriff etched into it. As expected of the sheriff, a gun belt hung around his waist.

"Been waitin' on you all mornin'," the sheriff said, a scowl warping his face and seeping into his words. Bright eyes glared from a pudgy face. "Quit your prancin' about and get up to the courthouse!"

"Was just headin' up now, Sheriff. Grimluk here's a demon hunter. Helped me out last night with that whole business with my boy. Wanted to show him and the little miss here the Harpy and get his weapons."

"Don't give two shits about the goblin, Duncan."

Grimluk bristled at *goblin* but kept his face as placid as he could.

"Least you was smart enough to get the weapons off him first. Get on with it."

Jed gave a wave to Grimluk and Gwen and made his way up to the courthouse while Stockburn grumbled something about lazy deputies and turned back to Grimluk.

"Listen up, goblin. I don't have time to deal with any bullshit so you keep that poor excuse for a nose clean or you'll find out why they call Fenton the Hangin' Judge and join the others on the gallows, ya hear me?"

For a moment, Grimluk debated bending down and asking for Stockburn to repeat himself. "We'll be out tomorrow morning. Just passin' through."

Stockburn eyed Gwen for a moment. "And what on Arkod are you doin' with this little girl? This gobby fucker steal you from your folks?"

The sudden focus caught Gwen off guard and made her jump. "N-no!" She looked away and inched her way behind Grimluk's leg in attempt to hide from the sheriff's perpetual scowl.

"Gwen is safe and well-cared for, Sheriff, I assure you."

Stockburn eyed Grimluk for a long time. "You speak out of turn again and I'll slap the cuffs on you myself." With that, Perfection's sheriff stormed off, following Jed's path back to the courthouse.

"I liked Mr. Trilgor a lot better than him," Gwen murmured.

"That is some truth, little one."

Chapter 3

The Happy Harpy was modest but well kept. The owner, Rosie, eyed Grimluk and his young companion for a moment but finally shrugged and led them to one of the empty rooms. Grimluk felt a twinge of disappointment upon learning there were no orc-sized beds, but that was hardly a strange occurrence. Rosie gave them a corner room with a window that looked out onto what amounted to the town square and across a smaller road where the livery stood. The bed looked fairly comfortable, covered in a thick, red blanket and two fluffy pillows. A small dresser and high back chair were the only other pieces of furniture in the room. More than enough for an overnight stay.

Their stomachs growled in hunger, prompting them to return downstairs to inquire about food. Rosie pointed them across the street to the Sapphire Saloon. The place was mostly empty, save for one lone dwarf behind the bar. The gray-bearded bartender must have had a platform behind the bar given the whole top of his torso was above it. Everything was clean here, too. Even the spittoons were polished bright. Grimluk's throat rumbled in thought. Clean streets were a surprise anywhere but a clean saloon was down-right strange. And he knew strange. The thought floated away though as the smells of the kitchen wafted out to meet them when they approached the bar.

"What'll ya have, bub?" the bartender asked.

"Depends on what's cookin'," Grimluk replied.

The bartender broke down their options. They could have beans and biscuits with a few slices of buffalo meat or boar. Gwen opted for boar, saying she was still excited about the buffalo herd from the days back. Beer was also off limits during the day but they had plenty of very fine sarsaparilla. The whole thing came out to twenty cents. Grim-luk thought about just paying a bilt but he had enough pennies to do it. He dropped handful of bronze coins fell into the dwarf's hand. Food cho-sen, they stood at the bar and waited.

"You folks stayin' long," the bartender asked when he returned from the kitchen.

"Just the night and then on up to Eagle Point."

"Ya might keep the kid out of the square when ya finish your food. Hangin' today."

Grimluk lifted Gwen up to sit on the bar so she could drink her mug of sarsaparilla. "So I've heard. Reckon it'll be soon?"

"Should be. It's about ten now." The bar-tender picked up a mug and inspected it, deciding whether he needed to wipe it down or set it aside.

"Judge Fenton likes to keep his schedule, er, well, tight."

Grimluk nodded and led Gwen to a table. The bartender brought them their food shortly and they ate in silence, trying to kill time. As they crossed the street back to the hotel, most of the town's inhabitants had gathered around the gallows. A man in a clean white suit stood at the edge of the platform, addressing the crowd. The man's graying hair and mustache were perfectly groomed. Two prisoners in rags stood restlessly behind him, nooses trailing up behind their slumped heads.

"Law," the man declared with authority. "The rule of law is the only thing that keeps this gods-forsaken province from falling. The rule of law brought order to this town."

Grimluk hurried Gwen along, eager to get her inside. They could head to the general store in an hour or so. That'd be plenty of time for the peace-keepers to get the bodies taken down. He had no doubt, in truth, that Gwen could handle the sight of them but, for now, he preferred to keep her eyes off any more of the dead if he could help it. They bound up the stairs and back into the room. Grimluk pulled the curtains closed on the window that faced the courthouse.

Gwen spent some of that time looking out the other window and, as a half-hour neared passing, she turned abruptly toward Grimluk. She stumbled forward, bracing herself on the bed, as her body trembled. "No, I don't want you to talk!" She seemed to struggle with something, doubling over.

"I need—" came the Spirit's altered voice, almost crackling as Gwen fought to keep it suppressed.

Grimluk rushed over as she collapsed into the floor and scooped her up, setting her on the bed. “Little one...”

“It's...trying to...but I won't let it...” Gwen looked up at Grimluk, one of her eyes the onyx of the Spirit's. A moment later, the other eye turned as well.

“Hunter, we have little time,” the Spirit said hastily. “Give the child that fool Selbie's amulet. Now.” Its message delivered, the Spirit faded once more, releasing its control over Gwen. She fell to her knees in tears, a pained cry warbling from her throat.

Grimluk caught the sound of the posse stomping into the hotel, connecting his instincts and the Spirit’s words. He hastily reached into his bag and pulled out the amulet, tucking it into one of Gwen's inner coat pockets. A moment later, the door to their room whipped open. Sheriff Stockburn sauntered into the room, followed by a red-haired dwarf and Jed Duncan.

“By the authority given to me by Judge Fenton and the province of New Gilead, I'm placing you under arrest for kidnapping, murder, and fraud. Do yourself a favor and come along peacefully.” Stockburn’s face said he hoped the orc wasn’t so peaceful.

Grimluk held up his hands and stayed quiet. No sense in giving the man a reason to get violent.

Gwen looked frantically from the hunter to the sheriff, tears still streaming down her cheeks. “No!” She hopped down from the bed and clung to Grimluk's leg.

"Duncan, get her offa him and grab their things. Donal, shackles."

Jed did as he was told but it was clear he was conflicted about the whole thing. Donal pulled Grimluk's hands down and set to work locking the shackles around his thick, green wrists. Two more deputies were waiting in the lobby of the Happy Harpy to escort their new prisoner. Gwen tried her best to get Jed to listen, to get any of them to listen, but it was no use.

The courthouse loomed ahead, its jail waiting underground.

The cell door slammed shut, closing Grimluk's new cage, one of six identical blocks of cold stonework serving as both the foundation and basement of the courthouse. Oil lanterns adorned support pillars, casting enough light to keep the space in a comfortable dimness that filled the cells with shadow. The back end of the room had a door covering most of the wall. The whole thing felt more like a dungeon than a jail.

"The Judge'll be along shortly," Stockburn informed him before he and the posse disappeared back upstairs.

Stripped of everything but his pants and shirt, Grimluk surveyed the cell as best he could, letting his eyes adjust. A bucket sat in the corner, grimy but empty. He felt a small pang of gratitude that the cell wasn't so small that he was cramped near to claustrophobia. He leaned back against the cool iron bars of the door and gathered his thoughts, everything stillness and silence.

No, not total silence. He could hear the faint sound of wheezing coming from across the way or maybe in the cell next to his. It sounded like a death rattle.

"You talk, big guy?" a voice called. Might have been a human woman. Or maybe an elf. Elven voices could be fairly androgynous most of the time.

"I do." He turned to look out into the lantern light and saw a pair of fists gripping the cell across from him.

"Whatcha in for?"

"Stockburn claims kidnapping, murder, and fraud. Not sure how I pulled that off this morning."

A low whistle echoed off the walls. "You're right fucked, stranger. You know what they call Fenton, right?"

"Reckon so."

"S'pose ya seen the gallows, too, then, from earlier."

"I did."

"See the wheels? They don't take it down, just wheel it out when they need it."

The hunter remained silent. He'd never heard of a gallows on wheels before.

"So who'd ya kill, stranger?"

"Only demons to my count."

The other man laughed bitterly. "Man's in jail for murder and kidnapping and says he only kills demons. You say true, stranger?"

“I do.”

“Bullshit,” came another voice, this one deeper. “Ain't no way you hunt demons and ne'er kilt no one.”

“Think what you like,” Grimluk said with a shrug.

The deep voice huffed and silence descended on the jail, save for that labored wheeze. Grimluk returned to his thoughts, chief among them whether Gwen was okay. He wandered to a corner and slid down, resting his head on the wall. The stones were cold against his mostly-shaved scalp. He closed his eyes and waited.

Sometime later, a chorus of footsteps prompted him to open his eyes again. He wasn't entirely sure how long it'd been but figured an hour or so. Lantern light cast its orange glow across a white suit. The man from the gallows. The man stood outside the cell, taking in the jail for a moment before facing him. Stockburn and the dwarf deputy stood behind the man in white, their revolvers out and ready. He recognized the dwarf as Donal, the man who'd shackled him. Donal unlocked and opened the cell door.

“Thank you, Deputy,” the man in white said, stepping into the cell. “You, stand up.”

“Judge Fenton, I presume,” Grimluk said as he rose, towering over the man.

“Judge *Parker* Fenton, and you will speak when I tell you to. I understand you're a kidnapper and a murderer as well as laying claims as a demon hunter.” The judge tsked. “Charlatans are a special kind of disorder. And you felt confident traveling with a child of my kind to boot."

"The girl is family," Grimluk said coolly.

Fenton held a hand out. Stockburn dropped a club into his palm with an amused grunt. Fenton stuck the club under Grimluk's jaw and pushed it into his throat. "You speak out of turn again and I'll make sure you don't say anything else for a good long while. You understand me, boy?"

Grimluk growled low in his throat but said nothing. He hadn't forgotten the guns trained on him.

"Good," Fenton said, lowering the club. "Sheriff, keep your gun on him. If he gets out of hand, shoot but don't kill him. Now, I'm sure you can *explain* yourself right quick but I'm a man of truth. I see through the lies your kind spills so here's what we're going to do. I'll ask a question, you'll lie your big green ass off, and then I'll correct you. Understand me?" Fenton tapped Grimluk's chest with his club.

Grimluk growled.

"I'll take that as a yes. Where did you steal the girl from? She's not local."

"I stole no one. I—" Grimluk grunted as Fenton's club slammed into his stomach.

"First lie, goblin. Care to try that again?"

Grimluk stared into Fenton's eyes, giving no sign he'd even been struck. "The girl is family."

Fenton struck again, bashing the club into each of Grimluk's tree-trunk legs. "That's two strikes for two lies. I'll repeat myself. Where did you take her from?"

Grimluk looked down at Fenton with measured eyes. "You call me kidnapper and murderer. Either show me the proof of your accusations, lawman, or get the fuck out of my face." He turned around, crossing his arms.

"Don't you turn away from me, you filthy fucking goblin! I'm the law around here and you will show your due respect!"

A grimace of pain shot across Grimluk's face as the club slammed into his ribs, then another shot to his back. He spun, lightning quick and caught his attacker's hand. Fenton's face was a mask of anger, his lip curled in an enraged sneer. A twist sent the club clattering to the floor. Grimluk released Fenton's hand.

Stockburn stepped forward, cocking his revolver. "Time to die, fucker."

"Sheriff, you kill that man and I'll leave you in here with the corpse," Fenton said, a growl coloring his words. He bent down and picked up the club. "He has attacked a judge of the province, adding to his transgressions. Justice will be served."

"Justice? I wonder if that word tastes bitter on your tongue, old man," Grimluk replied as Fenton left the cell. "Most folks out in the Borderlands, and even the Wastelands, can get along fine without someone pushin' his will as law."

"I see your wickedness runs deep. I'll have to break you. Take him to the room, Sheriff."

Stockburn and his deputy slipped into the cell once Fenton had exited, jamming the barrels of their guns into Grimluk's back and directing him to the end of the jail, toward the huge, wooden door. Fenton pulled it open, revealing the darkness inside, save for what cast inside from the lanterns, and stepped in. A moment later, two lanterns on either side of the doorway lit up, dispelling some of the darkness. The room was half as long as the jail itself, mostly bare but for a table with a crank on it and three pairs of shackles that hung from the back wall. The shackles glittered vividly in the lantern light. Mithril. Grimluk cursed inwardly as Deputy Donal slid each shackle around his wrists and locked them.

Fenton stood in the doorway, a grim look of determination upon his face. "I'm not sure if you're strong enough to break iron, but you're sure as shit not strong enough to break mithril. Until I say you're ready for trial, this is your new home." The others shuffled out, slamming the heavy door shut and bolting it, leaving Grimluk in solitude.

* * *

Gwen looked around the judge's office. She'd never seen an office before but this seemed to meet her expectations for what one would look like. A large, wooden desk sat in front of her along with a high backed, red leather chair. Behind all of this, looking down on her from the wall was a silver bull's head bust. Deputy Duncan had left her here after they'd arrested Grimluk. She'd cried at first but eventually, after waiting for so long, her tears had ceased and she'd calmed. At some point, after she'd been sitting alone for who knows how long, she started to doze off, worn out from the stress.

Finally, the door opened, waking her from her nap, and in walked the man in the white suit. A rough face regarded her silently for a moment before he licked his fingers and smoothed his mustache. “I'm sorry to have kept you waiting, child. It's been a busy day. I'm Judge Fenton. What's your name?”

Gwen looked up at him, fidgeting in her seat. “Where's Grimluk?”

“Don't fret, child, your kidnapper has been put away for now. You're quite safe in my care.” He gave her a smile.

Gwen didn't like the smile. It seemed mean and sad all at once and didn't go near his pale green eyes. “He didn't kidnap me. He promised to take care of me.” Her lip quivered but she took a deep breath.

“Did he hurt you? Gods know what he planned on doing with you.” Fenton took his seat behind the desk.

“No, no, no! He didn't hurt me. He protects me!” Gwen began to stammer through what happened, that Grimluk was a demon hunter, how he'd saved Greenreach Bluffs but her brother had helped the demon and got away. Enough of the details that she could stomach to give. “He promised Momma and Daddy and he made me his sister and he showed me bufflows. Let him go, Mr. Fenton, please.”

Fenton looked at her with appraisal, eyes hard with judgment that drew creases in his forehead. “It's clear that not only did the beast kidnap you but he's brainwashed you as well. What you're really saying is this so-called demon hunter utterly failed to kill the thing he was hired to and took you from your family. I swear to you, I will help you and he *will* be punished properly. In the end, you'll see the monster for what he is. In the meantime, I will take you under my personal care." He stood once more and stepped out of the office. "Stockburn," he called.

The sheriff came over quickly. "Yes, Judge?"

"Would you be so kind as to escort this child to my home?" He tossed Stockburn a key ring. "Until we can get the truth and a trial out of the orc, I've decided to serve as her protector."

"Yes, sir. Come with me." When Gwen didn't move, the sheriff yanked her up and pulled her out the door. "I said come with me."

Stockburn led her out of the courthouse, dragging her to the right and around the corner of the building. A little ways behind the courthouse sat Fenton's house, a simple, one-story wooden structure. He jammed the key into the door and shoved Gwen inside the empty home before slamming and locking the door back.

* * *

With one swift motion, the knife slid across the rabbit's neck. Hot blood poured out, filling the simple wood bowl, splattering here and there. After the last drops fell from the confines of the animal's veins, the carcass was laid neatly behind the bowl. A single finger dipped into the blood and moved smoothly across the bull's silver tongue leaving a glistening trail.

“My lord, taste this offering of blood and know I serve you. The vessel is prepared. Speak and command me.”

A lone bubble inflated in the center of the blood, soon joined by others. A low growl filled the room as the blood boiled, giving off a metallic tang. The first bubble grew large, shimmering sickly in the dim candlelight, rippling as something spoke through it.

“I taste the blood and I am pleased. I command you.”

“Command me, oh lord.”

“What is it, Fenton?”

“A demon hunter and his charge,” Fenton said, looking into the bubble now. “I seek council.”

“I already see you have imprisoned the orc. What of his charge? There is a spirit of some kind in her. I can feel it straining against me. It is weak. What do you know?”

“She's young, from the Wastes. She seemed normal enough when we spoke, no sign of this spirit. Though one of the deputies mentioned she’d helped the orc with another spirit outside of town. Apparently the ghost of his boy. Was it the one that you’ve been holding back?”

“No. That is a different spirit and still nothing of concern. Its presence amuses me.” The blood bubble rippled in long, low vibrations accompanying a long growl. “I want you to find out more about the spirit in the girl. If it is something than can serve me. If you are unable to turn her, I will feast on the child and the spirit within. Though its power pales compared to my own, they would still give me great strength."

"And the orc?" Fenton asked eagerly.

"He hunts my kind. I smell their deaths upon him. Punish him but do not kill him. He could be used to make the girl serve me. And he could be a powerful servant himself."

The judge wrung his hands anxiously. "My lord, the hunter is…obstinate. He'll die before he serves."

"Do you doubt, Fenton?"

"No, my lord, of course not. Never. I am yours to command. How shall I bring your order to the bastard?"

"Make him weak, break his body. When he's ready, we may bend his will fully. He will know subjugation as only his ancestors have properly known."

Parker Fenton bowed his head deeply. The bubble shrank and descended back into the bowl, giving a pale green flash that left the blood charred. He gathered the bowl and the corpse and left his office. Tomorrow, he would begin a new tutelage for the hunter and the child. A lesson in violence and obedience.

Chapter 4

Grunts of effort echoed off the walls, mingling with the soft clinking of the chains against the stone. Grimluk strained, trying to pull the shackles that bound him free from their fittings. Try as he might, he couldn't gather enough momentum. The chains were too short for him to bend his hands back and try to wrench them away. He finally gave up after hours of fruitless effort. His wrists started to swell along with thick bruises. If he'd been human, he'd have collapsed from exhaustion already.

Instead, he focused his mind, trying to formulate a plan. He couldn't break the mithril, he couldn't pull the shackles from the wall, and his captor had Gwen. He scanned the room, wondering if he'd missed anything in his initial observations. Everything was the same. Chairs, table, lanterns, the door. Grimluk sighed and wondered if it wouldn't be prudent to try and sleep.

Sleep came hard, rolling in fits and starts. He'd made do sleeping on the ground more times than he could count, even slept in a few trees, but trying to rest standing up, chained to a wall, was something no one was prepared to handle.

The door's latch called out, rousing him. Morning already? Or was it noon? His wrists ached sharply, throbbing with each movement. He never made a sound. Especially with Fenton sauntering over.

"Good morning," the judge said as friendly as could be. "Have a nice night?"

"Where's Gwen?"

"Safe from you. Safe from your mind-fuckery. Poor child wouldn't sleep until she was sure I had left."

"She's a good judge of character. Maybe you should hand your job over to her." Grimluk replied flatly.

"Well-rested and ready to begin your lessons then," Fenton replied coldly. "I'll call the sheriff and we can begin. Oh, and we'll be improving your accommodations. I had a special treat built for you."

As the judge walked away, Grimluk's mind started working. If they were moving him, that could give him the opening he needed. If he moved swiftly, he might be able to break through them and only take one or two bullets. If Stockburn or Fenton got near him, he could use one of them as a shield. Halflings were easier to carry than humans but no one would risk a shot at Fenton. A loud slam pulled his attention away from escape.

"Watch what the fuck you're doin', ya nearly dropped it on my foot!" The voice echoed through the jail and back to him.

"Sorry, never carried anything down steps like this," the voice's partner replied. It sounded like Deputy Duncan.

"Both of you morons shut the fuck up and get them stocks in there for that gobby piece a shit." That one was Stockburn.

After more cursing and nearly-crushed toes, Deputies Duncan and Donal finally brought the stocks through the big door. Fenton had them set it down in the center of the room and strode back over to Grimluk. "I'm sure you think you'll grab one of us and break out but I've got some bad news. Sheriff." Stockburn handed Fenton a small cup and a knife. "You see, you aren't the first goblin I've dealt with. You're all tough, I'll give you that, but most of you aren't very smart. So here's how it's gonna go down. I'm gonna take this knife and open you up. Oh, don't worry, it'll just be a little bit. Just enough to fill this cup. Then Duncan here is going to unlock you and you're going to very calmly get in those stocks. And then I'm going to use your blood and seal you in the damn thing."

"I was polite yesterday but I'm a mite cranky today, so you're welcome to try it that way and see how it works out for all of us," Grimluk said with a growl. "I can't break the shackles, but I can still break you."

Fenton smiled curtly. "As I said, none of you are very smart." He lowered his voice. "You're going to do exactly as I say or I'll march straight out of here and put a bullet in the girl's head. Do I make myself clear? You so much as bleed wrong and I'll hang her body up above my bench before your trial."

After a moment, Grimluk nodded slowly. Only a twitch of his cheek signaled that he felt anything as Fenton dragged the knife across his forearm. Blood welled up thick, rolling down his elbow and dripping into the cup. Once filled, the deputy unlocked him from the shackles and marched him over to the stocks. He could see an assortment of runes burned into the wood around the holes. As he knelt, laying himself into position, he felt his guts drop when the stocks slid shut. Fenton smeared his blood into the runes, bringing forth a sharp flash of red light that faded into the faintest of glows, burning with a low hum.

"There, all settled in?" Fenton asked, positively oozing with insincerity. "You're free to move as much as you'd like, if you're able."

"All due respect, sir, fuck that. I'm gonna split this gobby fuck's back open," Stockburn said enthusiastically.

"By all means, Sheriff. Put your back into it," Fenton said with a cruel laugh. "Where there's a whip, there's a way."

Grimluk strained against his bindings. Every muscle in his body tensed as he tried to move, to break free of the stocks. He watched helplessly as Stockburn pulled a sapling branch from his belt and moved behind him. Lightning shot across his shoulder blades as the sheriff struck. Fresh blood trickled out of the wound.

Grimluk let out a slow breath. He'd had worse.

"You're real tough, ain't ya, goblin, but we'll see how that holds once I've pulled the skin off your back." The switch whistled as it sliced the air and snapped against flesh again. "And don't you worry none about the wounds goin' sour. We'll have someone patch you up when we've finished."

Grimluk set his jaw and braced for another strike, grunting as it hit. He growled low in his throat, inaudible over the sheriff's laughter and mocking. Anger began to bubble deep down in his heart. He was protecting Gwen though. A little blood would keep her safe and that was a small comfort.

After a while, Stockburn finally tired out. Grimluk watched as the sheriff and his deputies left. Deputy Duncan looked back at him. He stared the man down.

"I guess that'll be enough for the day," Fenton said, strolling over from his place against the wall. "You learned your first lesson today and that's what's important."

"I learned you get off on hearing yourself speak," Grimluk rumbled.

Fenton gave an exasperated sigh. "This is my fault, really. I keep giving you too much credit, keep showing too much compassion. I had planned to send the doctor down here soon, along with some water and food but you can wait. You clearly need time to reflect." As the judge began his exit, pulling the big door shut, he paused for a moment. "You'll learn. You're still looking at me like you're above the law. I'm the law around here. Eventually, you *will* bow to the law."

* * *

Gwen slept little the night before. In the morning, after Fenton fixed them breakfast and left for his office, she collapsed, completely exhausted and slept most of the day away. She'd gone to sleep in the guest bedroom Fenton had given her, sleeping hard and dreamless. When she woke up, however, she was laying on the dining room table. In her sleepy haze and confusion, she failed to notice the table was floating high above the floor until she swung her legs over to get down and couldn't reach the chair. She blinked rapidly, trying to pull herself fully awake.

"H-hello? Um...can you put the table down, please?" she asked. She could feel the presence in the room with her now. "I'd like to get down. I'm hungry. We can talk if you want." She looked around and with the veil of sleep falling away, she caught the vague shape. The silhouette reminded her of Owen's spirit. She gulped. "Owen?"

It growled and faded completely from her sight.

The table spun around slowly, Gwen's legs dangling in the air as it turned. Finally, it halted and settled on the floor. Gwen climbed down onto the chair and then hopped off, landing with a light thud more from her boots than the impact.

"Thank you." She looked around again, trying to spot the shape. "I guess you're like Owen then? You can't be him 'cause he…" She realized she didn't really know *what* had happened to the boy's spirit. “Well, he went into his grave, I guess. Um, please don’t climb on my back. You'll hurt me.” She turned in a circle, still looking for a sign from the spirit. “But we can talk. I know you’re angry. I can feel it. I felt it with him, too.”

She stood in silence, waiting, listening. Gwen took in a deep breath and sighed. Her visitor appeared to be holding its tongue. While on the table, she'd spotted a bowl with apples on the counter. When she turned towards it, she jumped back. A clay plate floated in front of her, flipping slowly. It stopped and jittered, before flinging itself into the ceiling and slamming flat without breaking. Gwen caught her breath.

“Please don't do that. It might make the judge man angry. I don't think he's a nice man. Um...can you help me get an apple?” The plate zipped back down to the table, landing flatly with a thin sheen of ectoplasm. A moment later, the bowl of apples flew off the counter-top, crashing into the floor before sliding across it towards Gwen’s feet. Several of the apples dumped out when it stopped suddenly.

“Thank you,” she said, bending over to gather the apples back into the bowl. The sides were slightly sticky from ectoplasm, prompting Gwen to wipe some of it on her coat before she put one in her mouth. As she bit into it, an assortment of dinnerware began to circle over her head. Cups and plates, a coffee pot that was thankfully empty, and a variety of utensils. Gwen watched, nibbling gingerly at the apple. One of the knives floated down as one of the apples floated up. The knife burst through the apple and carried itself into the far wall behind her with a dull thud. The thing was angrier than the boy's spirit had been but it felt more controlled, too.

As Gwen munched on her apple, watching the floating objects overhead, Judge Fenton stepped through the door. She froze, teeth embedded in the apple's skin.

He looked at Gwen, then up at the swirling items. Fenton started to speak but never got the words out as everything in the air turned towards him slowly. A moment later, he slammed the door shut as it all rushed at him. Utensils stuck in the door with sharp thuds, while plates chipped and shattered.

Once everything had settled, the door inched open. Fenton stepped in cautiously, checking to make sure nothing was about to attack him again. He locked eyes with Gwen. "Well, it seems we need to have a talk about what you're capable of."

* * *

A roar shattered the stillness of the forest, sending animals scurrying and birds flying. Thunderous hoof beats filled the air, vibrating everything underneath them. A young orc ran towards the sound, his size belying his years. He gripped an old revolver in one hand and a beat up knife in the other. Fear and purpose covered his young face. He stopped in a clearing, scanning it as the hoof beats grew closer.

Across the clearing, the trees snapped and fell. A monstrous bull emerged from the brush, letting loose another roar. The boy's mouth fell open in awe. The bull watched him with shifting, yellowed eyes, pupilless and maddeningly focused. Its body was flowing blood given a bull's shape. Everywhere the blood touched, it hissed and popped and burned up in quick flashes of green flame.

The boy swallowed and took aim, hands shaking with fright that all but destroyed months of practiced aim. He took in a breath and let it out. He tried again, slower this time, and released it slowly as well. His hands began to shake less. The bull laughed. The gun barked, spitting a bullet at the beast. The boy cried out in triumph as the bull's left eye exploded but it just laughed again, a hard, cruel noise. The boy fired again and again, hitting the bull between the eyes and in the cheek. Another shot rang out, this one chipping one of the massive, bloody horns that spread from the creature's head.

The bull walked slowly towards him, wounds healing, reversing themselves in wet smacks, leaving no sign of injury. Two more shots connected, both under the creature's right eye. It snorted, ignoring, or just unable to feel the shots, and loomed up over the boy, covering him in its shadow. The bull-thing's yellow eyes bored into the boy's. He tried to look away but they were everywhere. They called him and he had no choice but to answer.

The universe fell out from under the boy's feet as he fell into the thing's eyes. He expected hatred or rage but there was only apathy and cold. He tumbled for eternity, into nothing and everything. He wondered if he had fallen into madness.

A bloody hoof fell across his body as the bull crushed him.

Grimluk jerked back to consciousness with a yell. “No!”

He was panting and covered in sweat. Bandages covered his back in long strips while dried blood flaked away or beaded up with the sweat and rolled away. He looked around but the door to the dungeon remained closed. He felt no movement and heard no one else. The lanterns were burning low, threatening to give up their fight against the dark. He slumped in the stocks, momentarily relieved despite his position.

“That's not how it happened,” he mumbled. He remembered the forest, it’d been his first test. But there was no roar. No hooves like thunder and no trees crashing. No yawning madness.

“That is how it will be.” The voice had no body, no mouth. He wasn't sure if he'd heard it or felt it.

“Worst thing about this job. You assholes are always getting in my head.” Grimluk spat in disgust. He tried to gather his willpower and force the thing out of his mind.

“You hunt us and yet show disgust when we fight back?” The voice was more curious than accusatory.

“You're a plague, demon. You infect the living and the dead alike.”

“The same was said of your people once. The Orc Horde, riding out wherever your master bid you.”

Grimluk sneered.

"Ah, yes, you were slaves then. But you are free now," the demon mocked. "Is that not right? Which is why you are continuing the now ancient tradition of hunting my kind down to atone for the sins of the Horde all those centuries ago. How many orcs take up the mantle even now?"

"Enough that you're threatened even when I'm bound."

Silence washed over the room. For a moment, Grimluk wondered if he'd managed to shut the demon up. Then the laughter started. It started low, a staccato rumble in the shadows. The laugh grew, stretching out long and sharp.

"Threatened? Do you really think so highly of yourself?" The lanterns' fires grew huge, bathing the room in orange before nearly snuffing out. The shadows coalesced in front of Grimluk, taking a vaguely elvenoid shape. Two yellow eyes burned in the darkness. "I am not threatened by you, Grimluk. I am impressed by you. You have such passion. Such potential for destruction. Parker Fenton has proven himself useful since he called me but he is weak. You are no such thing, even if you also cling to your petty ideals of law and order and honor."

"What are you talking about?" Grimluk growled and rattled the stocks again.

"I felt your rage bubble when he threatened the girl." The shadow bent down, close to Grimluk's face. "You want to end his life. You crave it. You reek of the desire for death. Your chance will come. I have such plans for the both of you. But shhh, it will be our little secret." A swirling, insubstantial hand reached out for Grimluk's face.

He tried to jerk away, forgetting about the stocks. He felt a dull buzz as the hand rested across his nose and eyes, at once weightless but as heavy as Owen Duncan's specter had been. White heat erupted behind his eyes and, for the first time in as long as he could remember, Grimluk's body filled with savage pain. He let loose a howl to match it before it was choked off, the stocks shaking as his body convulsed. Something was in his throat. He convulsed one, final time before vomiting up a pile of maggots and worms. The shadow swirled out of being in a fit of laughter, its disappearance allowing the lanterns to return to normal. Grimluk looked down, expecting to see a puddle of bile and a writhing mass but saw nothing. A shudder ran through him.

* * *

"I think it's safe to assume I know why the orc took you now. Or did he do this to you? I suppose it's not important either way." Fenton closed the door behind him, looking over the wobbling knives and forks. "Mighty rude to attack me while eating my food though."

"It wasn't me! It was the ghost!" Gwen scrambled to her feet as panic rose in her guts.

"Gwendolyn, I understand what that savage did to you and that you're compelled to lie for him. That stops now."

"It wasn't me, I'm not lying!"

You must escape, child, the Spirit whispered in her mind, detached but insistent.

"It was the ghost! I woke up on the table and it was floating—"

"Shut up!" Fenton yelled, slamming his fist into the door frame. Silence rushed in, filling the void between them. "No more lying for him."

Gwen's eyes were wide as fear filled her tiny body, her heart pounding rapidly as she tried to hold in tears. She dared to close her eyes for a moment to take a deep breath. When she opened them again, she was moving rapidly away from the judge, who looked on slack-jawed as she flew away. A moment later, the door to the guest bedroom flung open and then slammed shut, flashing with an ethereal light. After moments of stunned silence, she could hear footsteps as he ran after her. The doorknob shook for a moment but stopped with a disgusted gasp.

"Gwendolyn," he began, "open the door please. I just want to talk."

Gwen sat on the floor, utterly silent, staring at the door like she was a thousand leagues away. She blinked slowly, barely registering his words. All at once, she snapped back at the sound of a loud bang from an impact against the door. Instinctively, she scrambled to her feet and found a far corner to curl up in, tears streaming down her cheeks. Another bang thundered across the room and, this time, she saw the door undulate for a moment. Ectoplasm began to seep out of it in thick waves that swirled in pinks and purples and whites, covering it fully. She waited for another bang but it never came. A low growl filled the room and she heard a heavy thud and a yelp. The door creaked loudly and seemed to move in its frame. Whatever was happening, frantic footsteps seemed to be the end of it. She didn't hear any more bangs or growls.

As Gwen wiped her eyes, the monstrous shape moved outward from the door and hobbled toward her. A long growl rumbled from it. She nodded at it slowly, still feeling far away as the shape faded from sight once again. Exhausted, she curled up and drifted back to sleep.

* * *

Having been run off, Fenton set about retrieving his cutlery from the front door and putting his kitchen back in some semblance of order. He would leave the girl be for now and figure out how to deal with the unexpected development with the door later. The substance covering the door, viscous and pulsating, had attacked him after it had formed. Or tried. A hand had thrust out at his throat, sending him running. His master would want to know about this. In the meantime, he could get some work done and maybe press on the orc some more.

He paused for a moment. The orc. The girl wouldn't cast away her loyalty easily. He could use that. He tapped the fork he'd just freed against his palm. What if he offered to take her to him, let them speak? It should show the girl he was benevolent and provide an opening for swaying her. Given the potential power the girl seemed to hold, he felt it imperative. She would be more useful as a servant than a sacrifice. Maybe a gift and a hot meal would help sell her on his offer to speak with the orc. Fenton nodded to himself. Once everything was put back up, he left the house again.

Chapter 5

Hours later, Gwen awoke to the sound of her name. She let out a big yawn, the memory of what had transpired not yet returned, before looking up to respond only to see the ectoplasmic shell covering the door. Everything flooded back. The judge was on the other side of the door, calling her name. The door was still pulsing and sealed tight, which relieved her quite a bit.

"I can hear you moving. I know you're awake."

"Go away!" she shouted, a spark of panic lighting up.

"Gwendolyn, please," he replied, sighing with a hint of exasperation. "I'm sorry I lost my patience. You must understand, it's very hard for me to see such a sweet child under the thrall of such a monster. I only want what's best for you."

"Then let Grimluk go and let us leave!" Her stomach growled, reminding her that food lay outside of the door.

"I can't do that. He is a wicked man. But...I'm willing to compromise. I understand you're still under his thrall so in effort to help you get past that, I'm willing to take you to see him."

Gwen sat in silence considering the offer for a moment.

Do not trust him, Gwen, the Spirit spoke up in her mind. *He means to use me through you.*

"Shut up!" she screamed in her own head. "Shut up, shut up, shut up! Everything is your fault! You could've warned him! You could've warned them! Shut up and go away!"

When Gwen never answered, the judge continued. "Well, think about my offer. In the meantime, I'm leaving you a pork chop and a gift at the door. I want you to trust me and maybe these will help you see that I'm not your enemy."

You are exasperating, child. I am a part of you now. You must trust me if we are to survive.

"No! Go away!"

A grand sigh filled her head, and then silence. She remained silent for the rest of the night, eventually crawling to the bed. It was soft and, while unfamiliar, also strangely comforting. Gwen wrapped the bedding around herself and curled up as tight as she could. And she thought. She thought about the gift outside the door and the judge's offer and how much she missed Grimluk and how badly she wished he would hold her and tell her it was okay. She thought about the buffalo and her parents.

Her parents.

She missed them so bad she thought her heart would split and shatter into more pieces than she could count. She missed her mother singing to her at night. She missed her father's stories about things he saw while guarding their town. She even missed her brother, Nicholas, despite watching him murder their mother.

A sudden thought occurred to her. When Grimluk first talked to her, over a month ago now, she'd told him she'd dreamed that her brother had done something to her one night and then she'd started saying the strange things. She thought it had been the demon, who Grimluk told her called itself Priskus, trying to scare her. She'd learned later that the demon fed off of fear, so it made sense.

What if it had really been her brother, Nicholas? What if he'd been the one to put the Spirit in her? The thought festered in her young mind and she realized, deep down, she was right. With what he'd done to their mother, it wasn't so difficult a conclusion. The thoughts rang so true she couldn't ignore them. And she hated it. Hated Nicholas. Hated the Spirit within her. A knot of pure rage took seed in her guts with this realization. The anger hurt though and she wanted to forget it. Her stomach growled again. A perfect diversion.

"Um, ghost?"

The monstrous shape appeared at the end of the bed, hands pressing down on the footboard. It growled.

"I want to see what Mr. Judge left me. Can you please open the door?"

Silently, the door opened and the items slid in before it closed back. There was the pork chop on a plate with a small potato and, next to the plate, a small wicker basket. A bottle of sarsaparilla and a cloth doll sat in the basket. The doll's black, button eyes seemed to look up at her as she took the bottle and looked it over. It was plain brown glass, big enough for a single person, sealed with a cork. She picked up the doll as well and wandered back over to the bed, studying the judge's peace offerings.

Gwen took her time deliberating on the offer. Fenton would leave plates of food outside the door each time he made himself a meal and try to coax a response. She sat and thought, turning the doll over in her hands like the manifestation of her thoughts. The Spirit tried several times to advise her but each time, she fought the thing, doing her best to stuff it into some dark corner of her mind. Several days later, she decided to take Fenton up on seeing Grimluk. Ultimately, he simply asked, after they saw the hunter, that she sit and talk with him, to answer his questions about her apparent powers and why she was so attached to Grimluk. The thought of talking to this man like that almost turned her away from the decision but she agreed. He left her alone after that.

* * *

Blood trickled from Grimluk's forehead, covering his face in a mask of crimson. He spat a heavy wad of saliva and blood and looked up at Stockburn. The halfling stared down at him, panting and seemingly purged of his aggression. Even covered in blood, Grimluk remained strong, mocking the sheriff's efforts without so much as a word.

"I'd cut them fuckin' eyes out if the judge would let me, goblin," Stockburn said after a moment. Worn out from his work, the words were sluggish and low but still full of malice. "Duncan, get the witch and clean this piece of shit up."

Grimluk remained silent, the hint of a smile creeping across his lips. He hoped the sight of his blood-covered face put a measure of fear in the sheriff's heart. Given their power imbalance, he doubted it.

"Sure," Jed replied. He started to leave but stopped. "Sir, do you think Fenton will want him fed?"

"Gods-damn it...yes. Bring food, too." Stockburn rubbed his face in frustration and after Duncan left, he struck Grimluk again, sending a blood splatter across the floor.

Grimluk began to laugh.

"What the fuck's so funny, ya gobby bastard?" Stockburn grabbed one of Grimluk's ears and pulled. "Huh? Let's hear it!"

Grimluk swung his head and bit Stockburn's hand, crunching down as hard as he could, snapping bone and ligament. He grunted as Stockburn swung with his other hand trying to make him release.

"Let go of me, you bastard! Let go!" He was practically screeching.

Grimluk bit harder and released, his mouth now full of blood. Stockburn writhed around in front of him, clutching his bloody hand and growling. Grimluk began to laugh again as Deputy Donal rushed in, gun drawn.

"What happened?" he shouted.

"I told him a joke," Grimluk said, spitting Stockburn's own blood back at him.

The dwarf knelt next to Stockburn and looked him over. "Shit, boss, you're bleedin' everywhere."

"I fucking know that, you moron! Get me up!"

Donal hoisted Stockburn to his feet and walked him over to the table Fenton had brought in. "What should I do?"

"Go find Duncan and tell him to get his ass back here with the witch. Now."

The deputy nodded and took off, leaving Grimluk and Stockburn alone again. The sheriff breathed in sharp hisses as he pulled out a handkerchief to stanch the bleeding. "Oh you're gonna pay for that. I can't kill ya but I'll repay ya in kind."

"It's a payment well worth the price considering I now know what halfling tastes like."

A few minutes later, the deputies returned, a grizzled old dwarf woman in tow. Graying hair and sideburns wrapped in loose braids behind her shoulders, muddy-brown eyes surveyed the room, prompting her to inquire about what happened. Stockburn told her and demanded she patch up his hand. She cawed.

"Only you would put your hand near an orc's mouth after you got done beatin' on him." She pulled the handkerchief away and inspected the wound. "Small blessing you have such dainty hands, Sheriff. Any bigger and one of them tusks might've cut right through. Guess you'll be using your other hand to play with your pecker now."

Grimluk thought he saw Stockburn turn pale but it also could have just been the blood loss. He grinned in satisfaction either way.

Stockburn growled at her though and yelped when she pressed a sour-smelling substance into the wounds. "I swear to the gods, woman, you must be half-demon!"

"And still too much woman for you, Stockburn. Quit your belly-achin'." She wrapped his hand in a clean bandage and gave him a small bottle a little bigger than a shot glass. "Drink this with your next meal and your hand should be right again in a few days. And leave it dressed."

Stockburn grunted and relaxed once his hand was free. "Clean him up. And Duncan, get him a loaf and some water."

"Get him a *steak* and a loaf. He'll need a decent meal to heal up as well, you twits." She sneered at them. "And bring me a bucket of water, for fuck's sake. There's blood everywhere. And you, stop bleeding all over the place. I'm getting sick of cleaning it up."

"Yes, ma'am, I'll get right on that," Grimluk said. Deputy Donal returned shortly with a pail of water while Duncan left to fetch food. The healer set about wiping away the blood and cleaning up his wounds. Before long, she began to rub the same sour-smelling substance into the gashes across his back and forehead, working roughly with no real regard for his comfort, not that he'd have minded. Given his current circumstances, her bedside manner was downright pleasant.

Jed returned with his food and the witch gave him another bottle from her bag. “Give him this after he eats.”

“Where you goin'?” he asked as she passed.

“My job's done, you idiots can feed him your own damn selves.”

Stockburn fumed in his chair. “If she wasn't so useful I'd put a bullet between her eyes.” He got up and began to leave. “Feed him, Duncan.” Donal followed him out.

Jed Duncan looked back at Grimluk and sighed. “I'd really rather not lose my fingers to you.”

“You can keep them if you answer me one question,” Grimluk said, giving the man a hard look.

Jed rubbed his jaw in thought. “Yeah, fine. What?”

“You always turn on folks that help you?”

Jed studied the hunter's face for a long while, eye contact made a touch difficult as Grimluk’s left eye had begun to swell. He finally dragged a chair over in front of Grimluk and sat. “No,” he said quietly. “I have always endeavored to pay back kindness with kindness.”

“Then help me get out of here.”

“I won't. I told you, Judge Fenton helped set this town right and encouraged Stockburn to deputize me after my son passed. Serving the law gave me a purpose again. And despite what happened, I don’t *know* you. You don’t have my trust. He does.

Now be quiet and eat."

After being fed, Grimluk fell into a fitful nap, once more seeing the bloody bull in a dream constructed of a tainted memory. He started awake, growling and angry at having his mind invaded again. He began to call the demon out in protest and defiance, a threat ready upon his lips, but a wave of nausea slammed through his stomach before he could get the words out. His eyes rolled back as his tongue lolled out of his mouth. Gwen walked out of the shadows, yellow eyes shining with twisted glee.

"Now, now, friend, you might regret those words," the demon-Gwen chided.

The demon released its hold on him. "Get out of her you piece of sh—" His body seized and his jaw clamped shut.

"What did I just say?" Demon-Gwen sighed, sounding like a child exasperated with a frustrating adult. "Whether or not I am in your little friend's body or just a figment of your mind is irrelevant anyways. I wanted to talk a little more, really solidify our inevitable friendship. And really, I am surprised at your rudeness. You seem such an amiable sort."

Grimluk felt the demon lessen its hold on him. His muscles relaxed but his jaw remained shut. Fury burned in his eyes as he looked into the shining yellow orbs staring back at him. "What do you want?" he said through gritted teeth.

Gwen stepped forward and took hold of his

face, a smile spreading across the young face at once both cruel and affectionate. "You. I want you. As a vessel or a servant. I want you to kill for me. I want you to taste blood for me. I want you to worship me."

"Never."

"You say that now, Grimluk, but I can be very persuasive. Ah, but I suppose you could use some time to yourself. Maybe that will help." The demon turned to leave but stopped. "Oh, silly me. I have a gift." The child leaned forward and kissed his forehead. "Farewell for now, dearest hunter."

Grimluk's body convulsed again as the same white hot pain ripped through his skull again, spreading down through his body. A silent scream etched itself on his face, unable to give itself sound. His head jerked back and forth in slow, jagged movements. For the second time, he felt something in his throat, writhing, slithering as it came, cutting off his air. A hiss emanated from his throat. Scales pulled roughly against his tongue as the thing pushed its pointed head out of his mouth. The snake held itself aloft and turned to face him, holding his gaze hypnotically.

It continued to rise from his throat, taking purchase across his face to continue its journey. When the viper's body was free of his throat, he sucked in a deep breath before retching. Violent coughs followed as a thick wad of ectoplasm spilled out, slapping the floor. The snake curled around his neck languidly. Another spasm rocked him, bringing up more of the disgusting slime. The pain and coughs subsided, leaving Grimluk panting, sweat rolling down his brow in thick drops.

The snake hissed, opening its mouth wide. Grimluk yelled as it bit into his neck, felt its venom flush through his veins like fire. Within seconds, blackness engulfed him as everything fell away.

* * *

Gwen sat silently at the table, watching her host intently. He was busy preparing their dinner and, though she'd agreed to the judge's terms for seeing Grimluk, she remained wary, ready to bolt if he made the wrong move. Her stomach growled though, betraying her interest in the meal. The chicken had been roasting for some time, permeating the whole house with its smell, making her mouth water. She ignored the hunger and maintained her guard.

Do not trust him.

She ignored the Spirit's words.

When he finally set out their plates and laid out the food, she thought the smell would drive her mad. She held her vigilance and refused to eat until Fenton had taken several bites from his own plate and swallowed them. Gwen tore into the chicken leg with zeal and practically shoveled the boiled vegetables down her throat. He set a corn muffin on her plate, melting butter sliding off its crown. She snatched that up as well, all the while only taking her eyes off him long enough to look at what she was doing and take a drink.

"So, Gwendolyn," Fenton finally said, "I was

hoping we could discuss your condition some before we go to see the orc."

Gwen chewed slowly, looking away.

He continued when she gave no reply. "What exactly is it? Magic? Something inside you?"

Her eyes darted up to him for a moment. She reached for her cup, taking a slow drink from it, trying to procrastinate answering. "I don't know. Grimluk said it was a spirit. Not a demon."

"I see. And what sort of things can it do?" Fenton ate his own food idly, more focused on his questions.

"It used to tell people things," she said quietly. She tried to fight the flood of memories.

"What kinds of 'things?'" he pressed.

"Bad things," she replied deliberately, trying to keep from explaining. She could feel a tremor in her bottom lip. She loathed the thought of letting the judge see her cry. She thought of the buffalo and pushed the rising lump down.

Fenton sighed and tore a chunk of chicken from the bone. "We had a deal, Gwendolyn. I would take you to see the orc if you answered my questions. Do you still want to see him?"

"Yes..." She kept her focus on the plate.

"Then please, stop being so stubborn. What kinds of things?"

Gwen felt herself go far away. Her body was there but her mind retreated, letting her mouth work by itself. "It would tell people they were going to die and how. It told Grimluk that everything would burn down, and then a dragon burned it down. And Daddy, too." She felt a twinge of pain in her heart but like her mind, it was muffled and distant.

"A prophetic spirit? Interesting. Deputy Duncan also told me you and Grimluk brought the ghost of his son home and helped it on to the next life. He said you were talking to it and keeping it calm. Is that true?"

Gwen nodded, still staring at her plate, hoping that she would disappear.

"So, I suppose that means you were telling the truth about the ghost here then, hm?"

She nodded again. A growl filled the room, shaking everything with its rumble. If Fenton noticed it, he didn't react.

"Can you get rid of it as well?"

"I don't know. It's really angry. I think at..." She stopped, hesitating. The thought of it had brought her back to herself. She stared at him hard.

"Yes? Angry at what?"

Before Gwen could finish the thought, the judge's chair jolted away from the table, sliding into the sitting room before twisting and dumping him out into the floor. Fenton collapsed in a heap and turned to look back at what had happened.

"It's angry at you, Mr. Judge."

"Well," he said as he stood back up, "if you're finished, let's go get this unpleasantness over with. It's getting dark." He did his best to straighten his clothes.

Gwen got her coat and followed the judge to the courthouse. As they walked, she tried to focus on not being far away again so she could talk to

Grimluk. She was so focused on returning to herself that she missed the walk entirely. Suddenly, she was standing in front of a large door and the judge was asking if she was ready. She nodded but, in that moment, she had no idea what being ready meant.

Parker Fenton opened the door wide. Gwen gasped at the sight of Grimluk pinned down in the stocks. The judge stepped in ahead of her.

"Orc, I'm allowing you a special treat tonight. Gwendolyn is here to see you." He motioned for Gwen to enter.

She stepped into the dim room, studying Grimluk more than she would have had she not been trying so hard to disappear in herself. Had she been more present in the moment, she might have rushed forward and hugged him and tugged on the stocks. Instead, she stumbled towards him.

"Grimluk?" she asked cautiously, like the room and the huge man weren't real. He watched her, silently, his eyes looking a little glassy and distant as well. Gwen reached out gingerly to touch his shoulder.

"No!" he shouted, startling her. "Stop tormenting me, demon! Take your puppet and leave me be."

Gwen jerked her hand away. She stared at his growling face for what felt like years before the lump and quiver she'd stifled at the dinner table finally caught up to her. She burst into tears and ran out of the dungeon. She slid past the judge and ran for the stairs that led back up into the courthouse, her eyes burning the whole way. As Gwen neared the judge's front door, it ripped open. She felt herself drift into the air upon entry and as before, her ghostly companion whisked her away to the guest room, slamming the door and sealing it as it had done before. The ghost sat her in bed. Great sobs racked her, voicing every ounce of her sorrow.

* * *

As soon as Gwen started to cry, Grimluk had realized his folly. He tried to call after her but his throat tightened. He hung his head in shame while his captor gloated.

"I couldn't have planned that better myself." Fenton crouched in front of Grimluk, a malicious smile spread across his face. "I think you've just sealed her fate. Now she'll understand me, see the truth that you were just a monster that took her unwillingly from her home. How does it feel?"

The rage he'd felt when the judge threatened Gwen to get him in the stocks flared up, knotting his stomach and giving his mind an unpleasant pulse. Desire tore at his guts. In that moment, he wanted to kill Parker Fenton. He'd never wanted to end someone so badly in his life.

"I suppose it won't hurt to lay things bare now though. My master demands your service. Hers, too, because of that thing in her. And here's the kicker...you don't serve, I will make you watch as I destroy that child. I will put you front and center as the master chooses her fate. He'll have you both or you'll both die and you'll watch, trapped and helpless in those stocks as I end her. What say you to that?"

Grimluk bucked in vain, trying to break his stocks once more.

Stars burst in front of Grimluk's eyes as the judge kicked him. He tried to look up at the man but the stocks inhibited his gaze. He spat blood on the judge's pant leg. He wanted so badly to end that man. He couldn't stand it.

The judge snarled at the blood on his pants. "Savor your rest, Grimluk. I'll take the cost of that out of you myself tomorrow. You will respect law and order."

Chapter 6

Gwen hid in bed. Why had Grimluk yelled at her? Didn't he say they were family? Hadn't he missed her? She didn't know what to think. The judge kept saying Grimluk was a monster but she'd never believed it. Then she gets to him after a week of separation and it all went so wrong. The whole thing felt so unreal. Occasionally, she posed her questions aloud, wondering if her ghostly guardian would, or could, answer. The most she would get were strange ripples in the ectoplasm on the door.

The Spirit tried to speak through the noise of her mind. *It was not his fault,* it tried to reassure her. She ignored it. Barely registered the words.

As Gwen sat and wondered, doubt boiling away, the judge tried to coax her out. She'd been so lost in thought she hadn't heard him approach. His voice startled her, making her heart drop for a moment before thumping rapidly in her chest.

"Gwendolyn," he cooed, "are you all right?"

She looked at the door, conflict washing through her mind. Tentatively, she answered.

"No."

"Would you like to talk about it?"

She very much wanted to talk about it but she held her tongue, wondering at the right answer. "Maybe," she finally replied. It seemed the safest answer.

"I understand, child. If you want to talk, I was thinking of making some custard, maybe a pie. You could help if you wanted."

She curled up as small as she could, hoping to disappear. He sounded so soothing and custard sounded so good. She hadn't had any since before Grimluk arrived in Greenreach Bluffs. She squeezed her eyes shut, trying to hold back the tears and the memories of her mother's lemon custard pie. Lemons were one of the few fruits they could get to grow reliably even with the town magician's alchemical help. Her mother would let her lick the mixing spoon before dinner. Nicholas had always been a little jealous of this, saying she'd never let him lick the spoon.

"No," she thought. "No no no no no." The word repeated in her head over and over again in a desperate effort to try and drown out the memory of her mother's voice. The judge interrupted her thoughts again, most likely guessing that she wasn't going to answer.

"I'll be in the kitchen."

This time, she heard his footsteps trail away. She sat up, wiping away little tears that'd formed in the corners of her eyes. She sighed and came to a decision.

"Ghost?" she whispered. The door rippled.

"I...want to go talk to Mr. Judge. If you can let me out. And watch me, please?"

She moved toward the door. The ectoplasm rippled sharply and she noticed the shape of a face press out for a moment. The goo bubbled and shifted but finally sank back into the door with a growl. It slid open. Gwen slipped out and tiptoed to the corner where she peeked to see if the judge was where he said he'd be. He was. She took a deep breath and slipped silently into the room, pulling her coat tight.

"Um, Mr. Judge?" she mumbled. He seemed focused on the task of gathering what he needed. She repeated herself, louder this time and he turned.

"Ah, Gwendolyn, if I'd have known you liked custard, I'd have offered it to begin with. Come in."

She hesitated for a moment but her confusion spurred her forward. She needed to figure things out and he seemed to be her only option for help now. She climbed into a chair at the table and sat quietly, watching the judge prepare the custard. The words would rise in her throat but he would turn to look at her and she'd stare blankly as they fled.

After a few instances of this, he finally spoke instead. "Child, you clearly have something to say, please say it."

The request surprised her. The words stumbled out. "Why did Grimluk yell at me?"

Without pausing his work, he replied very plainly, "Because brutes like that prey on the weak.

I've seen it time and again in my work through the years. So-called *demon hunters* seem especially prone to it."

"But I remember what happened...don't I?" Visions of her mother and father filled her mind, the former covered in her own blood, the latter wearing Grimluk's coat after being burned alive by the dragon, both already dead but alive again from the amulet he'd shoved in her coat pocket. She suddenly felt its weight against her chest, heavy and sharp against her heart.

"I'd wager he used some sort of befuddlement on you. Some curse or charm to turn your memories to his own devices. More than likely, the bastard murdered your family and meant to take you for some nefarious purpose. Ritual sacrifice, food, maybe as a toy. You can't know for certain. His type lies, Gwendolyn. They hate law and order and thrive on chaos and misery."

She looked at her hands, fidgeting uncomfortably. "But, he showed me bufflow...taught me about berries and how to know animal signs. I tracked a deer and a rabbit and he held me when I woke up crying. He said we're family." Her words were sad and unsure, as if saying them out loud was the only way to reassure herself they were true.

"Maybe," Fenton said. "Maybe he did those things. Maybe he made you think he did. Even if he took the time to teach you or feign affection, it was disingenuous. You're not the first child I've seen taken in like that."

Her confidence in her memories was waning. The table shook gently but she barely noticed. She looked up, sullen and red-eyed.

"But what about my brother? What about the Spirit?" Gwen's breath appeared in a faint wisp of chill air, puffing out for a moment and then disappearing as warmth returned. "I remember."

"Do you though? He's come close to admitting the wrongs he's laid upon you, child." He continued on after Gwen let out a gasp. "As for the Spirit, I suspect he is the cause of it, though the consequences were clearly unforeseen. If you could allow me to speak to it—"

"No! I hate it! I won't let it out again. It's always taking me over. It's why Momma and Daddy are dead!" As her anger rose, so did the table's tremors. It budged, its legs scraping against the floor lightly. The air in the kitchen grew cool, rapidly dropping to a slight chill. "I wish it would just leave."

"Are you so sure, Gwendolyn?" He finally stopped what he was doing and turned to face her.

The eye contact drained her of emotion. Was she sure? Could she be sure? The tremors and cold vanished. The last of her willpower draining away as he spoke.

"Let me speak to it, child. Perhaps I could persuade it to leave you be, or find some way for you to control it." He crossed his arms. "I can't help you unless you let me."

Finally, she gave up. Gwen retreated inside herself and let the Spirit step forward. Her body shivered. Onyx blackness took over her eyes. Something altogether not Gwen looked up at Parker Fenton with the girl's face and spoke in a voice both Gwen's and not.

"I do not mind staying within her mind but it is nice to be out every so often." The Spirit held up a hand and looked it over. "It's nice to be able to move of my own accord sometimes."

Fenton smiled, though there was little warmth in it. "Greetings, Spirit."

"Greetings, Judge Parker Fenton. I understand you have been inquiring about me." The Spirit stood from her chair and walked around idly as it spoke. "How can I help you?"

"What are you?" he asked.

"A spirit, just as she has said."

"How powerful are you?"

"I do not know."

"The child said you were capable of prophecy, is this true?"

"I see the paths and possibilities of time. Why do you ask?" It smiled to itself at this. The touch of irony amused it.

"I would make use of you if I could. The knowledge you possess could prove invaluable to bringing order to the rest of New Gilead and the Borderlands. Maybe one day even the Wastelands." A subdued hunger shadowed his words. "Tell me what you see, prophet."

It regarded him for a moment, seemingly scrutinizing the question and the one who asked. "You will not like the answer, Parker Fenton." While the Spirit spoke, Gwen's features seemed so ancient and knowing, so alien. Something Grimluk had called eerie.

His eyes narrowed, studying the face. "What

does that mean?"

"It means what it means. You will not like what I see. The knowledge will upset you greatly." The Spirit's tone was that of an adult explaining something to a confused child.

"Maybe you should tell me anyways and let me decide on that, Spirit."

They stared at each other for some time before the Spirit nodded and spoke. "You are going to die a very bloody death, Parker Fenton. By the hand of Grimluk or another, I cannot tell but you will die. I see that much quite clearly."

The Spirit smiled quite politely.

* * *

Silence and shadow filled the dungeon but Grimluk wasn't alone. Not really. He could feel the demon's presence hovering around him. It stepped forward, coalescing from the shadows.

"My dear hunter, do you know the true history of the orcs?" the shade asked.

Grimluk gave a disgusted grunted as he attempted to ignore the demon's words. It had been taunting him for some time now, making him relive the night before. His guilt at not seeing Gwen was truly herself rolled through him in waves as he attempted to ignore the walking shadow. In his years as a full-fledged hunter, he'd never had things go so wrong.

"Rhetorical question of course, I know what you know. Your people have done a commendable job at passing the tales down through the centuries but there are many details you do not know, cannot know. And how could you?" The person-shaped shadow walked idly around its very captive audience. "For instance, you have no idea if your oppressor was even a mortal being, do you? Elf, human, dwarf; certainly not a halfling, I can assure you of that. Maybe even an orc! How marvelous would that have been? I could tell you. I will not. Not yet. Maybe one day. But I will tell you that like our friend the judge, they were obsessed with bringing *law and order* to this world."

"I suppose," Grimluk started before he could stop himself, "that you mean to tell me Fenton is the same as that ancient bastard? That through you, a new conqueror will rise?"

The shadow made a sound like the clucking of a tongue. "Fenton? No. I would make you that conqueror. And it would start with one very simple act."

"Let me guess. I swear my eternal allegiance to you?"

"Oh no, much, much simpler." The shadow moved, bringing its mockery of a face next to Grimluk's ear. "Extinguish his life. I know it is what you want. For the humiliation of having you trapped down here. For threatening the child. I can feel the *desire* rolling off you. If I could get what you call 'shivers' I would get them just thinking about that sight." The shadow moved away, letting out a low growl.

Grimluk sat quietly, reflecting on the truth of the demon's words. He'd wanted to end Fenton as violently as possible. Considering the level of raw strength he possessed, such an act could be gory indeed. The thought was dichotomous. As violent of a life as he lived, he had truly always endeavored to never end another mortal's life, even when they sought his death. The rage that bubbled in his guts had grown powerful though, and his desire to protect Gwen and punish the judge fueled it. Parker Fenton served a demon, had threatened to murder Gwen twice now, and was doing gods know what to her while he was trapped with a demon and a sadistic halfling for company. The part of him that wanted to end Fenton's life wanted to end Stockburn's as well. The thought was sobering.

"Guess I'll just have to disappoint you then, demon."

It laughed sharply, like hot points being shoved into his ears. "Oh, my good hunter, you will not have a choice in the matter. When the moment comes, your mind will seize to the task and you will fall into my arms where you are *destined* to be. When you taste his blood, you will become my right hand of doom, my favored servant, my champion."

"I'll tell you exactly what I will do. I will fight you until I breathe my last, demon. We were slaves once, never again." He rocked in the stocks, a renewed vigor filling him for a moment; hope that the effort would free him this time bubbled up. The stocks held though. The runes glowed from his effort.

"Such willpower. You are a thing of beauty, Grimluk. Truly, you will be a trophy. In the meantime, you have company on the way." With that, the shadow lifted, returning the natural luminescence to the dungeon.

Grimluk heard the door to the jail slam open. A moment later, the dungeon door did the same. Parker Fenton stepped forward wearing a mask of utter rage and contempt on his face. The judge raised his hand and pointed Grimluk's own revolver at him. It shook erratically, clearly heavy in the man's hand.

"I've just been given some distressing news from that thing inhabiting the child," Fenton said.

Grimluk let out a laugh in spite of himself. "Let me guess. I'm gonna kill you, right?"

Fenton ground his teeth together. "That's right. It's time to step up your execution."

"Then shoot, old man, if you have the iron. Aim true." Grimluk pointed a smile down the fidgeting barrel, watching as Fenton pulled the hammer back. Still the smile remained.

"Any last words, orc?"

"Reckon so, you iron-fisted little tyrant. Pull the gods-damned trigger and go fuck yourself."

Parker Fenton sneered. "Typical." He pushed the barrel into Grimluk's grinning face, denting his forehead with the muzzle, before pulling the trigger. The hammer slammed down with a loud click but nothing happened. An empty chamber? He tried again but the result was the same, steel glancing off steel. Again and again and again and again, every chamber remained silent. Frantically, he flipped the cylinder out. Six cartridges stared back him, glinting faintly from the lantern light, untouched in any capacity. He dumped them out into his hand. Each was still live and ready to fire.

Grimluk let out a mocking chuckle. “Well, what's the matter, Judge? Thought I was a dead man? There was no way you could miss this close.”

“How?” He fumbled the brass back into the chambers and tried his hand once more. Every shot was a dud. Furious, he screamed his question again and swung the barrel at Grimluk’s jaw.

Grimluk laughed outright, his jaw beginning to swell and darken. “You think I'm some kind of amateur? It's *my* gun, it's bound to *me*. Guess if you want me dead, you'll have to get your hands bloody.”

Fenton roared in anger and slammed the gun down in front of Grimluk before storming off like a petulant child with a bruised ego. The dungeon door crashed closed, echoing off the walls for a long time after. Grimluk stared down at his gun. If he could only get free of the stocks, he could make six shots work. He could find Gwen and they could escape. If only.

Chapter 7

Fenton's anger about the gun and the Spirit's words refused to cool. The next day, he ordered Stockburn to be more creative in his methods of torture, saying Grimluk must suffer but still remain alive and easily healed. The sheriff took his instructions with zealous glee and immediately made good on his promise to repay Grimluk for his hand. The tool of choice was a stiletto dagger. Stockburn took his time for once, pushing the needle-like point of the dagger into his captive's hand, replicating the tooth-marks left from Grimluk's bite. To his chagrin, Grimluk never made a sound. The silence just seemed to piss Stockburn off more.

After three weeks, the judge decided it was finally time for a trial. It would be no more than a show. A mockery of the system he claimed to uphold so fervently. Grimluk would be allowed no advocate, no defense at all, in fact, and would not even be allowed at his own trial. The whole affair barely took a full half-hour, mostly due to formalities than the actual trial. Judge Parker Fenton, bedecked in his robe, gavel in hand, led the procession. The prosecutor laid the case out simply for the attending audience: Grimluk had murdered Gwen Quinn's family, kidnapped her, and made camp for months in the area before finding Jed Duncan's child and kidnapping him as well. To top all of this off, when the young boy had finally escaped, the *goblin bastard* murdered him and waltzed into town, proceeding to the good deputy's house with claims of a ghost in an effort to conceal his actions. And all of this under the claim of being a demon hunter.

The evidence was irrefutable. The original search party couldn't find a single trace of Owen Duncan, but his favorite toy had been found, blood-stained, in Grimluk's bag. Jed's solemn fidgeting on the witness stand made it all too apparent to the crowd that the subject still pained him and they all agreed that the judge's sentence would be too good for such a cruel beast. Gwen was spared the trial, with Fenton declaring that the poor child was so traumatized by the whole affair; she could barely get out of bed most days.

In the end, the defendant was declared guilty and sentenced to death by hanging. Stockburn let it be known, loudly, that he hoped the goblin's neck held strong when the door dropped. Let him suffer for such grievous crimes. Some of the locals quietly agreed.

Fenton broke the news to Grimluk shortly after the event ended, letting him know he would die in a week unless he decided to serve his demonic master.

* * *

In the weeks after Gwen let the Spirit speak, she had resigned herself to the judge's words. She hadn't even bothered to keep her consciousness far enough forward to listen to what it had told him, but when she resurfaced some time later, Fenton was there, telling her he understood why she hated it so much.

"It's nothing but lies and malice, just like the orc," he'd told her. "It's clear now that you're in need of greater protection than I realized. I will accept the role as your new guardian and give you what that abomination falsely promised."

The words had seemed far away. She'd nodded and wandered back to her room. The weeks blurred together as she started doing choirs and eating meals with the judge. She responded to him dully, never quite present, always slightly outside of herself. He never seemed to really notice. She did what he told her and the disturbances from the ghost had all but ceased. Sometimes, at night, she'd awake and the door would have a thin sheen of ectoplasm with a face pushing out at her. Sometimes the hulking shadow faded into sight like a dream. It never lasted for long though.

The night Fenton told Gwen the news about the trial though, she awoke from a nightmare. She'd dreamed that Grimluk had escaped the dungeon and rescued her only for Fenton to capture him again. The dream forced her back into reality. Everything since the week she'd met Grimluk outside the general store in Greenreach Bluffs with her brother and mother filled her mind. She watched the ectoplasmic face, focusing on it and her memories, and began to dissect the months prior.

All the traveling, the lessons about the world around her, basic knowledge about magic and how people can react to it in certain situations. She looked at her hand as she remembered Grimluk teaching her a simple spell to start campfires. She held it out like he'd shown her. She pictured sparks and flame and tried to focus her will.

"Spark-a-dark, what's my desire? To lay, to stay, bless this camp with fire." Like that first time, a shower of sparks backed by a small flame shot from her finger tips, flashing into, and right back out of, existence. She repeated the words, bolstered by her success, and watched a second flame roll from her fingers, bigger and brighter. She didn't remember wrong. Grimluk had taught her things, taken care of her. She started to panic. She had to escape the judge. Had to get Grimluk out of the dungeon. Had to hug him. They had to run.

Focus, Gwen, the Spirit told her. *Focus and keep sharp. You must be ready.*

For a moment, she thought about telling it to be quiet again, about unleashing all her anger and pent up emotion. But she knew it was telling her the truth. She sighed. Her breath came out in a puff and she looked at the door. The ectoplasm had swollen back up. The face pushed towards her, much farther this time.

"Can we help the ghost talk to us?" she asked the Spirit.

You calmed and spoke to the first one. I see no reason it would not work again. It has formed a connection to you and seems to be responding to your renewed sense of self. Maybe willpower is the key.

She thought about this for a moment. "Please come out and speak to me," she finally said. "I need your help to save my new brother."

An eldritch light permeated the door. The towering shadow pushed out towards Gwen, taking steps on invisible feet from legs that seemed to disappear at the knees. Like Owen, it began to shrink, take on a more natural shape but, ultimately, still taller than her by several inches. The ghost began to solidify further, gaining details from its former life. Shoulder-length hair came into view, seemingly always there but just out of focus. Unblinking eyes rolled around and locked on to her.

"Hu—" The voice was faint, like a murmured echo.

Gwen's excitement grew. "Yes?" She had to keep herself from shouting.

"Hullo," the voice whispered. It realized suddenly that its voice was audible. "Hullo!"

"Shhh, we can't wake up the judge." The momentary panic made the ghost flicker but Gwen seized on the sight of its face and focused as intently as she could. "What's your name?"

"Name? Name...what was my name?" While it thought, more details started forming, still very much translucent but clear. A headband seemed to hold the hair in place and something resembling a simple dress took shape on the ghost's body. The voice grew sturdier, taking on a tone similar to Gwen's but full of echoes. “Leh...Leigh. My name was Leigh Fenton.”

“Fenton? Were you...were you the judge's daughter?”

The ghost of Leigh Fenton twitched as some measure of memory seemed to return to it. “Yes...Parker Fenton was my father. And...and...” Her eyes went wide and then suddenly, the ghost was growing monstrous and grotesque, no longer a vague shape. The temperature in the room plummeted.

Gwen reacted on pure instinct, reaching out and grabbing at the girl's arm, forgetting that her hand would simply pass through the insubstantial form of the ghost. Ghost and girl were both surprised, however, when Gwen's hand touched and held on. Indirectly, she could feel the ghost's weight. And the mountainous wrath swirling around. Understanding filled her mind. And memories.

“He was your father...and he killed you,” she whispered, looking up into what should have been the terrifying sight of Leigh's transformed features. “He sacrificed you to the demon.”

The ghost, nearly touching the ceiling, dripping ectoplasm everywhere, nodded dumbly, appearing very much like the child she had once been in life.

Images filled Gwen's mind as she saw through Leigh's eyes. Parker Fenton hugging his wife, Letty, Leigh's mother. Letty Fenton making dinner, letting Leigh taste it. The three of them going into town. Letty Fenton reading Leigh a story for bed. Then the judge looking down at Leigh with red-rimmed eyes and a weariness that seemed to fill his bones as he told her that her mother was gone. No sense to it. She'd simply vanished.

Parker Fenton returning a month later and telling Leigh with a detached joy that he knew how to reunite their family and that they could do it right then. She'd been so excited. Leigh had grabbed the favorite of the books her mother had read to her, a collection of stories about the mythical Fay, to take with them.

Gwen watched in horror as the judge picked his daughter up and sat her on an altar and began the recitation, uttering a prayer of offering to the demon. She let go of the ghost's arm, fleeing from the final image of Parker Fenton picking up his knife and moving it towards his daughter's throat.

The ghost's fury bled into her and now her own anger mingled with it in maelstrom for the desire of righteous vengeance that was not her own. She tried to regain her composure. The enormity of it threatened to overwhelm her.

"Have to…calm down," she said to herself and Leigh. Gwen panted and trembled.

The two of them sat in the floor, Gwen fighting to exercise her own will while Leigh shrank back down.

"I need your help to free Grimluk," Gwen finally said once they were both calm. "He can stop your dad and kill the demon. We need a plan though. Grimluk said you always make a plan first." Gwen closed her eyes for a moment, trying to think of the best way to get to Grimluk. She was exhausted but filled with determination.

The amulet, child, the Spirit said.

"What about it?" Gwen thought.

You must hide it. You will be caught. Parker Fenton cannot be allowed to have such a powerful item.

Gwen couldn't argue with that bit of truth but she seethed at the notion that she would be caught. "I won't get caught and we'll rescue Grimluk, just you watch!" She climbed back to her feet and fished the amulet out of her coat pocket. She'd never looked at it before. Bone and silver, covered in runes, with an eerie purple gemstone set in its center. The amulet had been the means of saying goodbye to her mother and father but she knew it was dangerous. Grimluk had explained how Kenton Selbie, Greenreach Bluffs's mayor, had used it, raising the town's dead to serve as aggressive puppets to defend him against Grimluk. He'd even managed to raise a long dead dragon. That dragon's fire had taken her father.

She took a deep breath, holding back the tears.

"Leigh," she finally said, her voice still shaky, "I need you to hide this. I don't know where. Up in the roof? A tree? Somewhere no one could accidentally find it." She held the amulet out to the ghost. "And hurry. If...if we do get caught, he can't have this. It's very dangerous."

Leigh nodded. The amulet floated away from Gwen's hand. The bedroom door swung open silently and the ghost vanished, warmth rushing in where the specter had been a moment ago. A chill signaled its return, followed by the door closing back. "It's safe."

Gwen slipped her coat and hat on. "We'll go get Grimluk now. He's in the jail dungeon room. If we can get in there, maybe I can break the stocks open. If any of the deputies are there, can you scare them off?"

Leigh hesitated. "I believe so. Until you got here, the demon had kept me quiet."

Gwen pondered this. "Okay...that's okay. Just try your best and we'll come back and help you and stop your dad. I promise."

* * *

Muscles flexed and strained against the bonds that held them. Grimluk was once again trying, however futilely, to break free of his blood-sealed bonds. With a week to live, the only thing he could think to do was struggle harder against the magic that held him. The demon, once more dressed up as Gwen, watched with an amused look on its face.

"I sincerely hope you put this much effort into destruction when you are mine," it said, an air of longing in its words.

Grimluk stopped struggling, instead falling into his thoughts. Thoughts he couldn't quiet. "You're doing a damn fine job here," he thought with a sigh. "First Greenreach, and now your promise to Gwen's parents. You'll die and that fucker will probably feed her to the demon."

"That's true," demon-Gwen said nonchalantly. "I will probably eat that girl before your body is even cold."

Grimluk's head snapped up. "Stay out of my head, demon!"

"Shhhhh, it's okay. You know how you can protect her. All you have to do," it bent over, face to face with Grimluk, "is serve me."

"No. I'll find a way. I'll stop Fenton and kill you."

"No. You will join me and kill Fenton and then you can keep the girl. You could make her a ruler in my name while you conquer the whole of this ridiculous little world. Just picture it." A malicious finger pressed itself between the hunter's eyes.

An image rushed into his mind. He rode a black, skeletal steed, dripping with poison, an army of monsters at his back. Everything around him was a sea of fire and death. Ghouls swept through villages, devouring all inhabitants. Nightgaunts, black as oil, faceless and horned, fought over the remains while great, writhing beasts, all teeth and claws and too many eyes, burst through cities, ripping and slashing and howling with fury. Vampires fed in the streets, gorging themselves on more blood than they'd ever dared to dream of before their mighty conqueror led them to victory. All the while, the corruption of the Wastelands spread farther and farther and, with it, all the creatures that haunted the shadows of nightmares came rushing forth in dizzying power, seen and unseen, to bring pure chaos.

The vision made Grimluk weep. He felt the heat of the fires, the spray of blood. Heard with total clarity the screams of the dying. It hurt him to the core of his being, the thought that he would ever be responsible for so much suffering. But then he wondered, hadn't he already tasted that with Greenreach Bluffs? Hadn't that been why he'd been so eager to leave at the first opportunity? He'd failed the town. Up until that point, he'd never failed a mission. Each bounty had been completed, the demon sealed or destroyed and sent back to the Abyss.

But not Greenreach Bluffs. He hadn't even stayed to help clean up the bodies of the dead Selbie had raised. Some of the town's citizens had been afraid of Gwen, sure, but he should have helped. Should have made absolutely sure that Gwen's brother hadn't fled. The boy had bound himself to a demon, made himself its host and anchor. No mere demon knight, the two were inseparable now and his wounded ego had caused him to run back home with a child he'd adopted both out of compassion and guilt.

The demon smiled as it watched the war in Grimluk's mind unfold. "I will leave you to your thoughts, Grimluk."

Moments later, the demon appeared in Fenton's mind, rousing him from sleep. "He's ready. And your bait is on her way. He will serve."

* * *

Gwen hurried through the house as quietly as she could and slipped out into the still night air. Despite Fenton's house sitting behind the courthouse, there was no back door to the building. She took the only way she could, creeping around the side of the building. Clouds hung thick, obscuring the moon and making the night that much darker. Gwen was surprised to find there was no one watching or patrolling. Here, in the heart of New Gilead, far from the Borderlands and farther still from the Wastes proper, there wasn't a great need for Watchmen. She slipped easily around to the front of the building and made a quiet entrance with Leigh's help.

The courthouse was empty and dark. She vaguely remembered the direction Fenton had taken her to get to the dungeon. It helped that there was only one staircase leading down. She crept down and through the jail. She struggled to pull the big door to the dungeon open for a moment but Leigh offered a ghostly hand and it swung open easily. Grimluk looked up at her, his face the very portrait of confusion and inner struggle.

His eyes lifted above her, going wide and then squeezing with anger. For the second time, he shouted at her. “Run!”

A hand seized Gwen’s shoulder and spun her around, making her yelp in surprise. Parker Fenton peered down at her with a grim satisfaction. “No visitors allowed, dear Gwendolyn.”

“Leave her alone, Fenton!” Grimluk strained once more against the stocks, the runes glowing at his resistance.

“You have two choices, child. Return home or prepare to die. Unless, of course, your guardian can stop me. Hm, Grimluk?” Fenton looked at his captive in disgust.

"Let her go. I'll do anything you want, just don't harm her."

Fenton regarded Grimluk warily. Gwen took the opportunity to kick him in the shin before running to Grimluk. Fenton grabbed a hold of her before she could get far though, gripping a fistful of her hair and yanking her back with a growl. Grimluk was shouting again but Gwen didn't quite hear the words until Fenton stopped moving.

"What? What did you say?"

"I'll serve your master if you keep her safe. I'll do whatever you ask."

"No! He killed his daughter for the demon! You can't!" Gwen was shouting now. A moment later, she realized her breath was coming out in icy puffs. Leigh came roaring through the back wall, having turned monstrous again. Freezing cold filled the room with her rage.

"Papa!" The ghost rushed towards the man, seemingly losing whatever anchor of humanity Gwen had revitalized, and tried to pounce on him. Vengeance would be done.

Parker Fenton squeezed Gwen's throat. "Enough! Stop her, child, or I'll snap your neck." Gwen froze and it was enough to falter the ghost of Leigh Fenton. She came to a stop, a rush of clarity hitting her as Gwen's eyes pleaded. Ghost, hunter, child, and judge all stood in silence, taking measure of the situation.

Parker Fenton broke the silence with a decree. "In light of Gwendolyn's little excursion, I suspect we need to do this tonight. I'm taking the child with me. When I return, we're going to have a little ceremony to solidify your decision to serve the master. And you, my sweet daughter, stay where you are. We will deal with you as well." He disappeared with Gwen in tow.

An hour later, Fenton returned with Sheriff Stockburn and Deputies Donal and Duncan. The judge carried a bowl with a piece of rolled up paper in it, having given guard duty of Gwen over to Stockburn, who had foisted her off on Duncan. Grimluk watched anxiously. If he could just get them to let him loose, he could grab Gwen and escape. Stockburn and his deputies had been informed of the ghost's presence but even still, she unnerved them.

"Now, Grimluk, we will seal your service in blood. I'm sure you thought I'd just welcome you to the fold but even now I can see the stubbornness in your eyes. I'm sure you thought I'd let you loose and you'd grab the girl and be free of us. No such luck. Gwendolyn wasn't lying. The ghost was my daughter and I killed her. What do you think I'd do to a child who wasn't mine?"

Grimluk growled as Fenton stepped forward and produced the bowl for him to see. He opened the paper, taking a small knife from his belt and grabbed Grimluk's hand. The knife bit into the orc's flesh with shallow slices from fingertip to palm on each finger. Fenton pressed the paper into the blood, producing a crimson handprint. The judge laid the paper into the bowl and commanded Grimluk to spit on the paper, the weight of the blood and saliva holding the paper in place. Fenton set the bowl down in front of Grimluk.

"Hunter, orc, mortal who answers to the name of Grimluk, I speak to you now in blood and oath. With your word, I bind you in service to the master of this ceremony until your final death and removal from the mortal realm. Once released from your current binds, you will forevermore belong to Cholem. Do you swear your service?"

Grimluk looked at Gwen for a long moment and then bowed his head. "I swear."

"Ia!" Fenton struck a match and dropped it into the bowl. The contents lit up in blue fire. "The oath is sworn. Cut the runes and release him, Sheriff."

Stockburn did as he was told, scratching away at the runes on Grimluk's stocks with his knife. The glow faded and popped as the magic released. Energy crackled and shifted as the blue flame erupted and engulfed Grimluk's entire body.

Chapter 8

The blue flames burst into a blinding tower, consuming Grimluk. The top board of his stocks blew away, smashing into the ceiling, bounding away into the back wall. He rose slowly, the fire swirling around him but not burning him. Cholem appeared in front of him, a grinning shadow no one else seemed to notice, and smiled.

Pain shot through Grimluk's bones as they shifted in unison, creaking underneath the flames. His vision went white as his jaw slacked, gums burning as his teeth cracked into jagged points. Joints crunched and ground, tendons stretched, muscles cramped tight as they expanded. Bony protrusions pushed out of his brow, sending a cascade of blood into his eyes. He roared in fury and pain. Unbidden and still blind, he stepped forward, knocking over the base of the stocks. He snatched the wood up only to smash it into the floor, shattering it into chunks and splinters. Stockburn and his deputies looked on in fear. Fenton looked on with smug satisfaction.

"Oh, my dear hunter. The time of your ascension has come," Cholem whispered in Grimluk's mind.

"Orc!" Fenton called.

Grimluk's head snapped towards the sound, a string of drool hanging from his lips. His vision began to clear. The blue light of the flames casting flickering shadows everywhere. He stepped forward, shaky at first as his muscles continued their fiery transformation. His fingertips itched as his nails forced from their beds in sharp points.

"Orc, I have an order for you." He motioned to Stockburn, who stepped forward with Gwen. Fenton took her by the shoulder and shoved her towards the wall of blue flame. "Kill the girl for your master."

Jed Duncan looked at the judge in utter shock. "What the fuck do you think you're doing?"

Fenton ignored him, his attention utterly fixed on Grimluk. "Master Cholem commands it! Kill her!"

Grimluk looked down on Gwen, drooling and growling. She looked up into his bloody, snarling face, frozen. Her mouth hung open and her eyes were like saucers.

"This is the moment, my dear Grimluk," Cholem whispered to him a second time, the mystical flames dissipating in a rush of hot air. "Now is your time. Protect the girl. Kill Parker Fenton and take your place as my general." The demon nearly squealed, utterly enraptured.

Grimluk looked from Gwen to the judge and back. Despite the dim light of the dungeon, he could see in perfect clarity. Gwen reached out with trembling fingers and took Grimluk's hand. Angry eyes looked down at the tiny hand holding his and softened for a moment before Fenton screamed his order again. Grimluk roared. Bloodlust coursed through his blood while violence and hatred threatened to drown him.

Jed looked at the sight and swallowed hard. Quietly, he drew his club. He bashed Deputy Donal in the back of the head, sending him crumpling to the stone floor in a heap. Stockburn turned around and received a club to the face, breaking his nose. He fell backwards, screaming. Parker Fenton turned, shocked out of his apparent victory, looking from the fallen, bloody halfling to the source of the commotion. Jed shoved him hard into the dungeon where Grimluk caught and spun him around. Fenton looked up into the eyes of what he thought was his new slave and saw he held no control whatsoever. They were the eyes of a predator.

Cholem giggled with sadistic glee.

"Grimluk!" Gwen shouted. "Don't!"

Grimluk held the man by his neck tight enough to labor Fenton's breathing. All he had to do was squeeze. Or crush. Or snap. Or bite. Or pummel him into a sticky paste. He tried to respond to Gwen, to explain that he was protecting her. That he would punish Parker Fenton for everything he'd done to them. "Kill," was the only word he could get out.

Gwen pushed on. "No. Home. Take me home. Please. You're not a killer. You could've shot Mr. Mayor but you didn't."

"Home." Grimluk thought about Hunter's Hollow. How long had it been since he'd left? The thought floated away, replaced with images of Fenton's death.

"Yes, don't be foolish. Listen to the child!" Fenton stammered.

"Kill him!" the shadow hissed in Grimluk's ear.

A rush of chill wind slammed into the shadow, catching it utterly by surprise. Leigh had been so quiet and still everyone had forgotten all about her, even Cholem. The ghost-girl chose her moment and struck, flying off in a tangle of pale light and pulsing darkness. The demon's hold loosened and Grimluk regained a measure of himself. Gwen called his name again and he focused on it like a lantern in the darkest cave. What if he killed this man and became what the demon had showed him? Worse, what if the thoughts invading his mind made him enjoy it? Would he be able to stop himself from hurting Gwen? He was no killer, no slave. With a grunt, he shoved Fenton to the side, sending the judge crashing into the wall.

Jed watched as Grimluk gently nudged Gwen out of the dungeon, following behind her. He was bigger now. Taller, wider, every bit of him turned monstrous, making him duck and twist through the dungeon door. As they passed by, Donal flopped onto his back, dazed and far away.

"Come on, you two," Jed implored.

A shot rang out as Jed neared the stairs, sending him scrambling up them. Grimluk scooped Gwen up in one massive arm as two bullets slammed into his back. He barely noticed, practically leaping up to the door. The trio burst out into the main level of the courthouse as Stockburn screamed and fired three more shots that bounced off the door and into the main room while another struck Grimluk in the shoulder.

"Bag," Grimluk half-shouted. "Need bag."

"No time," Jed implored.

"Help. Safe." It was so hard to talk.

Jed nodded and ducked into a side room, returning with Grimluk's bag. Jed led them out towards the livery. He found the biggest horse in the stable and led it out. To his surprise, the horse remained calm when it saw Grimluk.

"I don't have time to throw on a saddle or reins, you'll have to ride bareback." He watched as several of the other deputies and a few drunken stragglers wandered towards the courthouse to investigate all the commotion. "Go on. I'll try to hold them off, say you attacked us."

Grimluk sat Gwen up on the horse's back and held out his hand to Jed. "Thank you." Jed gave his hand a quick shake and implored them to leave again. Grimluk heaved himself up onto the horse, who grunted in protest but stayed steady. Jed smacked the horse's rear and they were off, galloping down the main street and out of town.

Jed Duncan breathed deep and started back for the courthouse. Stockburn came stumbling out with two other deputies, an elf woman and a human man, in tow. The sheriff's face and clothes were a bloody mess. As soon as he saw Jed, he started screaming for them to arrest him. Jed remained still for a long moment as he watched the deputies run toward him. He snarled and tackled the clearly confused elf. Jed broke his fingers on her jaw before the man clubbed him.

The road would eventually curve northeast towards Eagle Point but the town was still a day's ride. They didn't have that kind of time. Grimluk could feel the initial power from the spell and adrenaline waning. He had to act before he was too weak to keep riding. Gwen couldn't handle the task. He slowed the horse and handed Gwen his bag.

"Help." It was still hard to talk but he made a concentrated effort to make his mouth work like it should. "Meh...medallion. In bag."

Gwen nodded and started digging through the bag. Somewhere in the bottom, her fingers brushed against a piece of metal with a strange texture. She brought it out and showed it to Grimluk. "Is it this?" It looked like a larger version of a gold glut coin. Runes filled the edges while a sigil sat in the center.

Grimluk took the coin and nodded. "Knife?"

Gwen dug through the bag but returned empty-handed. His knife was still on his gun belt. Gwen gasped and pulled out the small folding knife he'd given her from her coat pocket.

"Good. Don't look." He drew the open blade against his left forearm, spilling his blood out in a thick line. Quickly, he ran the medallion through the blood, covering each side in a layer of crimson.

He had to cut a second time to finish the job, making sure to coat the whole thing. It started to glow white, faintly at first but rapidly gaining brightness. He pointed it ahead of them.

A bolt of energy lashed out from the medallion and split the air, appearing to slice the very fabric of reality. The horse protested for a moment but Grimluk gave its neck a pat and urged it forward. It did as it was bid and entered the shimmering portal.

Traveling through the portal was instantaneous. One moment, they were passing through, the next they were standing outside of a large wooden gate lit by two huge lanterns. Grimluk gave a great sigh as the portal closed behind them. His relief was short lived, however. As someone called for him to identify himself, his body seized up. Cholem was screaming in his mind, drowning out everything else. The world turned sideways as he crashed off the horse, his body a symphony of pain as the demon demanded he obey and return.

Grimluk refused with everything in him, walling off his mind in desperation.

* * *

Gwen screamed Grimluk's name as he fell. She looked down to see if she could slide off the horse without hurting herself and slipped down with a grunt. She knelt next to him but a commotion from behind the gate pulled her attention away. Gwen ran toward it and before she could do anything, it opened up.

"You have to help him!" she shouted all at once, not knowing who or what was coming.

Out stepped a thin orc, even taller than Grimluk usually was. Gwen gasped and watched as they led four other orcs to Grimluk. Quickly, but gently, they lifted and carried him inside, dripping a trail of blood along the way. Gwen started to follow them but the first orc stopped her and bent down to her, strands of dark hair swishing across their forehead. Lamplight glinted off of amber eyes. The orc reached out, arms bare, and took Gwen's shoulder gently.

"What's your name, kid?"

The voice was higher than she expected, almost like her mother's but gruff like Grimluk's. "Gwen. Is Grimluk gonna be okay, Mister?"

"I hope so," they said. "And I'm not a mister. Or a miss. Why are you with him?"

"He adopted me after my parents died. He's my new brother."

Surprise danced on the orc's half-shadowed face but so did a measure of amusement. "I see. Then I guess I should welcome you to the family, Gwen. I'm Bakhor. Grimluk is my son. Let's go in." Bakhor stood and led Gwen inside.

It was dark but the area was lit with a slew of lanterns and tall torches. The gate reminded her of home, standing taller than Greenreach Bluffs's but similarly designed for comfortable defense. As she looked around, she found both the familiar and unfamiliar. The immediate area was mostly empty yard. Beyond was a big building that looked like the apartment buildings from home. Lanterns shimmered far behind it but that was all she could make out. She could see the shadow of one building hugging the wall off to her right with another ahead of them.

Bakhor led her to the building, where the other four orcs had taken Grimluk. They'd laid him in a heavy cot, on his stomach, and were heading back out as Gwen and Bakhor entered. A black-haired, pale-skinned elf was on the cot's opposite side, hastily covering Grimluk's back in a thick green substance, spreading it out and packing it into the myriad lash-wounds that had reopened.

"What the fuck happened?" The elf was calm despite the urgency. "Only time I ever had to work so hard on the boy was when he took on that werewolf bloke. What happened?"

"Don't have a damn clue," Bakhor said very plainly. "He came in using his medallion, on a horse no less. Must have been bad whatever it was. You know he doesn't ride willingly."

"I can tell you what happened," Gwen said, stepping forward hesitantly.

"Out with it then," the healer urged, staring at her with eyes the color of deep ice. His voice was whiskey-rough but still soothing.

Gwen started at the beginning but Bakhor stopped her. "What happened immediately, Gwen? Why the emergency?"

"Oh," Gwen said and then rushed through what had happened that evening.

Bakhor had appeared nonchalant about the sight of hir son bleeding everywhere but a visible snarl spread across hir face at the mention of the spell. Ze walked over and bent down next to Grimluk's ear. “I'm proud of you, kid. Pull out of this or I'll kick your ass.”

“I'll get him patched up,” the elf responded, still spreading bandages and salve across Grimluk's back. “He's lost a lot of blood but thankfully he’s a stubborn sod. I'll let you know when he's stable.”

Bakhor nodded and led Gwen back outside. “He'll be fine. Mint’s a fine alchemist and healer, quite experienced. Four hundred years of knowledge in that head. Do you know about alchemists?”

“We had a magician at home who made potions.”

“Just like that. Why don't I take you in and introduce you to my partner and get something to eat?”

“I know it's late, but are there cookies?” Gwen asked.

Bakhor snorted. “If there aren't, Urgroz will use you as an excuse to make some. Come on.”

* * *

Grimluk was vaguely aware of his mother's words but they were merely echoes in the blank eternity he found himself walking. He was also dimly aware of a pain that filled every inch of him but it too was far away. He concentrated, trying to remember what was going on. His memories began to fill the void. Parker Fenton's spell. Jed Duncan's assistance. The horse. The portal. He'd fallen as the nightwatch had called out.

"Gods-damn it, I'm lying in the grass bleeding out." He growled in frustration.

"Not quite, dear Grimluk."

Grimluk grunted. "Won't even let me die in piece, demon?"

A faded shadow appeared in front of him, towering and immense. "Never. Though I am very disappointed in your cowardice at the...what do you call it? The courthouse. You felt everything you could have done. I saw it all pass through your mind before that girl and that weakling's daughter interfered."

"I made my choice. Either let me die in peace or free me so I can recover and come find you."

"You are not dying, I can assure you of that. I am not entirely sure where you are but I can still feel you and I can still speak to you. You are *still mine*. You will endure your wounds, however. They are punishment for disobeying me. Until you keep your oath and agree to come back to me, we are going to spend a lot of time together."

Cholem snapped its shadowy fingers. A flurry of chains shot out from all directions and Grimluk found himself suspended with his limbs stretched taut, unable to move.

"The first thing you need to learn is that disobedience has consequences. I wonder if all orcs are so stubborn or if you are unique to your kind. Questions for later, I suppose. Let us *dig* in, shall we?" Cholem's great yellow eyes seemed to gain strength as it moved nearer. "Your will is formidable indeed but your struggles are pure vanity. You swore an oath."

Grimluk shook as the demon struck him and tried desperately to will his attacker away. His physical body tensed from head to toe. One final twitch and he went still again. He tried to fight, tried to kick, bite, punch, headbutt, run, even argue his way away from the demon's growing influence. He was too tired, too weak from his wounds and the stress of his transformation and his mental defenses started crumbling. A booming growl filled the landscape of his mind, shaking everything. Grimluk knew then, without one single doubt, that he was trapped inside his own mind just as the demon had promised.

* * *

Gwen followed Bakhor into the apartment building, uneasy in the silence but not knowing if it was aimed at her or if the big orc was just quiet. Bakhor opened the door and let Gwen enter first, following with a bent head under the door frame. The main room was mostly dim save for a few lamps speckling the darkness.

"Urgroz, my sweet, are you awake?" Bakhor's tone was suddenly saccharine. A scoff came in reply. Bakhor continued farther in, moving between various pieces of furniture with apparent ease. Another orc met them.

"'My sweet,' you say. What on Arkod has happened now?" He motioned for a kiss with a sausage-like finger and Bakhor leaned over to oblige. Urgroz was fairly shorter than hir, shorter than Grimluk by a few inches as well, with a big belly and thick limbs. The sight of the kiss made Gwen laugh to herself and she thought he looked a little like Wesson, the old blacksmith from back home.

"A great deal, it seems but the most imperative is that our son is currently laid out in Mint's tent, unconscious, bleeding, and apparently gone monster from a gods-damned blood oath spell."

"Grim? Shit." Urgroz looked towards the door, contemplating heading outside to check on Grimluk.

"And he came into town on a horse with this one." Ze motioned for Gwen. "That would be the next bit of news. Say hello to Gwen. Our new daughter." Bakhor smiled to hirself as Urgroz's jaw dropped.

"A horse? A daughter? Fuck." The conflicting information seemed to whirl in his mind for a moment. "You said you were never having any more after Grim...and she appears to be human."

"Adopted, my dearest. It seems our son took her in recently. Given that he was bleeding all over the ground, I didn't have time to question either of them about it but now we have time. Though it is late, and I'm sure Gwen is tired."

"I'm okay, miss...mister...um, Bakhor. But..."

"Yes?"

"Will Mist-oh, um, are you a mister, Urgroz?" She thought it best to ask after her confusion with Bakhor.

"I am."

"Okay, well, Bakhor said that if I asked, you would make cookies if we didn't have any. And I would really like a cookie, please. If that's okay. Sir."

"Did ze now?" He looked at Bakhor with a grin. "My love, are you trying to make me fat?"

Bakhor let out a sharp laugh at that and kissed the top of Urgroz's head.

"Well," Urgroz said, running a hand through a loose mess of long, dark hair, "I'd say cookies are in order then, kiddo. Sounds like you've had a rough time. It just so happens I made a batch earlier this evening, so why don't you two have a seat and you can tell us your tale."

Bakhor took Gwen back into the center of the room and lit a few more lamps, turning their wicks up for full light. Ze motioned to a leather couch that looked positively massive. She climbed up in it, marveling how tiny she felt, and watched as Bakhor sat down across from her in a large leather chair that had clearly been made for orcs as well. With both arms lying flat out, she saw clearly the stump of Bakhor's left forearm. She tried not to stare.

Urgroz joined them, sitting on the other side of the couch. A plate of cookies went down between them. Gwen's mouth fell agape at their size. Her mother had only ever made tiny cookies, and rarely at that. Treats were hard to justify out in the Wastes. These were as big as her face. She looked up at Urgroz as if to say, "Are you sure?" He nodded. Gwen took a giant cookie in both hands and held it up. It was soft. She took a bite and nearly started giggling at how good it tasted. The giggles choked off when she noticed the glowing eyes watching her from a still-dark corner of the room. She froze.

The eyes came towards her and as the light touched the creature, it revealed long, overhanging teeth and wide nostrils in a black nose that led up to sharp, wolfish eyes and thinly furred ears on what looked like a bare skull. All of this stood on the stout, dark-furred body of a colossal wolf. The eyes held intelligence. The creature licked its chops as it moved towards Gwen, huge and curious and frightening. It sniffed at her and opened its mouth as if to take a bite.

"Fang," Urgroz said sternly, "you know you're not allowed to have cookies, ya damn idjit. They give ya the shits and they're bad for your heart."

The creature looked at Urgroz and half-growled, half-whimpered at him.

"I know you *like* cookies but they're *bad* for you. You remember what happened last time you got one?"

It huffed and yipped a few times.

"Well if you'd let her eat the damn cookie and lie down, she'd tell us what happened to Grim." He looked over at Gwen. "Wargs. Big babies the lot of them. She's harmless. Mostly."

Fang gave a halfhearted growl as she wandered over to Bakhor, laying her head in the orc's lap with a sigh.

"He's right, you know," Bakhor said, giving Fang's ear a little rub. "We'd make you clean it up but you don't have hands. So, Gwen, I stopped you before but now you're very much free and welcome to tell your story in full."

Gwen gave a slight start at her name and

looked down at the cookie and back to the warg before blinking several times and remembering where she was. She leaned back, pulling her feet up, crossing them, and took a deep breath. She started slowly.

"My name is Gwen Quinn. I was born in Greenreach Bluffs, in the Wastelands. My parents..." She faltered and took another bite of her cookie for strength. The story came spilling out once again, just like it had for the judge. Every detail wrung her heart out but unlike before, each time she felt the tears start to well up, she took a bite of the cookie and it eased her nerves. This giant piece of baked dough and chocolate chips and sugar and butter gave her some measure of comfort that had eluded her for so long now. It was a shield. A *delicious* shield, but a shield all the same. When she finished the story, she finished the cookie as well and let out a long, deep sigh that made her sound decades older than she was.

Urgroz blinked slowly, seemingly working through everything he'd heard. Bakhor continued to sit quietly, petting Fang's head. The warg had turned during the story and sat in attention. They all sat quietly, the light from the lamps dancing across their faces. Fang whimpered and walked over to Gwen, towering over the child. Very slowly and gently, she lowered her head onto Gwen's lap and gave a little high-pitched whine.

"Kiddo...how are you not just crying in the floor all the time? You've told us everything that's happened but not how you've felt or how you've dealt with it. Fuck. How old are you?"

"Seven," she replied meekly.

"By the gods and all our ancestors. And the thing in your head, is it being decent? Can we do anything for you? More food? A bed?"

Gwen ran a hand across Fang's head. Her head was definitely a skull but it was fuzzy and strangely soft. She stared off into space, thinking. "The Spirit is quiet. It's pleased we made it here. And, um, Grimluk...let me sit in his lap sometimes and rocked me. Could—"

"Of course, kiddo! Come here. Please." He moved the cookies to allow her to crawl over.

Gwen laid her head on Urgroz's shoulder, smiling at how much like Grimluk he felt. She wrapped her arms around his neck and suddenly found her eyes heavier than they'd ever been before. Slowly, her eyelids sunk and moments later, she was breathing steadily and lost to sleep.

"So," Bakhor said after a length of silence.

"So," Urgroz replied. "Looks like we have a new kid."

"Looks like."

The pair took Gwen up to their room and put her in bed before slipping out quietly for coffee and a further discussion on the night's events. Bakhor wanted to figure out what was wrong with hir son as soon as possible. Urgroz agreed with a simple nod of his head.

Chapter 9

The smell of bacon tugged Gwen awake. Sleep clung to her, beckoning her back into the safety of dreams but the bacon was too tantalizing. Once she sat up, she realized she wasn't where she thought she was. She dressed and drifted out into a long hallway, growing more alert as she took in the surroundings. She walked the hall until she found a wide staircase. She was surprised at how quiet everything was but she wasn't sure of the time so wondered if maybe everyone was just out working. The stairs led her back down into the main room where she followed her nose to the kitchen where Urgroz was whistling a strange tune through his teeth.

"Ah, mornin', kiddo," he said when he caught sight of her. "Just in time for a bit of late breakfast. You a toad-in-a-hole sort of girl, hm? Maybe a tadpole-in-a-hole, eh?" Urgroz gave a laugh at himself.

"What's a toad-in-a-hole?" Gwen asked, wrinkling her nose.

"Well, I take a loaf and scoop it out and then

put some sausage and a pudding batter...no?" Urgroz grinned at the face she made, not quite disgusted but confused and uninterested. "Well here, how 'bout some bacon and an egg-in-a-basket."

"Is that like an eggy-bucket?"

"Fried egg in holed-out toast?"

"Yeah! Momma made us those sometimes when the chickies had lots of eggs." For the first time in a long while, the sadness at mentioning her mother didn't hit her right away. It crept in, and then she was distant, vaguely aware Urgroz was speaking but the words were an indistinct jumble. She jumped when he very gently laid one meaty hand on her shoulder. He was holding a fork and plate with her food on it.

"Recallin' your momma?" he asked quietly, pointing her towards one of the dining tables. She nodded. He pulled a chair out for her and set the plate down, scooting her up after she climbed into it. "You wanna talk about her?"

Gwen took a slow bite of her meal and thought about it. She finally shook her head, instead asking how Grimluk was doing through a mouthful of bacon.

"Bakhor came in this morning and one of Mint's apprentices was tending to him. Said he wasn't bleeding so much now but he was still unconscious. He's tough, kiddo. He'll pull through."

Gwen nodded and dug into her egg. There was more butter than she was use to but she didn't mind. It seemed to help keep her anchored to her body, like the cookie had. She couldn't float off.

"So, Bakhor and I were talking," Urgroz started tentatively, "and we want to throw a little shindig in your honor once Grim recovers. Something to introduce you to the Hollow locals, like Mint and Kort and Archel. Tell everyone that you're part of the family now. If you're okay with that. You've been through a lot this summer and we don't want to scare ya none."

Gwen thought about this while she chewed, rolling it all around in her mind. "Mr. Urgroz, can you make custard?"

"Best in fifteen leagues, if I do say so myself." He gave her an exaggerated wink and grinned. His tusks were wider than Grimluk's. "Reckon I can make any flavor you could want."

A big smile lit her face up. "Really?"

"Really really, kiddo. You leave it to me. I'll make you a feast that Governor Feely would be jealous of."

"What's a governor?" she replied after a moment of thought.

"It's like a mayor but for a whole province. There's still kings back in the old world though. But you'll get to those lessons eventually. Point is, New Gilead's governor likes his feasts."

Gwen's mouth scrunched in thought. "Are all mayors secretly bad people?"

"No, not all leaders are bad people. There are others who aren't so secret about it either but the sheriff of Eagle Point is a good woman. She basically serves as a mayor and she's proven herself a friend to hunters on more than one occasion. I'm sure there are others as well."

Gwen nodded and set about finishing her breakfast, asking if they could go see Grimluk after. Urgroz was more than happy to oblige and called for one of his helpers, a young orc girl with shining, gray eyes, chestnut hair in a topknot, and lopsided tusks, to watch the kitchen while he was gone. Gwen couldn't help but notice the girl's wooden leg. The dark grain was a stark contrast to the green flesh and someone had carved pretty designs into it for decoration. The girl smiled at Gwen before Urgroz led her out, holding the big door open for her.

Clouds were rolling in, not quite dark but heavy with the gray of potential rain. In the daylight, Gwen could see the other building behind Mint's clinic better. This was a town very much like hers. Smallish and built to be a home and a fortification in one, utilitarian form, like if Greenreach Bluffs had been built around the Watch instead of the mine. The sound of work and conversation filled the air. A hammer rang out against an anvil from somewhere she couldn't see, accompanied by raucous laughs. Back home, the only orcs she'd ever seen were Trilgor and Grimluk, and she knew Trilgor had only been half-orc. Hunter's Hollow was positively brimming with them. Various shades of green skin and tusks of all kinds of shapes and sizes filled her vision. Everyone was so big. She smiled. A strange blanket of calm covered her with the realization of just how safe she was here. If Grimluk was so strong, how much stronger would a whole town of people like him be?

As they approached Mint's door, Gwen saw a

strange symbol painted on it. It looked sort of like several triangles overlapping inside a circle with a leaf in the center. The little building stretched out beyond the door, filled with rows of sturdy cots built to hold heavy orcs. Mint was currently lounging in a wicker chair near Grimluk, eyes closed and arms folded across his stomach. In daylight, she could see the elf's mutton-chop facial hair and the twin warts on his cheek.

"Still not awake," Mint said without opening his eyes.

"I know. Bakhor told me but Gwen wanted to see him." Urgroz gently urged her towards Grimluk's cot.

"Just keep your wits, eh. Hop back quick if I need to get to him."

Grimluk was on his back now, which was presumably covered in bandages and salve. Gwen could see him breathing slowly, in and out, like he was merely sleeping, still looking like some sort of monster. She approached slowly, reaching out to touch his bare arm tentatively, thinking for a moment that he would open his eyes and ask how she was. Instead, he tensed for a moment, every muscle in his body squeezing, and then he was breathing slowly once more. She swallowed and laid her head on his shoulder, wrapping her arms around his arm in an awkward hug.

"Come back, Grimluk."

He twitched again, making Gwen jump but she just squeezed tighter. Mint grunted but made no sign of movement. Urgroz looked on, worry covering his face. Gwen held onto Grimluk silently for a time before kissing his shoulder and returning to Urgroz's side. Absently, she took his hand before looking up at her newly adopted father in contemplation.

"You okay, kiddo?" She shook her head. "How would you like to see the warg house? Fang's sister had a few pups in late spring."

"Pup?"

"Yeah, a baby. No dogs back home?"

"No, just cows and some goats and a few horsies. But the horsies were grown-up." She thought for a moment. "I saw a baby goat one time. Daddy said they're called kids but that's silly cause people call me a kid. I'm not a goat."

Urgroz smiled. "Got goats, too. A lot of goats that roam on the other side of the Hollow with the wargs. How 'bout it?"

Gwen wondered if maybe Grimluk would wake up while they were gone. She nodded and followed Urgroz.

* * *

Low branches scraped at his face as he ran. Crashes and shrill, trilling roars followed, spurring Grimluk on. Young hands fumbled the hammer back on his apprentice gun, pulled at the lever and pin that held the cylinder in place. He moved as quickly as he could but his hands shook and the old percussion revolver's parts liked to stick. He got the cylinders swapped and locked into place, allowing him to point his weapon at the creature chasing him. The gun barked just before a volley of razor-sharp spines dotted a tree next to him, the shot fouling the beast's aim. He broke right into a clearing and stumbled as his right foot found a hidden dip in the grass. The young hunter fell hard, an audible pop sounding from his ankle.

The unseen thing roared again, full of malice and fresh anger after being shot, and rushed into the clearing, leaping over Grimluk's prone body. Long, slender limbs, six in all, stretched from a slick, bulbous carapace. Rows of thin spines shifted across the demon's back, rippling in dizzying waves as pincer hands stretched from the creature's mouth, snapping in anticipation of its meal. Black eyes dotted the thing's head.

"Be still, dear kin." Cholem's voice echoed through the clearing, stopping the demon in its tracks. It looked around, chittering in protest. "I know, young one. The orc has been aggressive but you must forgive him. He knows not what he does."

Grimluk looked on in silent horror as the great, bloody, yellow-eyed bull manifested behind the spiny demon. His memory was wrong again but this time, all he could do was watch it unfold. Cholem was determined to taint his memories and continue infecting his very being.

The spiny demon chittered.

"Yes, he wounded you but are you not healed already? This young orc will serve me and thus you. This one measure of mercy will assure you and your offspring feasts for millennia."

More indecipherable chittering.

"I swear to you, my kin, he will be no threat."

The pincer hands retracted back into its mouth with a wet snap before it wandered away.

"I will never serve you!" Grimluk shouted, finding his voice. The gun barked again, shots staggering the spiny demon. Cholem merely sighed.

"Very well, Grimluk. I thought maybe I could show you a new way but it seems I need to let my sibling have a small measure of vengeance as punishment. Especially considering you have already killed them. Khryxnlx..."

Pincer hands erupted once more as it stalked towards Grimluk, spines erect and shivering, almost rattling in warning. He tried to back away from it, scrambled to his feet, ignoring his swollen ankle, tried to run, but the thing hissed and filled Grimluk's back with a row of spines. He felt the poison rip through his body, a red-hot rush of pain that tackled him into numbness. He collapsed like a felled tree, landing with a dull *thump* on his side. Khryxnlx reached out, mandibles clacking hungrily, and grabbed hold of his foot delicately with one pincer. The other pincer snapped around his swollen ankle, removing his foot cleanly, the only sound the quick crunch of bone.

Grimluk watched as the thing slowly devoured his foot, peeling the thick boot away from it like it was an apple skin. A faint voice filled his mind, telling him to come back but it passed, overtaken by the sickening sounds of the chittering thing feasting on his flesh.

* * *

In the waking world, Grimluk's body spasmed and a thin ring of blood appeared on his ankle, sparking Minthralvatra's interest. There had been no wound on the man's ankle prior and the continued spasms were worrying. It was beginning to become clear that the situation was worse than he'd realized. Mint dabbed the blood away, checking for a wound beneath. There was none. He grunted in thought as he wiped away the rest of the blood but more welled up moments later.

The healer wrapped both hands around the blood-ring and focused, gathering himself, aiming magical energies into Grimluk's ankle, not to heal but to give a thorough inspection. The wound was clearly supernatural in nature and would require the supernatural to mend but to do that, he had to figure out the cause.

The world fell away, leaving only Mint and Grimluk. Mint's ears, acute and sensitive in ways only elven ears were, went dull and quiet. A heartbeat, pounding rapidly, filled the silence. Slow breathing rolled over the heart, strangely calm in comparison. The wound-free blood felt exceedingly sticky and hot against his palms. Silent screams pulsed from the orc's muscles as another spasm rocked him. Mint noted that the previous wounds were weeping again. He might need to cauterize them.

Something flashed in Mint's mind, sickly and yellow. He felt it from Grimluk's mind and refocused his gaze there. He gasped as a startled yell overtook the sound of the heartbeat and breathing. A strange voice spoke.

“Who are...aaaaah. You are the one he knows as 'Mint.' Elf...healer...what are you doing in here? You are interrupting my work.”

“Demon,” he said matter-of-factly. “You infest the boy?”

“Hardly. We are growing closer, Grimluk and I. And you. Are. Interrupting.” Cholem's growl filled every fiber of Mint's being.

“Closer it says,” Mint replied with a hint of a laugh. “I says turn loose of this one ‘fore ya piss him off.”

“Leave us,” Cholem said. “You bore me.”

Before Mint could respond, his focus was shattered and his body was hurled away. He landed, conveniently, in his wicker chair, aching all over, head throbbing so hard he wondered if it would split open. Instead, a sudden rush of nausea ripped through him, doubling him over where he retched violently, ridding himself of his breakfast. He sat back, panting, one of his apprentices running over to check on him.

“Teacher!” the young orc boy cried. “What happened?”

Once the world quit spinning and Mint caught his breath, he answered. “Our boy Grimluk here is deep in the grips of that demon he was runnin’ from last night.” A shudder ran through Mint as he continued. “That's why he won't wake and that's why his wounds won’t stay closed. Seems pretty set on holdin’ on to him. The Oath means slavery or death.”

“What do we do?”

Mint swallowed hard, staring at Grimluk all

the while. “My boy, I don't have a fucking clue. But I'll set it right. We'll continue on but I reckon I need to have a little chat with the girl, Gwen wasn’t it? There's something off about her but last night wasn’t the time to deal with it. Be a good lad and fetch me some water and then find Urgroz. He was taking her to see warg pups."

The young orc nodded and set to his tasks. Mint rubbed his face, scratching his warts idly, and sighed. His guts still churned, threatening to attempt further revolt. He closed his eyes and began humming low and soft, preparing himself for meditation. His apprentice returned with a pitcher and ladle, setting the bucket down at his master's feet.

"Anything else, teacher?"

"No, Kane, thank ya kindly." Mint drank several fills of the water, slowly, letting it cool his stomach and refresh him enough to settle into a brief trance and determine what the best course might be. Thunder rumbled in the distance followed by a low gust of wind. The rain was coming. Kane returned a short while later with Urgroz and Gwen in tow.

"Urgroz, my friend,” Mint started from his seat, “I have some good news and some bad news. Which would ya like first?”

Urgroz eyed the gruff elf. “Uh, the bad news?”

“Well, it seems your boy is worse off than I originally suspected. That spell is a real ass-kicker. Won’t wake up, can’t wake up, actually. He's not healing properly, and he started bleedin’ from a wound he doesn't have. The demon he encountered in Perfection is the one doin' it all, or at least pushin' it all."

Urgroz stared at Mint with a mix of confusion and understanding. "Makes sense, I guess. From what Gwen told us." He looked over at Grimluk, a wave of worry for his son washing over his face. "Considering you're so relaxed about all this, the good news better be, 'But don't worry, Urgroz, I know how to fix him,' or I might slug you."

"Well, not as such..." Mint said, nonchalance remaining quite intact. "The good news is I'm feeling much better after the demon ejected me from the boy's mind." He offered a playful grin.

"Nope, I'm gonna let Bakhor hit you."

"Fair nuff. I know that's not great but I was hoping maybe this one here might consent to an examination and a few questions. She did come in with him and I've felt something off about her anyways. Maybe looking her over could help me help him. Just don't tell Bakhor yet. You know how hard ze can hit."

Urgroz sighed and ran a hand down his face. "Talk to Gwen, Mint, I'm not the one you're wanting to look at."

"Ah, right you are." The healer gave her a crooked smile, friendly and calm as still water. "Gwen, may I have a look at ya?"

"What are you going to do?" she asked, seemingly curious and unsure.

"Nothing invasive. I just want to give you a look over and find out more about what you went through in Perfection and if you've experienced anythin' strange."

"You mean like the ghost?" Gwen asked.

"Exactly. Ghosts or demons or anything else supernatural. We can start with the questions. I need a few minutes still to recover after inspecting Grimluk. Lookin' over someone magically and being kicked out by the thing working that magic tends to wear a person out, ya see."

"All right. Um...I guess I should tell you, um..."

"Yes?"

"There's a Spirit inside me."

"I see. That would be what feels off about you. Did the demon do this to you?"

"No, well, I'm not sure. Not the one in Perfection but the one from back home...I think..." Gwen frowned and hugged herself.

Urgroz put a hand on her shoulder and gave a little squeeze before speaking up for her. "It's like this, Mint," he said, sharing Gwen's story and sparing her from having to recount it once more.

Mint gave a long whistle by the time Urgroz had finished and he looked at Gwen with sincere sympathy. "Bless ya, child. Real sorry about all that. I...hate to ask but it might be important if I can speak to this Spirit."

"It's been really quiet lately. I can still feel it but I think it's hiding."

"That's partially to do with the wards protecting Hunter's Hollow. They severely limit or outright hinder any powerful entities like this Spirit of yours. Even put demon traps under all the cots, just in case. Probably the only reason

Grimluk hasn't tried to walk out of here. Long as you're here, you have complete control of it."

Gwen stared at Mint in disbelief long enough he started to grow a little uneasy.

"Gwen?" the healer probed.

"I have control?" she finally replied

"That's right."

She turned giddy and started giggling, twirling happily all the while. The giggles stopped suddenly though, her face scrunching up. "No!" Gwen shouted.

"No?" Urgroz asked. "No what?"

Gwen continued on. "Like you helped Momma and Daddy? Like you helped Grimluk? Like you helped me?"

Mint knelt down to her. "Are you talking to it?"

"It says it can help Grimluk," she replied, bristling with anger. "It lies. It always lies. It won't help. It just says bad things." Tears welled in her eyes. "Shut up! Just shut up! Shut up, shut up, shut up! I'm in charge here! Me!"

"Gwen, remember I said I could inspect you magically?" Mint said, bringing her attention back to him.

"Like you did with Grimluk before the demon kicked you out."

"That's right. I think I may be ready to do so again, for you now, if you'll let me. I'd quite like to speak with this Spirit. I need your permission though. I'd like to see what it knows and where it came from. What ya say, hm?"

Gwen looked up at Urgroz, who nodded his

approval. "All right...but I'm in control, right?"

"Yes, completely, my dear. I just ask that you let me speak and evaluate the Spirit's words, even if it makes you uncomfortable. But if you truly can't stand it, just say so and I will step away."

"I'm sorry if it says bad things to you. Don't listen."

"I'll remember that, thank you. If you're ready, just sit down here with me and try to relax." Mint dropped cross-legged to his butt. Gwen followed his example and let him take her hands. As before, he brought all his focus onto her, falling into her heartbeat, her breathing, looking her over for any bruises, cuts, or other physical trauma. Satisfied with her health, he delved towards her mind, shuddering for a moment as he did. A strange feeling swept through him, bringing with it the kernel of an idea. He could test the idea further after he got some answers. With a deep breath, Mint pushed into Gwen's mind.

CHAPTER 10

A door appeared before him, opening as he approached. Inside was a large room with a kitchen, a big iron stove, and four wooden chairs. Gwen appeared next to him.

"This was my home," she said quietly. A strange shape resembling a person flickered in and out of focus in one of the chairs. Gwen's ire suddenly exploded. "Get out of that! You, you—" The words faltered. "That is Momma's chair and if you don't get out of that, I will lock you under Brother's bed."

The Spirit moved away from the chair. *You put me here, child. This is your mind.*

Mint stepped forward. "Hello, Spirit."

Greetings, Minthralvatra. I understand the child *has granted you permission to speak with me.*

"That's right. Reckoned we could palaver, maybe figure out what you really are, hear what you had to say about helping Grimluk. I'd also mind your words. Gwen's the one in control of all this and if she says we stop, we stop. Understand?"

The Spirit seemed to bristle for a moment, shimmering in dark colors. *I do.*

"All right then. I suppose the polite thing to do is ask your name, if you have one. Do you?"

I…do not remember. I think I did, once, long ago.

"Spirit it is then. I got my suspicion as to why you seem to have taken up with Gwen but it's only a guess without knowin' what exactly you are."

Gwen watched the Spirit, a look of curiosity on her face in spite of what she'd voiced up to then.

I do not know, entirely. I am only spirit and the future shows itself to me. I do not prophesy, as some have said. Prophecies tend to be vague and self-fulfilling. There have been more prophecies about the end of this world than not.

"Ain't that always a kick. I heard a few in my lifetime, and seen them pass by unheeded." Mint thought for a moment. "So you are a spirit of premonition then?"

That might be the most accurate term one could conceive, I suppose. As I told Parker Fenton, I see possibilities.

Gwen listened, crawling up into the memory of her mother's chair. She hugged her knees to her chest.

Mint paced in thought. "And you say you can help Grimluk? How? I've never heard of a way to break an Oath spell. Especially ones made with blood."

The Spirit paced as well, its form shimmering once again, slowly this time, a sight at once immensely unusual but beautiful in its own way.

His oath cannot be broken. At least, not in the way you might conceive of. Cholem's influence is what binds him yet.

"Mm, I'd seen as much when I gave him a look."

Every command he disobeys wounds him despite the spell being cast in a blatantly coercive way. Grimluk gave himself to it and magic can be quite rigid at times, as I am sure you know, Healer.

"I do. But you know a way, don't you."

The Spirit's color slowly drained to darkness as it stopped in front of Mint. *I do. And it is old magic. Very old. Few remain who know of it and fewer still would think to use it but…*

"But it's the only way, ain't it?" Mint finished warily. The Spirit nodded. "Let's hear it then."

The ritual would allow him to free himself from the Oath and Cholem. There is a price though. Several. The first price is that he must be the one to free himself.

"And how's he supposed to do that when we can't even speak to him?" Mint crossed his arms.

The opportunity will present itself to him. We must hope he recognizes it and seizes it. It will be hard though. The penultimate price comes in the form of time. The ritual must be performed during the Witching Hour and must succeed before dawn.

"And the final price?"

He will be a shining beacon to all things immortal and spiritual. Spirits of all kinds will be drawn to him from all over. Maybe even some lesser demons. They will manifest and try to claim him for themselves. He will need substantial protection or his very essence will be utterly obliterated, his body free to be used for ill. It will leave all involved drained of their vitality, both physical and mystical.

Mint considered the information carefully, his mind bubbling with doubt and worry. He sighed and took up pacing again. Gwen watched in silence, her anger and curiosity having subsided, melting into visible concern and fear for Grimluk.

"And this is rightly the only way?"

It is the only way I know of. And it is the only option I can see that holds the possibility of Grimluk's survival. And… The Spirit hesitated.

"And?"

It is dangerous to reveal so much of what may come, Minthralvatra. Very dangerous but if Grimluk does not recover and live to face down Parker Fenton, that man has a very real chance of overrunning this New Gilead of yours. I have no doubt that there are many demon hunters as capable as he is, and even more so perhaps, but his presence will represent a great distraction for master and servant.

Mint paused and scratched his warts in thought, looking first at Gwen and then the Spirit. He smiled, ear to pointed ear. "Love the plan. I'm keen to be a part of it. I do have one more question, Spirit. Just one."

Yes, Minthralvatra?

"Is Gwen a spirit caller?"

The Spirit shimmered rapidly and turned to look at Gwen. It wandered near her, looking her over closer, too close. It made Gwen squirm in the chair.

"Stop!"

The Spirit faced Mint once more. *Healer, I*

believe you are correct. I do not know how I missed it all this time but it certainly explains a lot about her. About our bond.

Mint nodded slowly. "Then there's hope for this ritual yet. Thank you. And try to work things out with Gwen here, eh? For now, at least."

With that, Mint and Gwen were looking at each other in the flesh once more. Mint let out a long sigh while Gwen laid back in the floor. Urgroz stared down at her.

* * *

Bakhor took the news poorly at first, threatening to pay Mint a visit to hasten his mind towards the task of healing Grimluk. After Urgroz finished explaining though, with Gwen filling in her part of the story, however grudgingly towards the Spirit, ze calmed down. Ze paced the room for a time, adopted daughter and partner watching in silence, each chewing silently on leftover cookies.

"Gwen," Bakhor began, falling neatly into hir big chair, "I'm grateful you allowed Mint to speak to the Spirit. I hope you'll allow us to make use of it further. This ritual sounds like a big pain in our asses but if it's the only way…"

Gwen watched Bakhor lean forward on the stump of hir arm, gesturing with the other as ze spoke. For the moment, she preferred to avoid the topic of the Spirit. "How did you lose your arm?" The question tumbled out of her mouth. She felt ashamed at asking so bluntly but preferred the shame over acknowledging the Spirit any more today.

Bakhor stared at her, the shadow of perplexity on hir face. Ze looked at Urgroz, who replied in a soft shrug that said to let it go for now and tell the story. Bakhor sighed and nodded.

"I lost it on my last official hunt." Ze held the stump up, looking at the faint scar where Mint had patched the wound up all those years ago. "I relished the hunt, you know. I was good. Damn good. And while my son prefers his revolver, I used my body. As an apprentice, I trained under an elf from gods-know-where. He was so small but he could stop me with ease. To this day, I've never seen anyone else fight like him. The irony is he offered to teach anyone who wanted to learn. I was the only one.

"Anyways, I was," ze sighed, "pregnant with Grimluk, and while I love the boy with everything in me, that is an experience I wasn't keen on to begin with, much less after. So I took this job up in the northeast corner of New Gilead, near the mountains. Didn't think much of it, rumors of lesser demons mostly. Most rumors are just summons gone wrong or some poor creature suffering possession."

Bakhor paused, looking at Fang as she wandered closer to hear the story. "Most animals can't survive an exorcism. Wargs are one of the few. I've seen some old bears that could take it but most can't. Most of the time, we just end it for them. So I figure that's all this is. Just a dog or a cow or maybe even a fat imp. It wasn't. Not entirely. There were two dogs that had been possessed but the real problem, the one the town hadn't seen, was a full blown death hound. I know you don't know what the means right now, and you'll learn, but to keep it simple, they're huge and black and they have one nasty bite. I was caught off guard.

"See, death hounds don't just bite. If they're strong enough, they get inside what they bite, like an infection. I finished the dogs off quick. They hadn't been changed long, didn't have much power. Then the death hound comes at me, eyes burning, all teeth and muscle and malice. It plows into me, knocks me into a tree hard enough I see triple. It comes in close and I take a swing. Dumb move. Dumb. Should've kicked or gotten my hatchet. This one was strong. It got my hand. Just a quick nip but that's all it takes. I felt my hand go bad."

Bakhor sighed heavily, running hir hand over the soft flesh of the stump. "I did the only thing I could do to save myself and the little thing growing inside me. I got my hatchet and—" ze made a chopping sound. "That, my dear, is how I lost my arm."

Gwen's mouth fell open. She was sorry she'd asked.

* * *

Jed Duncan awoke in the corner of a cell, groggy and shackled, with what could only be described as one shit-kicker of a headache that elicited a dull groan. The world tilted to the side for just a moment before settling back in its rightful position. He had no idea how long he'd been out. The memories came back slowly. Grimluk being forced to make the oath, told to kill Gwen, his part in helping them escape. He couldn't have been in here long then, unless they'd given him something after he'd blacked out. Maybe they had. Or maybe he'd just fallen asleep after. He raked his face. "Least I'm square," he muttered.

"Deputy Duncan," Fenton said with an audible sneer and his own grunt of pain.

It made Jed jump in surprise. He looked up at the man.

"Before I hang you for insubordination, attacking New Gilead officials, and collusion with a prisoner and the escape thereof, I would like to know something."

"Why I did it?" Jed asked almost casually, reaching up to rub his head. The cuffs rubbed his wrists wrong.

Fenton grunted.

"I'm dead anyways so how's 'bout we trade. I answer your question if you answer mine. Call it a last request if ya like."

"I'm not an unreasonable man, though my patience is quite thin. Make it quick."

Jed rose unsteadily to his feet, everything sloshing around for more than a moment, leaving him reeling and leaning against the cell wall for balance. The feeling finally passed and he stumbled to the bars to look at Fenton face to face.

"Did you really sacrifice your daughter to the demon, Judge? After all your talk about *protectin'* Gwen and then tellin' Grimluk to kill her, I believe what she said. But I want to hear it from your mouth."

Fenton eyed the captive deputy for a long time, clenching his jaw, some thought or another visibly bubbling in his mind while he prepared his answer. "You're a dead man, as you say. Yes, I pledged my daughter to the master. My reasons are my own, however, and I don't expect some fool from the backwoods to understand."

Jed ran his tongue over his teeth, ignoring the growing double-vision. "Well, I reckon that's a good enough answer to return my own. That's why I did it. Because you sacrificed your daughter to a demon. Don't much care why in the world you would do such a thing. You did it."

Fenton learned in closer to the bars. "Deputy, I'll grant you one last favor before I declare your sentence."

"You only have one sentence and it's at the end of a rope. I know what's comin'."

"Deputy...Jed, I know what happened to your son. I took him. I laid him on my altar. I shushed his whimpering. I dried his tears. And then I slit his throat and let my master feed on his blood."

If Jed Duncan had been as strong as Grimluk, he might have broken his cuffs and strangled Parker Fenton right there. Rage surged through him the likes of which he'd never felt. Every ounce of grief and pain boiled over in an explosion that wound up popping his wrist out of place as the cuffs banged into the cell bars.

The Judge smiled maliciously while Jed thrashed and screamed, impotent in his wrath. "As for your sentence, Jed, you *will* hang, of course, but it won't end there, no. I will take your lifeless body and lay it out for you to become a ghoul. Most people don't know it but ghouls are demons inhabiting the dead. The demons themselves are weak, probably nameless even, but you get a swarm of them together and they can overwhelm anyone. So in essence, your son was mine. Your life is mine. And your death will be mine."

Jed spat in Fenton's face. "You better pray to your gods-damned master that my soul doesn't linger because I swear to you on everything I know and everything I am that I will make you pay. I will find a way, dead or undead."

Fenton took out a clean white handkerchief and wiped the saliva away. "If your wife wasn't already dead, I'd take her, too, and make you watch first. Enjoy what little time you have left, Mr. Duncan."

Footsteps echoed in the dimness of the jail, followed by the slow thud of the jail's door, leaving Jed Duncan alone with his thoughts and the slow crawl towards the end of his life. The only thing that approached the horror of knowing what had actually happened to his son was that he had spent so long working for the man who'd taken him, had even extolled the bastard's virtues in reshaping Perfection from a nameless shit hole plagued with bandits to the safe, comfortable town it was now.

As he wept, he cried out to any god or spirit or ancestor that might be listening, whatever would answer his plea for vengeance. He begged for the opportunity when the time was right to strike out at Parker Fenton and make him pay. He had no idea if anything answered him.

* * *

While Fenton and Jed had their chat, Stockburn and his deputies, aided by a swarm of imps, were out searching everywhere within ten leagues of Perfection. Despite his broken nose, Fenton had forbidden Stockburn from returning to him without some sign of Grimluk and Gwen, on pain of breaking something else.

He'd gone out straight away, stopping long enough for the witch to give him something for the pain before forming his posse and sending them out. Had Jed not gotten in the way, they might have given chase fast enough not to lose the orc and child.

One of the imps reported to him as he left a farm southwest of the town, its tiny, membranous wings flapping insistently to keep it aloft. "Tracksssss…magic," it said with a voice like hissing rattlesnakes, beckoning Stockburn to follow.

He pushed his pony back north behind the imp's lead, hoping the little bastard had found something worth returning for. Some of the imps could be utterly foolish, not knowing the difference between a simple backwoods witch and something more dangerous to their work under Cholem. More than once, he'd been alerted that the town witch herself was dangerous. He knew the cantankerous old dwarf was good for nothing but her skills with potions and remedies. She'd never so much as shown the inclination to use even the most basic of magics.

She did, however, like to run her mouth to Stockburn. Always the most infuriating comments. He would take great joy in silencing that mouth should she ever lose her usefulness.

The imp circled around, flapping back over to Stockburn. "Here. Tracksssss. Magic."

Stockburn climbed down from his pony, squatting to inspect what the imp had found. There were fresh tracks in the road. Thunder rumbled in the distance. Good timing, Stockburn thought. They would at least have a direction now before the rain washed the tracks away.

"Good work," he said to the imp. "We can tell the judge which way they went. They have a fair head start but they had no supplies and I know I shot the orc."

"No," the imp squawked impatiently. "Magic! Tracks end!"

"What the fuck are you on about?"

The imp gave Stockburn a look like he was possibly the densest mortal in existence and hovered over the ground a few yards ahead, pointing one taloned finger at the road. "Tracksss," the rattlesnake voice said.

The sheriff growled, ready to backhand the little demon from the air. "What?" he demanded, stomping over to the imp. A thick indentation had been made in the earth of the road, the whole of the groove burnt but not smoking or smoldering.

"What is it?" Stockburn asked the imp.

The imp gave a sigh that sounded more like a

hiss. "Magic. Escape. Orc gone."

"Gone? How can he be gone? The tracks are right he—" Stockburn cut himself off as he noticed one of the horseshoe impressions was split in half. Beyond the burned groove in the road, there were no more tracks.

"Magic. Escape," the imp repeated with a level of smugness in its voice.

"Gods-damn it," Stockburn grumbled. "Let the others know what ya found. We'll meet back at the courthouse."

He climbed back up on his pony and watched as the imp took off to relay his message to the posse. "Fenton's gonna be pissed," he said to himself before beginning his journey back to Perfection.

A few hours later, the other deputies returned behind the other imps. Stockburn had spent his time in the saloon, drinking watered down beer from a glass that was too clean. He loved the power working for Fenton gave him, could even tolerate the judge's demand for order in the town. He could never get used to the man's dislike of drink though. Could not fathom it in the least. At least if he drank a dozen, he could feel some sort of tingle. For the time being, it had to be enough. He gathered information from his men to add to his own and then tentatively knocked at Fenton's chambers.

"Get in here, Stockburn."

He pushed the door open. "Judge."

"I trust you did your job, Sheriff?"

"None of the farms had seen anyone in days.

We did find fresh tracks leading out of town, however."

Fenton nodded. "No doubt they'll have found a place to camp. How long do you expect to catch up to them?"

Stockburn swallowed hard. "We won't."

"Come again, Sheriff? Mayhaps my ears have gone sour after being thrown into a wall. It sounded like you said you *won't* be catching up to them."

"Yes, Judge. The imp you sent with me discovered their tracks and smelled magic. The road had been scorched and one of the tracks split right in half, with nothing fresh beyond."

"So what you're saying is you lost them." Fenton stared right through his diminutive lawman.

"It would appear so. Sir." No sense in excuses, if he was dead, he was dead.

"Fenton," a voice said.

"What?" Fenton replied harshly, looking to his door for the source of the voice. Instead he saw Stockburn staring up behind him in shock. He turned to see the silver bull's head looking down at him. "Master! I'm sorry, I thought—"

"Yes, I know what you thought, Fenton." Cholem's voice took on a metallic quality from the silver.

"Forgive my mistake, Master."

"Very well. Never let it be said that I am not benevolent. You should forgive the good sheriff as well. He is not at fault for Grimluk's escape, nor should he worry about the orc."

"Why is that, my lord?" Fenton asked

bemused.

"Because I am handling it. While he escaped back to whatever safety he had, and believe me, it is quite heavily warded against me, his mind is still mine to work upon. As we speak, Grimluk lies in a sleep that only ends in his abject surrender to my will or his death."

"I don't understand," Fenton said.

"Have you forgotten the ritual? You bound his service to me. Service or death are his only choices. And when he returns, you are not to punish him for daring to resist. I am meting out retribution as well. He will return broken and ready or not at all."

"I see. Excellent. And what of the child?"

"She will be the first he kills when he submits. He is with a healer who just attempted to poke his ears into our business. He will die as well as the rest of them. In the mean time, Fenton…"

"Yes, Master?"

"I hunger."

Without turning, Fenton flicked his hand dismissively. Stockburn disappeared, off to find a new sacrifice to satiate the demon's hunger.

* * *

As the sky opened up and finally let loose the storm that had been brewing, Gwen hurried out to Mint's clinic while Bakhor watched from in the doorway of the big house. Gwen stopped at Mint's door and looked back. Bakhor gave her a nod before heading out into the rain as well, off somewhere else. She slipped through Mint's door and found the healer hovering over Grimluk once again.

"If you're gonna ask how he's doing, he's bleedin' more. Not worse, just more," Mint offered before she had even formed the words.

"Can I sit with him?" Gwen asked quietly.

Mint finished checking whatever he had been checking and planted his own chair next to Grimluk's cot for Gwen and wandered off. She climbed into the chair and curled up, watching Grimluk for a long time in silence.

Gwen.

She stiffened as the Spirit spoke up.

Gwen, I know you are angry with me but he will—

"Just shut up. I know he's gonna die if I don't let you help. You know I know." She hugged her knees tightly and tried not to start crying. She was so sick of crying. The Spirit remained silent but stayed at the front of Gwen's mind, seemingly joining her next to Grimluk. A long, low roll of thunder rumbled across the sky.

"Spirit."

Yes?

"I'm gonna let you help but I want you to know something first," Gwen thought with a sniffle.

Of course.

"This is my body. Mine. And if we're stuck together, if Mr. Mint can't get you out of me, then you need to respect that."

Does this require that I stay locked in the back of your mind unless needed? I will acquiesce but that…

"But?"

Believe it or not, you have had a great effect on my existence. The longer we are together, the more I understand you and the more I understand what it is to be mortal. I...like Grimluk. I grow fond of him. And you.

Gwen remained quiet for some time, listening to the rain patter against the tin roof. She thought hard on the Spirit's words, wondering what her family, new and old alike, might advise her to do.

"Will Momma end up like Leigh because of Nicholas?"

I believe the one named Ivor Danshor saw to it that your parents would remain at peace.

"You promise? I wanna know if she's gonna be an angry ghost."

I am certain but if you do not believe me, we can go and check once Grimluk is better. If I was wrong, I will help you set her to rest. I swear, Gwen.

Gwen sighed. "Guess I ought to give you a name then. You can't just remain 'Spirit.'"

Oh. I see. Um...what...what would you like to call me?

"I don't know. I never named anything before. Maybe I could ask Bakhor and Urgroz to help me."

I would accept this. Should we talk to Minthralvatra now?

"Soon. If I let you stay up front, will you please let me tell him what you say? Momma would tell me to be polite and I'm trying but Mr. Mint said I have control here."

I swear to honor this, Gwen. Please consider letting me speak through you when needed though. I will have to explain a great many things for this ritual and I may even need to show the healer what to do. I will only do so with permission henceforth.

Gwen thought about it. "Deal," she finally replied.

Chapter 11

Bakhor sent a group of orcs out into the surrounding area to find the right spot for the ritual. The Spirit had relayed that it had to be a magically sensitive area where the veil between worlds could be worked properly. Mint had given each of the scouts a small talisman that would react under the right circumstances. When the scouts returned, one of them informed Bakhor and Mint that she'd found such a spot. The young hunter's talisman had glowed and pulled on its cord towards a small clearing surrounded by young trees several miles away from Hunter's Hollow. When she stood at the center, the talisman pointed to the sky and shown fiercely.

Next came the preparations. First, they would need to paint specific runes and sigils across Grimluk's bare skin. The Spirit explained that most were for protection but certain sigils in particular would be the primary catalysts for the ritual, needing to go on his forehead, heart, hands, and feet. After that, he would need to be wrapped in a harness that would be staked to the ground, both to keep him stationary and as an extra means of protection from whatever eldritch forces decided to come for him.

They had plenty of time to prepare while waiting for the true moon, when the moon was at its fullest and highest. The time was still several nights away. Close enough that it made the wait that much more arduous as more wounds opened up on Grimluk. The Spirit made sure to reiterate that despite the moon, they would be dealing with powerful darkness, though a new moon would have been all the more dangerous. Urgroz, Bakhor, and Gwen found little sleep that night before the ritual.

The next afternoon, Bakhor informed the other hunters what was going to happen before calling for Kort, the head trainer. "I'd expect Hunter's Hollow can make it without me for a whole night but all the same, keep the apprentices from getting into too much trouble. With a little luck, we should return tomorrow with my son."

Kort, heavy as Urgroz and bareheaded, gave a laugh. "The runts'll mind themselves as always. Good lot this year, if a bit small. Don't tell 'em I said that. They'd never respect me again." He stuck out a huge, meaty hand. "Bring Grimluk back. We'll be waitin'."

Bakhor shook Kort's hand at his wrist, almost too thick even for hir huge hand to encircle. "Either he comes back or I go get him and drag his ass back with me. I'll remind him where he gets his stubbornness from."

"Maybe the Fates will smile on you, if they still exist," Kort suggested.

"Fuck 'em," Bakhor said as ze walked off, ready to make the trek, "we are our own fates."

Kort gave another loud laugh.

* * *

They walked in silence, Urgroz and Bakhor carrying their still monstrous son's cot and most of the supplies in packs. They found the clearing easily, surrounded by the clustered grove of trees just as the hunter had told them. Mint commented on the buzz of magic immediately, even while the talisman gave its confirmation. Gwen could feel it, too. She wondered for a moment how much of that sensitivity was the Spirit's influence and how much was her own gifts that Mint had spoken of.

"All right, set him down. I'll get him prepared while you make camp," Mint said. "Gwen?"

She stopped looking around and moved to Mint's side. Everyone seemed so much bigger.

That is the magic. Do not be alarmed. The veil is very thin here. You are strong.

Gwen nodded inwardly and looked to Mint.

"Help your folks and have a bite to eat. We can start the runes when you're ready. There's still plenty of daylight left." He gave her shoulder a pat and shooed her.

Her folks. The sound of that was so jarring. Her *folks.* Still, the two orcs had welcomed her so easily. She found them so comforting, like Grimluk had been, especially since leaving Greenreach Bluffs. Her folks. She started to ask what she could do but her voice cracked. Urgroz knelt in front of her with a canteen and a stick of goat jerky. Tentatively, he planted a kiss on her head, one of his tusks bumping her slightly. The surprise made her laugh in spite of herself, expelling some of her nervous energy.

"Eat, kiddo. You're a growing girl and you'll need your strength for the night." He leaned in conspiratorially and whispered in her ear, "I brought cookies, too." He gave her a wink and went back to helping Bakhor.

For lack of any other clear idea of what to do, she took three steps back and dropped to her butt softly, sucking on one end of the jerky and watching everyone work. For a moment, she felt herself start to disengage from the world around her, but a wet nose against her ear anchored her. The nose pushed past her face and started for her jerky.

"Fang, that's not for you," Bakhor called out casually.

Fang gave a high growl in reply.

"You still need to ask her permission first. You're not going to steal her food just because it's easy to get to."

Fang let out a huff and circled around in front of Gwen, eying the jerky and licking her chops. Gwen giggled and broke off a piece of the jerky, holding it out. Fang's tail started wagging, swishing loudly against the grass.

"Thought you told the pup to stay home, Bakhor?" Mint asked, stripping off Grimluk's old bandages.

"You know how well she listens. If she were an apprentice, Kort would've run her 'til her legs gave out."

Fang looked back and gave a low bark. Bakhor let out a loud laugh in response.

"What'd she say?" Gwen asked.

"She said, 'He would've tried.' You can see why she's family. Damn warg's just as stubborn as the rest of us."

Gwen giggled and munched her jerky and stroked Fang's shoulder.

Hours later, much to its surprise, she let the Spirit take control to show Mint the sigils and runes for the ritual. She loathed to do it but after the sixth time she messed up the first sigil, she threw her hands up and swapped roles. The painting went smoothly once it got going and she let the Spirit continue helping so as not to waste any more daylight. They still had to wrap Grimluk in the shroud, which could thankfully be done by firelight if need be.

Bakhor and Urgroz lifted him up while Mint and Gwen, once more in control of her body, ran the wrappings around Grimluk snugly, making sure not to smudge any of the paint. Mint assured her it wouldn't smudge but she was scared of messing up again and asked to go slow just to be sure. Mint obliged her readily.

When they finished wrapping all that was left was to wait for the moon to peak. The sky was perfectly clear and filled with a soft orange as the moon ascended. The higher the moon got, the more restless Fang got until she began pacing around Grimluk in a wide circle, ears twitching in all directions.

Mint must say the words soon. Are you ready?

"No," Gwen thought, swallowing hard. "Mr. Mint, the Spirit says it's almost time. Do you remember the words?"

"I do." He took his place at Grimluk's head, lifting it into his own lap and looking back up at the moon. "Can't say I'm happy about the language, but I remember it."

A bag dropped next to Grimluk. "I think it's time we prepare," Bakhor said, pulling off hir coat and tossing it back toward the tent. "Better that we have it and not need it than the other way around."

Ze reached into the bag and retrieved a prosthetic arm that seemed to be mostly metal and strapped it to hir stump with a growl. Urgroz followed suit, pulling out a revolver and a hatchet. Gwen took a knife that looked like Grimluk's. In her hands it looked more halfling's sword.

"Watch yourselves," Mint said, worry creeping into his voice. "It's time."

Mint spoke the first words of the old Elvish language. The sound of it made Gwen's head swim and her tongue taste sour. He continued on and the ground rumbled. As the spell filled the grove, the moon began to glow red, covering the world in a blood light. Clouds started swirling in fast and dark but the crimson light held strong. The wind howled and whipped through the grove furiously. Mint spoke the final words and every ounce of paint on Grimluk's body lit up, clear through the red glow of the moon. In the heightened magic of the grove, Gwen felt Mint make the connection with Grimluk.

Fang's hackles rose on end and she started growling, still circling Grimluk before stopping towards the trees to the south. A hungry growl, like boulders grinding against each other, greeted the warg's ears as a troll lumbered into the clearing, dragging a huge tree limb club.

Bakhor stepped forward with a grin. "Urgroz, my love?"

"Bakhor, my sweet?"

"How long has it been since I killed a troll?"

"Oh, you sexy thing. Too long."

Bakhor held up hir hands in a fighting stance, loose but ready to strike at any moment. The troll lumbered in closer, its arm tensing to swing the massive club, eagerly growling and seemingly sure that it would crush its victim in one swing. The club went high and crashed down where Bakhor had stood a moment ago. Ze kicked the club free from the troll's hand before back-stepping and spinning to deliver another powerful kick to the troll's elbow.

The troll let loose a furious, bellowing roar from its drooling mouth as its elbow flexed the wrong way. It swung with the other arm, back and forth in slow, clumsy movements that Bakhor dodged and deflected with ease, showing outstanding grace in such a large body. Before the beast could react, ze'd circled around it and delivered a flurry of punches to its back. The metal fist struck the troll's spine hard, resounding with the distinctive sound of metal pounding dense, hairy flesh. The blow made the creature groan and shudder from the pain.

"Watah!" Bakhor let out a fierce shriek as ze loosed a spinning heel kick into the troll's thick ankle that took it down to one knee. In desperation, the beast swung its bad arm limply at what was no longer the opening course of a long dinner. The orc hooked the arm and yanked back, finishing what ze'd started with the kick to its elbow. The troll's shoulder dislocated with a sick snap that brought a satisfied smile to Bakhor's face.

Ze took to the air, using the troll's shoulders to vault back over in front of it, dragging its head down in hir landing and then striking hir knee hard to its face, one last blow that shattered its bulbous nose and sent a cascade of blood down its chest. It looked up at hir with dumb eyes, still focused on the potential meal, and grabbed a hold of the orc with its good hand. It growled, hungry and triumphant.

"Come on, darlin', you're just playing with it now," Urgroz called from behind. Gwen looked at him in shock.

Ze let out another savage shriek, "Wah! Ha!" and knocked the troll's arm away before slamming hir metal fist into the troll's eye like a cannonball, utterly crushing it.

The troll tried weakly to bite at Bakhor's face but ze simply hopped backward and answered with a loud "Kah!" and a spinning jump-kick that almost took the troll's jaw clean off its head. A simple shove pushed the huge creature to its back where it lay bleeding and useless. Bakhor walked to its head, the lone eye rolling around in its socket, trying to focus once more but its brain too addled to register the end coming as Bakhor lifted hir foot high into the air.

"Yah!" The troll's skull exploded inward with the force of the kick, creating a slick puddle of gore. One lone spasm rocked the creature's body before the last of its life fled.

* * *

Peter and Cassie Quinn watched Grimluk stagger into the cave, the temple where Ivor Danshor had lived and worked in Greenreach Bluffs. Peter's charred, hollow eye sockets, though empty, weighed on him nonetheless, while Cassie, dressed all in her own blood, glared at him from the center of the main chamber.

"You did this to us," Cassie said gently. "You carry our deaths on your hands."

"It was all your fault, Grimluk. If you'd have never followed Trilgor back here, we'd still be alive and happy with our little girl." Peter stepped forward, his skin crunching loudly in the uncomfortable silence of the cave. "Look at me, you goblin bastard! Burned alive by a dragon! A gods-damned *dragon*! All because of you."

"No, Selbie called that dragon," Grimluk replied, shaking his head. "I fought as hard and fast as I could to get to him and stop it!"

"You wasted time!" Cassie said, nearly hissing the words. "You could've drawn and killed him before he could've shot Sadie. Was it so worth it?"

"Won't ride a horse. Won't kill anyone even to protect a whole town. Some demon hunter you are." Peter huffed with a voice like parched desert.

Blood pulsed out in spurts from Cassie's chest, crashing out like flood waters from a broken dike. The crimson pool rushed and flowed around the trio before forming into the shape of a massive bull.

"My dearest Grimluk," Cholem said, "my, how you failed this little town. Of course, you never could have saved this woman even if you had ended Kenton Selbie's miserable and pathetic life. She was meant for greater things, freeing my sibling from that ancient cave. And with the help of her own son, how delicious. And why?"

One powerful fist broke the surface of the blood with a wet slap. Grimluk pulled it free and swung the other, again and again, alternating heavy punches, yelling all the while. "I tried so hard! I did everything I could to stop the dragon in time! To stop Selbie! To kill Priskus! I tried!"

"Lying," the demon said mockingly through each punch. "Tell the truth, Grimluk. Or do not. Give in to me and I will make you forget this. Nothing will ever prick your conscience again."

Grimluk started to throw another punch but a bright light split Cholem's form in two, causing the demon to scream in pain. When the light faded, Mint was standing there, panting.

"Mint?" Grimluk said unbelieving. "I…heard you before. What's going on?"

"No time, kid, you have to—" his form wavered sharply for a moment as Cholem fought his presence.

"I told you to mind your own business, elf!"

"Freedom, Grim—" Mint's body disappeared in its own blast of light.

Grimluk could still feel his presence, though dimly and far away. Peter and Cassie had vanished in the light as Cholem reformed its bloody body. "That hurt," it growled so low the cave seemed to shake. "I am going to make you murder that meddling pest when you finally accept your place as my general."

"No," Grimluk said, baring his teeth. "You'll free me, you troll-sucking abomination!" With a roar, he threw another punch. Cholem had begun to laugh dismissively but the punch landed hard, stunning the demon and choking the laugh. Its bloody skin sizzled and started to burn away.

As Grimluk raised both hands, ready to smash them down, Cholem rushed forward and knocked him away. He bounced off a wall and slid towards the temple's exit. A malicious roar ripped through the mental recreation of Greenreach Bluffs. The dragon, undead from Selbie's amulet, was finishing the job it started before Grimluk had commanded it back to death in a battle of wills.

"By all means, let us go and greet that beast," Cholem suggested with a hint of a growl. "I will show you what it feels like to be burned alive. Just like Peter Quinn."

* * *

Spirits swarmed around the camp, rushing towards Grimluk's unconscious body in screaming fits while Mint remained still with Grimluk's head in his lap. The red clouds above swirled in a howling vortex, directing anything that was close enough to care about what was happening to the camp. Gwen shrieked as a screaming skull flew over her head. A long arm reached for her from the dark only to be met with a hatchet from Bakhor.

Dark shades rose up from the ground under Grimluk, trying to rip him free of his confines. Urgroz grabbed a bag of salt from the weapons bag and slung a fistful out under his son. The salt sent the spirits fleeing from its burning touch. Two more trolls lay dead at each end of the clearing, one of them with a hatchet buried in its skull. The other was missing part of its face. A piercing shriek hit the group's ears as a banshee came screaming in from the north, stunning them with its cry. Gwen looked on in terror as it rushed her.

A banshee brings death, Gwen. You must command it, the Spirit said urgently.

The banshee's terrible wail froze her in place as the Spirit pushed her to action. She felt her legs go out from under her and the world began to spin and go black. The Spirit urged her to speak again. One word finally came out. "Stop." Barely a whisper. The banshee quieted down quite suddenly, a strange bewilderment washing over its ethereal face.

"Help, please," Gwen begged as the effects of the cry faded.

The banshee nodded slowly, suddenly keenly unsure of what she was doing. A tangle of spirits rushed in towards Grimluk once more and the banshee hurled herself at them, screaming with all her power, blasting the foul shades far away. Their howls of pain grew distant under the cacophony of shouts and screams still filling the clearing.

Gwen, you can command the other spirits like the banshee.

Before she could focus on the Spirit's words, a familiar shape dropped from the sky and landed in the clearing. The ghost of Leigh Fenton roared, injured and dripping ectoplasm, but monstrous all the same. The huge form jumped on another tangle of spirits and crushed them under the immense, angry weight of her wrath. More spirits continued to pour in from all around as Urgroz and Bakhor took defensive stances at either side of Grimluk, swatting them away as best they could.

A hard swallow and a deep breath and Gwen spoke. "Hey!" A lone spirit stopped to look at her for a moment before attempting to fly at Grimluk again. "Stop that!" she shouted, reaching for the spirit before she realized what she was doing. Like she'd done with Leigh, her hand gripped the incorporeal being tightly. The spirit looked at her, a sudden wave of shock filling it.

"I said stop," Gwen said with her most commanding voice. The spirits all froze, plainly unsure of what to do and probably even less sure of what it meant that this tiny human could touch them. "Good. You, sit down and stop being so rude. That's my brother you're trying to get to and he's very sick. And that goes for the rest of you, too!"

The spirit in her hand nodded slowly and sank to the ground where it was. The others, alone or entangled, all began to calm and join the first spirit in front of Gwen, looking at each other like toddlers afraid of being punished by their parents.

"Gwen," Urgroz called, "what's goin' on?"

"I'm making them mind. Like Momma use to do when I wouldn't listen. She'd make me sit down and ask me what I thought I was doing." She giggled. "One time, she found me sitting in a cabinet with all the pots and pans spilled out everywhere. I told her I was exploring."

One spirit latched on to that thought and tried to tell Gwen that *it* just wanted to explore, too, but she told it to just hush up.

"You're all going to sit there and think about why you're being so rude and if any more of you show up, you're going to tell them to join you or I'll...well, it won't be nice. When you're ready, one of you can tell me how I can *help* you and you can leave me and my family alone." She pointed at them in the best impression of her mother she could muster, wagging her little pointer finger at them all with one hand on her hip.

The spirits all nodded in agreement, totally befuddled at what had happened.

* * *

Cholem dragged Grimluk out of the temple by an ankle, anger boiling the blood that composed its body, which had shifted once more to walk on two legs, taking a more orcish face in further spite of its captive. The memory-dragon stalked over towards them, its black scales shimmering under a showy fireball. The demon tossed the orc towards it with a sneer.

"Here is what will happen, Grimluk." Cholem

rolled him over so he could look up at both it and the dragon. "You will suffer under the dragon's claw until I tell it to burn you. I suspect that the experience will finally snuff your life out. I would quite hate to see that but unless you honor the oath and serve me like you swore you would, your life is forfeit all the same. Serve or perish, orc."

A lone, green fist swung towards the bloody demon's jaw and missed. Cholem shook its head and motioned for the dragon. The beast let out a grave laugh before it crushed one of Grimluk's ankles under a taloned foot. In the waking world, Grimluk's body jerked. Vaguely, he could feel Mint focus on the damage, drawing on whatever energies were swirling around them to keep the injury under control. It didn't lessen the pain though.

The dragon turned and slammed its tail down onto Grimluk's chest. In desperation, he grabbed the shiny black log crushing him and bit into it. Had he tried that on the real dragon, his teeth likely would've shattered in his gums but this was not the real dragon and he knew he had the power to hurt the demon and its tools now, even if he didn't understand how. The beast roared and tried to pull its tail back but whatever strength Grimluk still had went into holding on and biting harder.

"How are you doing that?" Cholem roared. "You are under *my* command! I control your mindscape!"

The dragon finally managed to dislodge Grimluk with a savage whip of its tail, sending him crashing into one of the valley's rock walls. Greenreach Bluffs as a town had disappeared, replaced by the endless expanse of the worn out lake bed the town had been built in. Cholem rushed to catch him and pin him to the rocks, roaring in his face, demanding an answer to its question.

"Guess you're not as in control as you thought," Grimluk wheezed through gritted teeth. "I choose death."

"You would rather the girl, Gwen, be left to fend for herself? You would rather die here in your own mind than serve and save her?" Cholem pushed Grimluk deeper into the wall, gripping his shoulders with sharp fingers that dug into the mental flesh. "Would you really throw away your life so easily in the face of true power?"

A long, wet wheeze slipped through Grimluk's teeth as he reached up for Cholem's face. Grasping fingers settled around a bloody tusk. Then he ripped with everything he had left. Cholem roared in pain and hurled Grimluk back towards the waiting dragon.

"Insolent, arrogant, self-righteous little mortal! You will burn!" Cholem's bloody skin popped and hissed with rage. A bubble on its mouth popped as a new tusk formed. It loomed over Grimluk, hauling him up by the throat. The dragon drew close once more, flames licking its lips like hundreds of eager tongues. The demon spun Grimluk around to face the beast once more, one crimson arm hooked around his neck.

"If I could send you to the Abyss to be ripped apart by the uncountable masses of my kind for eternity, I would. This will have to do. Goodbye, my precious hunter."

The dragon inhaled deeply, planting its feet

into the desert hard pan. No, not hard pan. Now it was stone. As the flames rose in its throat, the valley disappeared and four stone walls slammed into place around the trio. The fire leaped from the dragon's maw, its heat making the air shimmer. Grimluk waited for the flames to engulf his body but it never happened. Before they could even so much as singe the hair on his arms, the black beast vanished as if it'd never been there.

As the ceiling slammed down overhead, Grimluk realized with astonishment that they were in Parker Fenton's dungeon again, right in front of the big door. It opened, the hinges groaning in protest as the judge himself stepped through, holding the bowl he'd used to perform the Oath with. A growl caught in Cholem's throat at the sight of his servant intruding. Parker Fenton looked up and gave an unsettling and uncharacteristically friendly wave.

Chapter 12

Parker Fenton looked around at the dungeon and at the bowl in his hands. He mouthed, "Oh," and gave a little nod to himself before stepping forward. His hands moved mechanically, performing the steps he'd taken several nights prior in preparing Grimluk and the ingredients for the Oath ritual.

"What is this?" Cholem asked. "What are you doing now, Grimluk? This is not me. Stop this at once!"

"Oh, this isn't our young friend, Cholem. And I'm not Parker Fenton. I'm merely—" he paused, rolling his hand conversationally and laughing to himself, "an agent. Doing my duty. Though truth told, I'm not even really that. I'm merely a…figment of his i-*magic*-nation." He snorted, blatantly tickled with his pun.

Grimluk snorted as well, in spite of his confusion and pain. This really wasn't the judge.

"I do not care *what* you are, you will stop this instant so that I may destroy this pesky mortal and continue on with my eternity," Cholem demanded, sounding very put out that it'd been interrupted but too confused to be totally angry still. His grip on Grimluk lessened.

"Tut tut, I can't oblige that request, my good devil." Fenton held the bowl up to Grimluk's mouth. "Spit, please."

"Uh…" Grimluk eyed the man suspiciously. Why would he go along with this gods-damned spell a second time?

"That's a good thought, young man. Why *would* you do this again?" Fenton shook the bowl, looking like he didn't have all day.

Grimluk, still quite confused, obliged and spit into the bowl.

"Oh, and you, you can stand here with me again. Gotta make this proper." Cholem's grip on Grimluk loosened completely and the bloody orc, once more a living shadow, appeared next to Fenton. The judge nodded and looked back at Grimluk, whose mouth was agape.

"I know, I know," Fenton said sympathetically, "so many questions. They'll be answered in time, if you know what to say to this next part. Hunter, orc, mortal who answers to the name of Grimluk, blah, blah, blah, blood and oath. I, in the form of the one who bound you, ask you once again if you will swear your eternal service to this soul-sucking bastard, on pain and death and on and on. What say you?"

Grimluk looked down at the bowl and back up at Fenton, who was smiling patiently, looking very much like someone's kindly grandfather and not the gallows-happy judge he really was.

"What?"

"Simple question, m'boy. And one you already answered. Do you, as you swore previously, pledge your service this demon?"

"Serve the demon?" Grimluk asked. "Serve that? I made that oath to protect Gwen! I would never serve evil filth like that! But what was I supposed to do, let Gwen die?"

"No, no, of course not. So you're saying, what? That you didn't mean it? That your heart just wasn't in it?"

"My heart? No! Fuck no! Every word in every dialect of Elvish, Dwarvish, and Manish for no! If the orcs still had their own language, I'd scream no in it, too. I just wanted to keep her safe."

Fenton stepped forward and gave Grimluk's shoulder a pat. "I know. You did what you had to under threat of the death of another. And you answered true, just like I hoped you would." He stepped away again and lit a match. "Good job, m'boy. Go get your answers."

As before, the match hit the bowl and erupted into a great blue flame that engulfed Grimluk.

"No! No, no, no, no! He is mine! You cannot take him from me!" Cholem roared and tried to run through the flames for Grimluk. Blue fire snaked around the demon's body, drawing screams of agony from it that drowned out all thought and sound before ripping the writhing shadow to pieces and expelling it from Grimluk's mind in an explosion of light.

"Time to wake up, Grimluk," Fenton said, slowly fading away. "And let your guilty conscience air out when ya do."

Sunlight exploded all around him like dawn, high noon, and dusk all at once, washing over him in bright warmth. He could feel Mint, weak and trying to urge him to wake up. He followed Mint's presence, everything around him fading quickly. He felt almost like he was rising back up to the water's surface after a deep dive in a lake.

Grimluk opened his eyes, slow and heavy, blinking away the morning sunlight as it shined down through the trees of the clearing. The sun was too bright and he shut it back away for a moment, trying to wake up. He vaguely felt the wrappings holding his body in place, unsure of what they were, or where he was, and what was going on. He knew Cholem was gone from his mind. For the first time in over a month, he was actually sure that he was awake and firmly in reality.

"He's awake" Mint informed them, moving Grimluk's head gingerly to lay on a rolled up bed roll. The healer stood, slowly, working his stiff limbs, producing loud pops as his joints resettled after so many hours sitting still with Grimluk's head in his lap.

"Too loud," Grimluk said with a groan. The pressure from the wrappings loosened little by little and a moment later, he felt his limbs go free of their confines as his arms splayed out. A wave of pain washed through him. Tentatively, he raised his hand and looked at it. No more sharp nails. He felt his forehead for the sharp protrusions. They were gone. He felt his tusks and teeth and sighed with relief. He was himself again.

Some foul stench assaulted his nose as he looked around, trying to adjust to the soft light of dawn, shifting his focus again.

"What," he started, coughing weakly and nearly gagging, "what *is* that smell, Mint? Smells like dead troll."

Bakhor stepped forward. "It is, my little hunter."

"Cenka?" Grimluk blinked at the towering figure.

"Me, too, kiddo," Urgroz said, stepping up next to his partner.

"Dakka?" A thought flooded his mind before he could say anything else and he sat up too quickly. "Gwen? Where's Gwen?" His head swam and everything went sideways, pulling him back down onto the bed roll. His muscles and his guts screamed at him for his foolishness.

"I'm here," she said, joining the others. "We saved you!"

Grimluk looked up at Gwen, blinking hard, trying to will everything to be still. A hazy shadow passed over him, twinkling lights of reds and yellows and blacks spread through it. He realized after a moment that spirits were looking down at him. One reached out for him.

"Uh uh!" Gwen said. "What did I say? We'll help you but no touching."

"Cenka, what the fuck is going on?"

"Well," Bakhor started, letting out a long sigh, "that's an interesting story. And I'm gonna let Gwen explain it cause I'm still not sure what the fuck happened myself." Ze pulled Urgroz away to help pack the camp back up as Grimluk looked at Gwen curiously.

"Heh, well, see, you wouldn't wake up and Mr. Mint said the demon was keeping you asleep and hurting you and your ankle was bleeding and you were still too big and he went in my head and talked to the Spirit and it said it knew how to help you and Mint asked if I was a spirit caller and then we came out here and did the magic ritual the Spirit told him about and I can talk to spirits and tell them what to do and we saved you!"

He looked at her in stunned silence, trying to process what she'd said. Memories bubbled up, half-formed and vivid all at once, pushing the need for understanding away. The tainted recollections of events past and all the accusations from Cholem swirled in his mind. The words rose in his throat as he remembered the vision of Peter and Cassie Quinn intermingled with the true memory of their goodbye. Not-Fenton's words echoed as well.

"Gwen," he said, voice suddenly shaky, "I'm so sorry. I failed you. I failed your home. I failed everyone."

"What are you talking about?" She knelt beside him. "Everything's better now. We fixed it."

"No, not that, little one. Not that. Your home, your parents. It was all my fault. I was cocky. Even after denying any arrogance. I knew Selbie was bad as soon as I met him. I should've killed him. I should've stopped him. I tried to tell myself it was just Priskus's influence but it wasn't. And I got your father and your mother killed cause I couldn't…wouldn't aim right."

"What? No! No, no, no, no! You helped us! You protected me after Momma and Daddy…and the Spirit and Nicholas…" Tears streaked from her eyes, glistening in the sun.

"And I didn't stop the demon. Your brother…your whole family might still be alive if I'd acted better and you wouldn't be stuck out here with us. You'd be safe. Least as safe as you coulda been in the Wastes. And I just ran. I was so ashamed at my failure that I just took you and left. I didn't even stay to help them rebury the dead. I could've let Trilgor speak to his mother again. Wounded pride got in the way. Please," he started, tears rolling away from tired eyes, "please, little one, can you forgive me? Can I ever make it up to you?"

Gwen inched her way toward him, laying her hands on his chest and choking back a sob. "Brother did this to me. Brother killed Momma. Mr. Selbie did those bad things, not you. You said we were family. Can we be family still? I want to be your family." She looked back at Urgroz and Bakhor as they packed slowly. "I like your family. Urgroz made me feel safe, like you did. He said we'd throw a party for me, to welcome me in the family. Fang let me pet her."

Gingerly, Grimluk reached up and wiped away Gwen's tears before pulling her down into a hug. "Oh, little one. Of course. I would never turn you away. I've done everything I could to protect you. I promised your parents I would keep you safe. I swore. I love you, little one."

"I love you, Grimluk." Gwen buried her face

in his shoulder and clung to him. When she loosened up finally, she sniffled and whispered, "Do you think I can have strawberry cake for my party?"

Grimluk gave a light laugh. "I reckon so."

"Oh, Leigh helped us. She's hurt though. And she said there's more ghosts like her. Oh, and the other spirits. I promised we'd help them. They're so fussy." She wrinkled her little nose at that.

As Urgroz and Bakhor finished repacking and smothering the campfire, Mint suggested they head back. "You seem free of Death's grip for the moment," he informed his patient, "but you still need to recover. And last night took its bloody toll on all of us. Reckon we could all use some food and a bit of a rest when we get back to the Hollow, eh? You hungry, Grimluk?"

"Not just yet." He grinned. "Don't have the spirit."

Urgroz barked a laugh. "My son." Bakhor and Mint groaned while Gwen looked on a bit confused.

After eating more of the jerky and a few cookies from Urgroz's pack, the orcs moved their son back onto the cot. Fang stuck her big nose in Grimluk's face, whimpered and licked him affectionately before growling and yipping at him to voice the worry she'd felt. He laughed and patted her head weakly, apologizing for worrying her. Gwen gave a final command to the remaining spirits to pay attention for her call when they'd all had a chance to recover. They all nodded dumbly, sitting in a pile in the clearing, still clearly confused and frightened of the mortal girl. After that, the group began the trek back to Hunter's Hollow with a ghost-girl in tow, dripping a trail of ecto-plasm behind them as they went.

After a long time of silence, Bakhor spoke up. "Grimluk."

"Cenka?"

"I'm proud of you. Proud of what you've done with Gwen and proud that you've tried so hard to only kill demons and monsters."

"Thanks…"

"And you need to stop being such a stubborn jackass and forgive yourself. Oldest rule of huntin', kid, you can't save everyone. You messed up. We all mess up. It's gonna happen. You were always such a serious child. I'd hoped after your training, once you got out in the world, you'd loosen up a little." Ze grunted, adjusting the leather strap ze was using to steady the cot.

Grimluk looked away, frowning and feeling frustrated.

"I know, that's not what you want to hear and you won't like this either. I tried to tell you before you left but you didn't want to hear it. In our line of work, eventually you're going to have to kill someone. And it's okay that you don't want to rush towards that but it's an inevitability. When it finally happens, it'll wreck you. And it should. Then you come home and talk to me about it."

The frustrated frown softened into one of worry. What if that time was approaching? Parker Fenton was an evil man. Selbie had been a fright-ened coward looking for immortality. Fenton wanted control. All of it. And he'd murdered his own daughter on his way to get it.

"Thank you, Cenka. I was thinkin'…I reckon it's time I finally add some real protection to my gear."

"Like what?"

"I want the seal."

"Heh. 'Bout damn time you took me up on that. Let Mint recover and we'll do it immediately."

"Good. I've had enough demons playing with my mind for one life. Now, maybe you can explain to me what rightly happened while I was out."

Bakhor sighed and attempted hir best to explain. Ze related the story as ze'd seen it, which turned out wasn't much more detailed than Gwen's version of events. It didn't do much to relieve Grimluk's confusion. He just sighed.

"The dead troll stench kept the rest of the critters at bay though. Dead trolls are good for somethin'," Bakhor said with a laugh.

"What'd she promise—? Gwen what did you promise the spirits?"

"Stop wigglin', boy," Urgroz said with a grunt.

Gwen ran ahead from Leigh to Grimluk's side. "I told them we'd help them with one thing they wanted, if it wasn't rude and hurtful."

He blinked, unsure of what to make of the news. "I get stuck in my own mind, being tortured by a demon and you develop magical powers. It's been quite the summer, little one."

Gwen giggled and smiled big for him, like she had when they'd first met.

The posse returned to a hero's welcome. Everyone who knew Grimluk told him how happy they were to see him back and still alive. After the fanfare died down, Bakhor and Urgroz helped him to his feet, returning Mint's cot back where it came from before taking turns helping him back inside the living quarters and into an empty bedroom where he collapsed onto the bed, exhausted and huffing. It'd been so long now since he'd felt a soft bed.

"Thanks, Cenka, Dakka."

"Always, kiddo," Urgroz said, leaning down to bump his son's forehead with his own. "What else are parents for?"

"Well, strawberry cake certainly wouldn't hurt. Gwen wants some for her party."

"Consider it done."

Bakhor smiled.

"One more thing, Cenka," Grimluk called as the two started to leave.

"Yes?"

"Call the Doom Riders."

A tug of surprise pulled at Bakhor's face but then ze grinned wickedly and laughed.

* * *

The courthouse shook as Cholem's mental link with Grimluk severed, blasting its consciousness away. Black ichor welled up in the eyes and mouth of the silver bull's head hanging in the judge's chambers, running down it in slow, thick drops that pooled together and fell to the altar below it.

The ritual had done more damage than the demon could have ever guessed. Pain was not a concept Cholem had known before. It called out to Parker Fenton dimly, a rasping voice in the man's mind, urging him to respond.

Fenton felt the tremor from his house, rousing from his sleep, rousing even sharper when he realized he could only just hear his master's call. He slipped on boots, too panicked to change out of his sleeping clothes, and rushed out into the early morning air. Few people were awake yet. The courthouse and the streets of Perfection were empty, save for its judge who flung open the double-doors and practically flew up to his chambers.

"Master?" he cried, stopping at the sight of the inky black mess spilling off the bust and puddling on the altar. The drops splashed, spreading out in speckles across the wood.

Blood…I must feed.

The voice was louder now that he was near the demon's anchor. There was so much black blood. Fenton rushed away, aiming for Stockburn and his deputies. The sheriff had built himself a small mound not far from Fenton's house, big enough to comfortably house himself but no one else. Fenton pounded on the door, prompting a shout from within.

"Who the fuck is bangin' on my door this early?" he roared, ripping open the door. "Oh… Judge. What can—"

"Cholem's been hurt. We need sacrifices."

"We just got one," Stockburn countered sleepily.

Fenton's hand snapped out, grabbing a handful of Stockburn's hair and yanked him out of the shack. "Sacrifices. Now. Or I'll feed you and your men to the master."

"I thought you said it only eats children!"

"I doubt very much that our lord would be so picky right now. Round up every child you can find. If their parents fight, arrest them or shoot them, I don't give a shit which."

Stockburn nodded his head, Fenton's hand still gripping his hair tightly. Once released, he prepared as quickly as he could. Rushing in fear to saddle up his pony and call his men to work.

Fenton hurried back into his chambers to find out what had happened, stammering the words as they rolled off his tongue. "What? How?" The ichor had finally slowed to a more reasonable drip but wasn't completely stopping. He suspected it wouldn't until the demon had fed.

"The orc," Cholem rasped in the bull's head, voice still thin and weak. "His elf healer…did something to him. It froze me, commanded me… removed me. The magic was old."

"What does that mean? Is he dead?" Fenton's mind was on the matter at hand but his eyes were locked on the puddle of black blood on the altar.

"The orc lives. Grimluk is free of the Oath." The demon let out what Fenton thought sounded like a wheeze. "It is time to prepare for war, Parker Fenton. It is time to rule."

"Yes, Lord. Stockburn has been dispatched to find you more sacrifices. Once you're healed, we can start."

"We may start now. You can begin the summons. Gather my essence up from the altar first. Take a finger of it from the mouth of my anchor and touch it to your head. I will give you instruction on how to form an Abyssal womb."

Fenton set straight to work. He snatched the bowl he usually filled with sacrificial blood and pushed the puddle of demon blood into it, spilling some onto floor in fat splashes that would stain forever. He stood, inky blackness covering his pajamas, and reached up to the bust's mouth, still trickling with Cholem's essence and touched a finger to it. It seemed to latch on to his fingertip. He looked at it for a moment. This really was the demon's blood.

The substance pulsed as he rubbed it across his forehead. Pulsed steadily, slowing his perception of time. The world slowed to a crawl. Fenton looked around. He could touch the shadows. Slice what little sunlight made its way in through the north-facing window with his palm. A bloody bull limped into existence behind him.

"Parker Fenton, loyal servant, partake of my knowledge."

Fenton swore that months passed but when he came to, nothing had changed except his mind and the skill he now possessed. He slid his sacrificial dagger into the waist of his pants and wandered out of his chambers in a daze, black-blooded bowl in hand. A young human woman, one of the filing clerks, edged her way into the courthouse as he made his way out.

"Judge, is everything okay, the doors—" she stopped cold. Her eyes went wide at the sight of him. "Did you spill a bottle of ink on yourself?"

"Yes," he said quietly. "Yes, everything is fine. Could you come help me with something for a moment?"

"Of course, sir." She followed him dutifully down into the jail.

Parker Fenton sat the bowl down quietly, out of his way, and then turned on the woman before she could react, smashing her face into the stairwell. He scooped the bowl back up along with a handful of her hair and dragged her stunned form across the floor and into the dungeon.

Supernaturally practiced hands moved swiftly and efficiently, drawing out the summoning circle and sigils in ichor across the back wall. The liquid took a sharper shape once the lines were completely connected, pulsing rapidly. Fenton stood the girl up in front of the wall.

"My dear, for all of your fine loyalty and service, I thank you. Serve me now one last time with blood." The knife blade dragged across the woman's throat with an imprecise fluidity brought about by a nervous hand. He pressed her into the wall and squeezed. Blood shot out, red and hot and smeared into the black ichor. "Ia! Ia! Shub-Niggurath, Black Goat of the Woods with Uncountable Young, I beseech thee! Resplendent and glorious Mother, grant me your favor and let the Abyss open wide!"

The sigil lit up in an eerie glow and began drinking the blood greedily, drawing it out of the wound in wet smacks like a child sucking on ripe berries. The circle would, in time, be able to summon demons from the Abyss itself. It would take seven bodies, drained of blood and slowly devoured to become fully charged and active. It would never be strong enough to summon another powerful demon like Cholem but it would suffice for the lesser orders. More imps, death hounds, maybe burrowers and, if enough bodies were supplied, an army of ghouls. The so-called womb would serve as a doorway for the judge's foot soldiers.

Once the magic had taken hold of the young woman's body, relieving Fenton of the need to hold it tight against the wall, he left, retiring back to his house for a change of clothes, stopping first to summon an imp to remind Stockburn to make a "hasty fucking return" with the sacrifices. Three hours later, the halfling and his deputies returned, each with a child in tow.

The sheriff directed his men to lock the other children up in the jail while he carried a wailing toddler to the judge's chambers. He watched wordlessly, apparently apathetic to the child but enthralled by the process or the low thrum of power that filled the room as Fenton sacrificed the child.

Like the budding portal in the dungeon, the demon drank its fill with a voracious hunger.

"Judge," Stockburn whispered, a touch of reverence in his voice. He dared not interrupt his true master's feeding.

"What is it?" Fenton replied coldly in the same hushed tone.

"We're startin' the war, ain't we?"

"Indeed."

The sheriff swallowed hard and looked up at the silver bull's head. "I wanna be stronger for it. I wanna be strong for the war. I wanna be a weapon."

Fenton gave a low laugh. "You really do love to hurt people, don't you? We'll discuss it later. Let the master recover. In the meantime, round up the town. There's a project downstairs that will need more sustenance. And we'll need bodies. Bring them all in."

"Yes, sir." Stockburn grinned malevolently, turning to head out and gather his men to make preparations for the next few days of arrests.

"Oh, and Stockburn."

"Judge?"

"Make sure Duncan's up and around when you finish. It's time to serve him justice."

Chapter 13

Everyone except Bakhor spent the next few days lounging about. The giant orc managed half a day of rest before ze got restless and went back to hir regular routine of helping run Hunter's Hollow and patrolling outside the walls. Gwen spent her time visiting Grimluk and keeping Leigh focused in her injured state. Amazingly, that effort was easier than one would expect. All Gwen did was chat with her about whatever topic came to mind. As they spoke one day, Mint came out and motioned for them. Gwen took Leigh's transparent hand in her own and led her friend into the healer's clinic.

"Leigh, Gwen, how are you two? Pardon the obvious question, Leigh."

Gwen grinned in spite of herself. "Um, I'm good. Leigh's still hurt."

"I would figure so. Even a spirit isn't gonna tangle with a demon without harm."

Leigh flickered for a moment, looking more gaunt and worn out. "It hurts to be here. It hurts so much."

"Yeah," Mint said with a sigh. "Sorry bout

that. The kid here's the only thing keeping you from being dismissed from the Hollow. The wards are pretty strong. We like to keep up our mystical defenses." He regarded the ghostly girl silently for a long moment. "Leigh, after Gwen explained what happened to you, I did a bit of research with our Loremaster. He's fairly sure you're no mere ghost. Ghosts are typically nothing more than death echoes. Sometimes, when folks pass on, they can leave a piece of themselves behind. Usually, that happens from a particularly violent death but sometimes it's from those who've inhabited one place all their lives. Leaves an imprint. Either way, it happens in a pretty specific place."

"If Leigh's not a ghost, what is she, Mr. Mint?" Gwen instinctively gave Leigh's hand a squeeze. After days of contact, she'd grown accustomed to the cold grip.

"Vatris figures she's a myling. They're spirits birthed from an unwilling sacrifice to a demon. Emphasis there on the unwilling. A myling is a piece of someone's essence left over. They grow wrathful if they're not put at peace immediately and have a habit of jumping on the backs of travelers. They do share a trait with ghosts though and tend to stick near the place where they died."

"I didn't die in that town," Leigh said quietly.

"Yes. You've stuck to your father. Almost like a poltergeist. Now, maybe Vatris's books have old information but…I wonder if you aren't trying to turn into a wraith. Maybe even spirit of vengeance."

"I feel Papa calling to me. His spirit." Leigh twitched. For a moment, the ghost's monstrous visage shined through again but Gwen squeezed her hand. "He has to make it right. He murdered other kids, too. Fed them to that thing."

Mint nodded slowly and sighed. "I was afraid of that. And unfortunately, I am ill equipped to heal you. I've spent a long time learning how to treat all manner of wounds but—"

"I'm dead."

"Simple truth. For what it's worth, you handle it quite well."

"Mr. Mint, what if I can heal her?" Gwen asked quietly.

The healer scratched his chin and seemed to consider it. "Reckon it couldn't hurt to try."

"Can I heal her, Spirit?" Gwen asked inwardly, looking at the strange gash shape across Leigh's torso.

I am…unsure. It is possible.

Gwen took a deep breath and touched a hand to the gash, doing what she thought Mint would do. Her eyes squeezed shut and she tried to focus on the spiritual wound. When nothing happened, one eye peeked open. Then the other. A frustrated grunt escaped the child's mouth and she looked to Mint.

He gave a low shrug. "Sorry, kid, maybe it can't be done. Maybe you should take Miss Fenton out of the Hollow. The wards aren't so concentrated outside the gates. Should provide a little relief. Take that fool warg with you for protection. She could use the walk. Urgroz is feedin' her table scraps again."

The girls sighed and Gwen led Leigh to collect

Fang and head outside the gates. She found Fang lying next to Grimluk's bed. He was sleeping soundly, one hand folded across his stomach. Gwen looked at her adopted brother for a long time, wondering how long it would take him to recover. No one was sure but Mint had said he doubted it would take too long. She bent down next to Fang and asked if she would mind to come with them outside. The warg looked up at Grimluk and back at Gwen and whimpered.

"Go on," Grimluk said lightly. "I'm okay. Watch her for me."

Fang gave a high whimper.

"I'm sure."

The lupine beast rose to her feet and lumbered out of the room. Gwen gave Grimluk a quick hug and followed after the warg. She looked back as she closed the door. He smiled at her and closed his eyes again.

* * *

It'd been days since Mint had wrapped his wounds, slathering the badges in the healing salve Grimluk had relied so heavily on for years, and given him a strong potion that smelled like troll fat and tasted like rotten berries. The salve had most likely already done its job but potions were slow work. His whole body was still in rough shape after his transformation under the Oath. His mind needed time to heal as well.

After almost two months of psychic attacks and several days of intense mental torture, reliving old memories made twisted and sharp, he needed all the rest he could get. He was doing his best to take that rest but he'd never really been so inactive. He was bored and growing more restless by the hour. Still, he'd need to get back to peak health before he could take on Cholem and Parker Fenton. He'd asked Bakhor to have the Doom Riders scout Perfection before coming to Hunter's Hollow. He feared what news the demon hunting duo would bring but he had to know. Perfection was his responsibility now.

He looked out his window to see the sun creeping into the sky. He lay in bed, staring at the trees beyond and finally whipped the blanket back and sat up. Fang, ever vigilant at the side of his bed, scooted out of the way and gave a low growl.

"I can't sit in bed any longer, girl." He stood slowly, testing his legs, keeping balance with one hand on the wall. "If I don't get up and walk around, I'm gonna lose my mind."

Fang huffed. Grimluk nodded to himself and stretched, long arms scraping the air just below the ceiling. Urgroz had provided some clothes for this very moment, when Grimluk had inevitably gotten sick of staying still. Loose denim trousers and a pale red shirt that he slid easily into, not bothering to catch any of the five buttons that ran from the chest to the collar. Fang nosed the bedroom door open and led Grimluk to the stairs. Once on his feet, he'd felt confident in his ability to stay upright and walk but the stairs gave him a sudden pause and he wondered for a moment if he would need someone's assistance.

"Fuck it," he muttered and took each step

meticulously, like a small child. Fang paced up and down the steps, watching him, short whines escaping her snout every so often.

His bare feet finally touched down at the bottom and he sighed. Good. He needed that. Small victories could go a long way. Fang let out a pleased yip and led him onward, toward the kitchen. Urgroz came out to see what she was yipping about and gave a big smile.

"You're finally up," he said, moving quickly to envelope his son in a tight hug.

Grimluk squeezed his father lightly, taking in the smells of the kitchen that wafted off him. Spices mixing with a heady aroma of meats and broths and a hint of yeast from bread.

"I missed you, Dakka."

"I missed you, too, boy." Urgroz pulled away, looking up at Grimluk, giving his face a light pat. "Come on, I'm sure you're starved. Even *my* stews can't keep you filled up in bed like that."

"Still good all the same." Grimluk's stomach let out a very audible gurgle. "Guess I came down at the right time."

Urgroz gave one lone laugh that shook his big belly and ushered his son to a dining table before sending Fang to find Bakhor and Gwen.

"How's Gwen been doing while I've been stuck in bed?" Grimluk took a seat, facing half towards the kitchen.

"Mostly, she's been trying to figure out how to fix that ghost girl up but, I think it was yesterday, Bakhor took her to Vatris's lessons and started her on learning her letters in between his history lessons with the apprentices."

"Oh, I bet he likes her. I'm sure she's asking more questions than the apprentices tend to."

Urgroz came back out of the kitchen carrying a slab of buffalo steak and a loaf of dark, crusty bread. As the smell of the steak hit Grimluk's nose, saliva practically flooded his mouth.

"Ayup," Urgroz replied. "He's quite taken with her. And Leigh, too. He was rather excited to take down a myling's story."

"I reckon so." Grimluk's brow furrowed. "A damn myling. Certainly explained a lot. How are Gwen's letters comin'?"

"She's takin' to 'em pretty quick. Maybe the Spirit's helpin' her. Said she wants to give it a name, too. Asked if we'd help." He dipped back into the kitchen to fill a pitcher with water from a pump, returning with a tankard in his other hand as well. "I haven't a clue what to name the damn thing. It says it doesn't remember having a name either."

"A name? I take it Vatris and Mint can't find a way to pull the Spirit out of her?" Grimluk asked, a touch of worry on his face.

"Vatris had never heard of a spirit living inside someone like that before. Or as he put it, 'co-existing.' Told her he'd keep looking if she wanted. I think she's getting comfortable with it though."

Grimluk sighed and broke off a chunk of bread. "She seems to be doing well at least."

"Mm, better than when you rode in on that horse. Guess that ritual helped her, too. If that kid decides to be a hunter, even just to work with wayward spirits, she could do a lot of good."

Grimluk shook his head. "No. No, she needs to stay away from hunting. The safer she is the better her life will be. She's suffered enough already."

"Boy, you know that ain't your choice to make."

Grimluk grunted and sighed. "Shut up, Dakka."

"Eat your steak, ya big, green ass," Urgroz said with a grin.

Grimluk tore into the steak with zeal, slicing chunks off and wrapping them in bits of bread. As he devoured the meal, Fang returned with Bakhor and Gwen in tow. Gwen took off running for Grimluk and barreled into his side with a squeal.

"You're out of bed!" she shouted, hugging him so hard he could have sworn she was trying to burrow into him.

"I am. I hear you're learnin' your letters. That's good. Vatris is a good teacher." He pulled her back and offered her a piece of bread. "Dakka says you're doin' good, too. How's Leigh?"

"She doesn't like being inside the walls very much. Mint says the wards hurt her. I wanted to heal her but I guess I can't do that." A frown formed on her little face. "I keep tryin' though. She helped us so much."

"That she did."

A thought blossomed in Grimluk's mind as he took another bite of steak. It occurred to him that he was forgetting something. Something big. Something very important. It struck him all at once. He turned to Gwen, panic rising.

"Little one…where's the amulet? What happened to it?" His eyes were wild. If Fenton got a hold of it, he'd make better use of it than Selbie had.

"Oh, that. Leigh hid it for me. I said to put it where no one could find it so I don't know where it is. I asked her to do that before we went to find you. She said it was safe."

Grimluk let out a huge sigh, practically deflating in the process. He dropped his head down into his hands for a moment, dragging them down his face as he lifted it back up. "Good, that's good. Smart thinkin', little one."

Gwen beamed a smile at him and twirled absently. When they'd met, she liked to twirl her little dress but now she wore pants. The dresses suited her personality but pants tended to be more practical. He doubted the twirling would leave her without some effort though.

Bakhor watched quietly, a small smile on hir face. "Good to see you up again, my little hunter. How are you feeling?"

"Still shaky. My dreams are still weird but I'm getting better. Was thinkin' about getting a gun in my hand again. Even just to clean it. I need to do something besides sit inside."

Bakhor nodded. "The Riders will be here in a week. Comin' in from a job on the southern edge of New Gilead."

Grimluk munched quietly on his steak. He had no doubt Fenton would be planning something big after his escape. They'd have to do the same.

"Reckon I ought to start gettin' myself back into fighting condition then," he said.

The food felt good and gave Grimluk fresh energy. He figured the best way to start his recovery was to walk the grounds. So, stomach full, he headed outside. It'd been five or six years since he'd last been to what amounted to his home. Most hunters wandered but he'd been single-minded in his desire to get out into the world and help. Logically, he knew it'd be a never ending job. There were always people like Selbie and Fenton or cults bent on bringing some demon or supposed god into the world. But there were good people in the world, too.

He stopped outside Kort's training area, musing on his thoughts. The apprentices were practicing their hand-to-hand skills. Kort himself had a distinct style built around his power. Archel, Kort's partner in training, was an old elf covered in scars who taught a style on the opposite side, based on speed and turning an opponent's strength against them. Grimluk thought back to his days as an apprentice and how many times he'd gotten flipped on his head for barreling at her thinking he understand how Kort could spar so evenly with her. "It was just strength," he'd thought. He had size and the natural, raw strength of his people. He charged, for weeks, and each and every single time he'd end up on his face eating dirt.

Kort, always hands on, walked through the current crop of apprentices, correcting their positions, offering encouragement or a growl of disapproval when needed. He spotted Grimluk and made his way over.

"My favorite pupil returns," he said, offering his hand.

Grimluk took his old teacher's hand. "Favorite pupil my ass. You gettin' soft, Kort?"

"Ha! The day I get soft is the day you give up hunting. Good to see you up and around again. Bakhor might finally calm down now. Ze's been pestering everyone, trying to keep busy." Kort turned and pointed towards one of his students, a young orc with a mop of black hair and a thick body. "Decided to try and teach a round of melee and bruised that one's ribs. Tough kid but I felt bad."

Grimluk grunted. "He looks a bit like Dakka."

"Ya reckon? Huh. Anyhow, kid'll be fine. Mint gave him a small potion and gave him a quick rub. You know how he does." Kort's face got serious as he did an impression of the healer. He clapped his hands together, rubbing them roughly before holding them out and letting out an exaggerated hum.

"Gets the job done, don't it?" Grimluk said with a shrug.

"That it does. Anything I can do for ya?"

"Maybe. I was thinkin' about gettin' back to a gun soon. Need to collect myself and target practice is a good place to start. Think you can set me up at the range?"

Kort shook his finger and nodded. "Consider it done, Grim, m'boy. You come back any time tomorrow and I'll have you a station ready."

"I'll need a gun, too. Anything'll do until I can

get something new forged and ready. Lost my gun and my knife."

"And ya rode in on a horse. Fuck me. It really was as bad as all that."

Grimluk looked down. "It really was."

"I'll take care of it. Nothin' but small groups since you left so there's plenty of spare pistols. Might even still have that old conversion you used."

"Thanks, Kort. Get back to your class before one of them gets bored and hurts themself."

Kort nodded and made his way back through his students. Grimluk gave a wave to Archel as she appeared to teach her portion of the lesson. She gave a stiff nod, the barest hint of a smile forming on her lips before focusing full on the students. Always business. He stood still, watching the apprentices, mostly young orcs, before finally wandering off towards the forge.

The forge was a slight misnomer. It seemed the best title for the operation. And the smiths *did* forge weapons but that old process remained entirely for bladed weapons. Mostly that consisted of knives of varying sizes and uses, from skinning animals to Grimluk's own knife, which served many roles. Beyond that, they had all manner of machinery designed for building firearms and pressing ammunition.

The two forgemasters were an odd pair. One was a towering orc. At least, towering over her dwarf companion. In truth, she was on the average size for an orc woman, which was still pretty big. They were affectionately known as the Forgemothers and their skill was known throughout New Gilead. That skill kept them supplied, which kept them producing for the Hunters.

New Gilead itself was an allied province, founded between the two primary nations of the Ornesean continent. The idea itself came from a young lord a century prior, looking to expand diplomatically. The Dwarven nation of Reddagia that occupied the north-easterly portion of Ornesea had little interest in expanding beyond the mountains but had no objections to lending aid. The elves of Westlynth, the founding nation, were eager to expand west, hoping to meet more of their native, tribal brethren. New Gilead would have expanded further west, providing citizenship and benefits to the settlers who'd left the region.

Then the Sundering had happened and all westward exploration and expansion had nearly ceased with the formation of the Wastelands. The Borderlands had risen instead, running all along the eastern edge of the Wastelands, almost into the Southern Territories. The need for demon hunters had grown bad enough that the previous governor had put out a call for any hunters who would settle and grant them official guild status. Hunter's Hollow had formed a few months later.

Now, decades later, two of the best smiths in the province, with a handful of apprentices, kept the soldiers supplied with weapons and ammunition. Their shop took up more space in the Hollow than one might expect but they needed room and plenty of machinery to keep up with larger orders.

That massive shop was quiet as Grimluk

approached though. For now, only one of the Forgemothers was active, entirely in one of the workstations that served as the entrance to the rest of the shop. Ythena, the orc woman, was grinding a knife out as he approached. "Hail, mother, strong as steel," he called.

She stopped and looked back. "Grimluk!" She set the knife aside and hurried over to him. "Oh, it's good to see you safe, boy!" Not quite as tall as Urgroz, she wrapped her strong arms around him and lifted him up in a massive bear hug.

"Thank you," he said, laughing, "but I'm still recovering and you might snap me in two."

"Oh oh!" Ythena sat him down gently. "Pardon. It's just been so long since you've been home and then everything that happened to you…word got around."

"I know. And more bad news."

She looked at him with sudden annoyance. "What?"

"Lost my gun and my knife. Gonna need replacements."

"Oh, is that all?" She waved him over. "A few of your peers liked your knife design so much I made a whole batch of them. Still have a few leftover. How'd the revolver treat ya?" She opened a drawer in the wall, revealing a pile of broad blades, seemingly just like his own, save for their wrappings and variations in size. Not everyone favored such a big blade like he did.

"Damn fine weapon. Served me well. Had to have the butt reinforced though. Was hammering too many ghoul skulls. Did you keep the plans for it?" Grimluk reached in and took a blade, unsheathing it. It was identical to its predecessor in every way except the pattern of the metal. The way the Mothers forged their blades meant no two were alike. The process combined mostly strong steel with a bit of cold-forged iron and touches of a silver alloy. He traced the twig-like symbol of the Elder Sign etched above the guard.

"You know we never get rid of a plan. Vatris would probably shoot us himself if we lost one."

Grimluk grinned. "Reckon so. Well, if that's the case, a copy of my gun would do nicely, reinforced butt, too."

Ythena nodded. "Your timing is splendid, actually. Flor's had a new idea. A hunter from Westlynth brought Vatris an old enchanter's tome a while back. All about blood runes."

"More blood magic?"

"Yar. She wants to line the barrels in runes. If she can find the right combination, she thinks it'll allow for the guns to be even deadlier to demons and monsters."

He nodded and his throat rumbled in thought. "Reckon I'll need all the help I can get. Build it. I'll give it a test when it's ready."

"Consider it done. Though it'll be a few days before we can start. Gotta finish an order from the capital."

Grimluk slid his replacement knife back into its leather sheath and nodded. "Figure we got time and this needs to be done right. I had to call in the Riders anyways. They'll be here in a week with news from Perfection."

"That bad?"

"That bad."

She nodded and sighed. "Flor'll be back tomorrow. We'll start as soon as we can."

"Thank you, Ythena." He tapped the sheathed blade against his chest and nodded, leaving her to her work once again.

As the sun rose the next morning, Grimluk crawled out of bed, attempting to reclaim some semblance of a daily routine. Normally, that didn't involve a bath but it'd been days since he'd cleaned up and he still felt a touch on the disgusting side. His time in the dungeon hadn't exactly been clean and he felt like a long soak might help. It did. He followed the bath with some time taking care of his teeth. He'd told Gwen once that orcs prided themselves on taking care of their teeth. Grimluk set about grooming his mouth vigorously.

Once he finished, he headed to the dining table and dropped into a chair for late breakfast with some of the new apprentices. One of them was older than the usual fair. Probably closer to Urgroz's age than Grimluk's, the man was human and introduced himself as John. They discussed training for a few minutes before John finished up his breakfast and headed for lessons with Vatris.

After Grimluk's own breakfast, he went for a walk around the perimeter of the Hollow, Gwen, Fang, and the ever quiet spirit of Leigh Fenton following him. After making his way around and back to the gates, he made for the practice range.

Kort was as good as his word. An old, single-action revolver sat holstered on the farthest bench with a box of a hundred brass shells next to it. A small table sat behind him, cleaning supplies and oil waiting for him as well. Grimluk flexed his hand. The revolver slid out of its holster with the smooth scrape of steel against leather. Two clicks of the hammer and he opened the loading gate, pulling out shells and slipping them in slowly, deliberately before closing the gate back.

Two more clicks of the hammer and the gun was ready to fire. He aimed down the range, a thick hay target pinned into a long dirt wall built somewhere around four feet thick. More than enough to stop the bullet. For a moment, his hand shook. He fired. The top-left corner of the target exploded.

He pulled the hammer back again, click-click-click-click. It was a comforting sound. He pulled the gun back to his ear, moving the hammer back to its start. Click-click-click-click. He smiled and held the gun back out. He breathed in. *Aim with your eye*, he thought, recalling his training so long ago. Make the bullet go wherever you look. The hammer slammed down and the gun barked. He breathed out. The target popped again, closer to center this time.

He lowered his arm for the next shot, like he was shooting from the hip. The other top corner of the target spat straw. Three more shots and it was time to swap in fresh shells. The plunger kicked out the spent brass into a little bin hanging from the beam separating shooting stations. Never waste brass, Kort had always said. Any apprentice who forgot this rule would be punished in a way that made sure they didn't forget a second time. The others would start dumping their shells on the ground while their offending peer collected the shells, cleaned them, and reloaded them.

An hour later, he'd worked through half the shells. His grouping had slowly started pulling back to center. The last six shots had stayed within the penultimate ring. One had even struck dead center. He nodded and dropped the shells into the bin, then dropped into a chair at the little table and set about breaking the gun down for cleaning. This time, he didn't have to argue with his hands or his eyes. They simply did their task. Grimluk let out a contented sigh.

Chapter 14

Hooves thundered across the Sapphire Plains as the Doom Riders made their way north towards Perfection. The two orcs, Eagle and Beast, sat astride two powerful horses that reflected their riders all too well, looking as if they were more than capable of fighting demons themselves. Riders and steeds alike bore the scars of those battles.

The pair wore matching pauldrons and bracers, all black steel and leather with studs and fanged skulls, and the loose denim, also black, that was common to most hunters. For the most part, the studs and skulls were for intimidation purposes. Mortal cultists tended to slow whatever dark ritual they were doing when the Riders appeared. The two were hulking brutes covered in spikes and black with tattoos on their faces. Eagle's tattoo was a stylized version of his namesake, while Beast's was something like a spider mixed with a skull.

Eagle cut ahead with a squeeze of his boots, heading for a smoking farmhouse in the distance. Beast followed. The pair slowed as they approached the house. The heat from the blaze was immense, rolling off in waves that combined with the heat of the late summer sun. Eagle directed his horse around the house. Beast took the opposite direction, meeting his partner in the front.

"Tracks?" Beast asked.

"Too many. Arson." Eagle scanned the flames. There was too much heat to get much info but the broken lantern outside the front door spoke volumes. "They was lazy, too."

"Reckon we oughta check the town and then head on. Grimluk's waitin'."

They approached the town more cautiously. Bakhor had given them a coded warning in the magi-tell message, letting them know to be extremely cautious in their scouting. Ze hadn't mentioned Grimluk by name either, just in case Parker Fenton somehow intercepted the message. Beast had wanted to bust in at first but Eagle reminded him that if they could trust anyone's advice towards caution, it was Bakhor's. Beast agreed and they'd set off.

They stayed in the relative safety of a copse of trees near the edge of Perfection and dismounted, their horses holding their position. Eagle took a spyglass from his saddlebag and crept along until he found a tree big enough to support him. Beast knelt at its base, keeping watch while Eagle hefted himself up into the branches to scout the area. The spyglass clacked as the brass body extended out.

Perfection jumped to his eye. He saw nothing. The main street was empty. Every buckboard porch was bare even of a lone rocker. A gust of wind kicked up a natural dust-devil that spun down the street unhindered for some time before dying out. He followed it, watching it dissipate near the courthouse, undeniably the only area in Perfection still active. Eagle collapsed the spyglass back into his hand, and stroked his handlebar mustache in quiet contemplation with green, meaty fingers before making his way back down.

He knelt next to Beast. "It's too damn quiet. Courthouse is busy but everything else is silent as the grave. I don't like it."

"Well, ya know somethin'? I think you're right. Let's haul ass to the Hollow."

They cut back south towards the farmhouse as an extra precaution and then due east, a mile south of the road, keeping far from it until they'd put plenty of distance between them and Perfection. The Riders cut back north in time to meet the crossroads that pointed them toward Eagle Point and the path to Hunter's Hollow.

* * *

Dakhor finished tapping the ink-tipped needle against Grimluk's bare, shaven skull, setting it aside and dabbing away any excess ink and blood. The seal was a pentacle, surrounded by another circle that was sectioned off at each star point. Sigils filled the sections with more sigils filling the space outside of the star itself. In the center was the five-pronged, twig-like shape, like the one stamped on his knife. What was known as the

Elder Sign. It was an ancient symbol of protection said to repel lesser demons and some monsters. The Sign being centered like that bolstered its power and combined with the sigils to create a powerful mental barrier.

He'd chosen the crown of his skull for the seal's placement both symbolically and logistically. Once his hair grew back in, it would blend in even with his usual hairstyle of a single strip over shaved sides. The seal sitting where it did was a declaration that he'd never have another demon, or a psychic for that matter, in his mind again. It would take something powerful beyond comprehension to break that seal. And, should he ever be captured like in Perfection again, the mystical nature of the tattoo meant it couldn't be removed by force. Besides, how often do you actually look at someone's skull?

Bakhor applied a bandage and off Grimluk went to the range, to join the apprentices for their afternoon shooting. The apprentices all but stopped when he arrived, watching him instead as he took aim. Grimluk certainly wasn't a legend but he was renowned. He thumbed the hammer back with those four familiar clicks and waited. He squeezed the trigger and the gun replied with a small thunderclap. The target popped, just a hair off dead center. He fired two more shots, expanding an already crooked hole. He emptied the gun, each shot similarly off, just a hair, but close enough that each had extended the length of the hole before it.

Kort barked at the apprentices after Grimluk finished his first round. "All right, maggots, show's over. Get to shootin' your own damn selves!"

They each took up their own guns, small bore for the first and second year trainees and big bore for anyone beyond that, or in the case of some of the rare, older apprentices, those who had some semblance of training already. The younger orcs did their best to emulate Grimluk, holding their guns out in one hand.

Grimluk tapped the shoulder of the kid in the stall next to him, startling him. "Use both hands to start with."

The boy nodded silently, slack-jawed, and did as he was told, the barrel of his gun shaking with nervous energy. The shots were wild.

"You'll get there," Grimluk said reassuringly. "Just breathe, take your time. Make every shot count." He gave the boy a pat on the shoulder before going back to his own shooting, alternating between arm out and from the hip. After a while, he found himself satisfied and sat down to focus on cleaning the revolver for the day. As he broke the gun down, Gwen walked up and climbed onto the fence that served as a back wall to the firing range.

"Whatcha doin?" she asked, her legs dangling lightly from her perch.

"Cleanin' my gun. What are you doin', little one?"

"I'm supposed to tell you that the…the Dumb Riders is here."

He snorted and looked at her. "Doom. Dee oh oh em."

"Oh!" She paused. "What's doom?"

"It's like bad things are gonna happen. If you say someone's doomed, it means the bad thing is inescapable."

"So are the Doom Guys bad? They almost shot Leigh. They're pretty loud, too."

"They're only bad if you're a demon. They didn't know about Leigh. None of us have ever really *talked* to a spirit before, little one. At least, not like you do."

Gwen watched intently as Grimluk jammed a wire brush through each successive chamber of the gun's cylinder. "Are you a Doom Rider?"

"Not exactly. That was just sort of a nickname they got before I was even born. They liked it and it stuck."

"Okaaaaay. I gotta go tell them I told you." She hopped down and took off, boots that were almost too big slapping the dirt with thuds that weren't quite heavy.

Once Grimluk finished cleaning the gun, he followed her trail towards the big house. As the door opened, the sounds of raucous laughter spilled out, reminding anyone who might have forgotten, that Eagle and Beast were around. Eagle stood up as Grimluk joined them.

"There he is! Good to see ya, kid. We were just tellin' your folks about the job down south before we came up. Whole pack of death hounds being led by a demon knight. What a rush!"

"A pack of death hounds with a knight? How on Arkod did you two get up here so quick then?" Grimluk couldn't contain his surprise.

"Took out the knight first. Stampeded right through the damn dogs," Beast replied. "Musta been recently summoned. Was too cocky, like he'd never heard of us."

"Never heard of us? *Us*?" Eagle laughed hard and slapped his thigh. "That cost him. We deviated septums, ripped out goozles, and knocked the yellow right off the teeth of that bastard."

"Confused the hounds. We took 'em down before they could get any sense back," Beast finished.

"Nothin' like a good fight to get the blood pumpin'," Eagle declared.

Grimluk shook his head in awe. It would've taken him a good deal of planning to take on a demon knight by himself like that and the Riders went in and killed it without any foresight beyond race in and pummel it. He laughed in spite of himself. He supposed sometimes you just had to attack.

"Have you been filled in on why I called you?" he finally asked.

"Bakhor gave us the gist of it," Eagle replied. "Gave us a big fat warning in the magi-tell message so we sent up somethin' big for ya. Should be here tomorrow. You're gonna love it."

Grimluk's throat rumbled in thought. "See anything in Perfection on the way up?"

"Town seemed deserted except for the big building at the other side of town. Didn't much like it. Beast didn't like it either so we hauled ass on up here."

"Yeah and what's with the spirit sitting outside the Hollow? Thing's bleedin' ectoplasm everywhere. And what about this kid here. Says she's your sister. She don't look like no orc."

"Spirit was the daughter of Judge Parker Fenton, the guy who runs Perfection. Name's Leigh and her loving—" he sneered, "—father sacrificed her to his demon master. And that's Gwen. Took her in a couple of months back after a job went bad. Thanks to those two, we managed to escape Perfection."

Eagle and Beast looked at Gwen who just gave them a big, proud smile. They looked at each other and nodded in agreement. "All right, kid, start at the beginning."

Grimluk took his time recounting everything that had happened since he arrived in Greenreach Bluffs. Gwen, having climbed into her adopted brother's lap, filled in her own parts where she thought appropriate. The Riders listened attentively, soaking in the information, arms crossed and faces set sternly.

Eagle had let out a mirthful laugh when Gwen started talking about slipping out of Fenton's house to find Grimluk. "I like this kid," he declared.

Beast chimed in. "You got grit, kid."

Gwen's brow furrowed in confusion. "I got dirt?"

"You're tough," Beast corrected. "Double tough."

"Your new sister's gonna make a great hunter, Grimluk," Eagle said, flexing a fist out in front of himself.

Gwen looked up at Grimluk with a huge grin. He refused to meet her eye and frowned instead. "No. She can be a loremaster, study under Vatris or even healing under Mint. I'd prefer she study under Dakka, be a cook, keep herself out of trouble."

Gwen's face dropped.

Eagle shook his head, a knowing smirk across his face. "That's what your folks said about you and look how you turned out. It's her choice to make though and I'd say she's proven herself."

Grimluk gave a low, annoyed growl. "Yeah, well, I promised her folks. Promised."

Gwen squirmed down off of Grimluk's lap and walked away. She'd managed to make it through the whole story without so much as a whimper but his sudden mood shift had clearly upset her. A heavy sigh filled Grimluk. He raked his hands down his face, guilt and sympathy gnawing at him in equal measure. Eagle cleared his throat and pointed one finger in Gwen's direction. Grimluk nodded his head wearily and followed after her. Cicadas pulsed noisily as he made his way towards the front gate, figuring she'd go to find Leigh. He found Gwen curled up against the wall just outside the gate, hugging her knees and sniffling. Leigh hovered passively nearby, quiet and foreboding. A sneer played at her ghostly lips.

Grimluk dropped down next to Gwen. "I'm sorry, little one."

"I just wanna help. Momma and Daddy said they were proud of me. Aren't you proud of me?" She looked up at him, tears sparkling in the afternoon sun.

Her face was so earnest it hurt to look at. "Gwen, of course I am." He wrapped an arm around her, practically swallowing her underneath it. "I just want you to stay safe. After messin' up so bad and promisin' your folks that I would keep you safe, I don't know what else to do. Fenton took you and used you against me. To control me. He could've killed you. *I* could have killed you..."

"But you didn't. We saved each other. Leigh and Mr. Duncan helped, too."

Grimluk sighed. "And Jed was probably killed for helping us. That's what this life is like. Nothin' but blood and pain, little one. Even when we help people."

"But you still help them."

"But only in violence. I have a talent for it but there's other ways to help. Alchemy, economics, even just listening to folks."

Gwen said nothing, just leaned into his side and attempted to hide her face. Maybe from him, or Leigh, or even the sun and anyone or anything else that might see. Leigh stared at Grimluk, the sneer fading as the ghost's eyes softened.

"I have to help people though," Gwen finally said. "Because of Nicholas. I have to find him. I have to stop him from hurting people. Have to stop him from...killing another person's momma."

With one arm, Grimluk scooped the girl up and pulled her into his lap, rocking her silently for a long moment. "That wasn't your fault. You don't have to make it your responsibility to find him either." The irony of the statement flitted in the back of his mind. The same could be said of the orcs after all this time. Cholem had even mocked him for that.

"But I need to. Brother hurt everyone." She let out a pained sigh. "He's bad."

"Shh, it's okay. Just…wait 'til all of this is over. Wait until I've stopped Fenton and *then* we'll talk more about you becomin' a demon hunter, okay? Please?"

Gwen sighed, wiping her nose her on sleeve. "Okay. Are you proud of me though?"

"Very proud, little one. You've been so brave. And you, too, Leigh. I know the wards hurt you and I know it's very hard to control what you are. Thank you."

"Gwen gave me back a piece of myself. I had to do it," the ghost said, its voice quivering. "I don't think I can stay near this place for much longer though. I can feel him pulling me. I need to punish him." Leigh's form bubbled, hinting once more at the true form beneath that burned with the desire for vengeance and wrath.

The trio sat quietly as the sun worked its way lower in the sky. Grimluk wrestled with his thoughts. He reckoned Gwen and Leigh were as well, each of them attempting to find some sort of solace.

* * *

Groans filled the Perfection jail. Every traveler in the hotel, every dancer, patron, and barman in the saloon, and anyone else with the misfortune of being in Perfection had been rounded up and imprisoned, one by one, two by two. At first, Stockburn came up with whatever trumped up but believable charge he could but after half the town had been taken, and half of them fed to the Abyssal womb, they stopped asking and just started wounding and dragging them away. The farms had followed shortly after.

All the children had been locked up separately.

With the last family secured, and their house in flames, Stockburn entered the dungeon amid screams and protests. He slammed the door for silence and watched as Fenton shoved the slit throat of yet another prisoner into the swirling energy of the womb. The old dwarf man twitched as wet, gurgling groans spilled out his mouth, spurting through what remained of his once bushy, salt and pepper beard. When the sigils took hold of the man's body, Fenton let go.

"Yes?" he asked, turning to face Stockburn. He pulled an old towel from his pocket and wiped his blade clean.

"Everyone is accounted for. We burnt some of the farmhouses down."

"*Everyone*?"

Stockburn hesitated. "Except the witch. Went for her first. Old hag just upped and vanished like a fart on the wind."

Fenton sneered. "How elegant, Sheriff. It can't be helped then. And how is the good Deputy Duncan fairing?"

"I'd say fat and happy if he was still among

the living. The ghoul seems pleased though. Eats and turns the loud ones, teaches 'em who's in charge."

"Never let it be said that you can't achieve competence when you put your mind to it, Sheriff." Fenton pocketed the knife once more, wrapped in the opposite side of the towel. "Is there anything else?"

"Just..."

Fenton crossed his hands behind his back and eyed the halfling. "Just?"

Stockburn suddenly remembered his hat and pulled it off quickly, holding it to his chest. "Just, I was hopin' once we rounded everyone up, you and I could finish our discussion about my request."

Fenton's eyes lost a touch of their annoyance. "Indeed. As it happens, I was discussing it with the master this morning. Cholem informed me that the thing behind me will be ready in a few days' time. It was suggested that we, ahem, partner you and your deputies with some of our forthcoming allies."

Stockburn's eyes darted to the sigil glowing behind the judge. "I hope you don't mean to feed us to it or make us lowly ghouls."

Fenton sighed. "Stockburn, you have been far too useful to turn into a simple shambler or sacrifice. No, the master would like to make you all into demon knights."

Stockburn processed the information, trying to remember what a knight was for a moment. It finally clicked and he practically beamed with pride, puffing out his chest and grinning. "Well gods-damned, boss. Me, a *knight.* Ain't that just a kick in the head!"

"Yes, well, try to show a little class to go with your new station, will you?"

Stockburn nodded, slapping his hat back on his head with a flourish and made his way out, ready to tell his deputies the good news. Fenton sighed as he went, shaking his head. A loud crunch popped from behind him, drawing his attention. A scaly, onyx talon shot out from the dim vortex growing under the old dwarf, punching through the body in an attempt to expedite the feeding. The corpse pulled in behind the talon, crunching and snapping while the demonic arm yanked. The spine finally snapped, bending the body unnaturally, and the corpse slipped through the hole. Dim howls slipped out of the portal.

* * *

Their talk helped settle Grimluk and Gwen. After a big dinner that night, they slept soundly, letting the cares of life slip away long enough to get some much needed rest. The Riders left for Eagle Point before dawn to fetch whatever it was they'd hauled up for Grimluk. He was recovering steadily, increasing his activities each day by doing more or pushing a little harder. Mint's potion and the quiet of the Hollow worked to mend him mentally as well as physically. He could feel his old strength returning.

A good many trips around Hunter's Hollow had Grimluk itching for some target practice. He found the range empty and set about his routine. A few dozen rounds later, he set the gun down satisfied. His hand felt steady once more. He decided to see just how steady it was and found an apprentice gun belt, slinging it around his waist and buckling it snugly. The butt of the revolver sat just at his hip.

He stepped out in front of the stall and stood there casually, replaying the last time he'd been stopped by highway thieves. One with a gun. Three with knives. Two ready to charge him with their blades. In his mind's eye, he saw the one with the gun cock the hammer. He slapped iron.

The shot hit high on the target but his draw had been smooth. He still wasn't the fastest but he was plenty fast to handle anyone who lacked more training with a gun. He'd need to switch focus to quick draws, regain his accuracy out of the holster again. He smiled to himself. This was good. He slid the pistol back into the holster and readied himself for a second draw.

"There he is! Hey, Grimluk!" Eagle yelled.

Grimluk looked back at the Rider heading toward him and his brow furrowed in curiosity. The two were heading his way with what looked like a huge, ornate coffin on their shoulders. He blinked, taking the sight of it in. The whole thing was filigreed with brass. The wood had been carved in looping floral patterns that ran up and down the sides. He wandered out to meet them.

"What in the world are you carrying?" he asked. "It looks like a coffin."

"Course it looks like a coffin," Beast replied.

"It *is* a coffin."

"Head back out where you were," Eagle instructed. "Told ya, you're gonna love this thing."

Once back out on the other side of the range stalls, the Riders set the coffin down, skinny end pointing down at the back end of the range. Eagle bent down and flipped a catch with a loud *shunk* and pushed the lid back revealing the mysterious contents. Grimluk looked down at a mass of gleaming metal. The lid housed eight tubes strapped down tight.

"A cannon?" he asked.

"Ha! No, even more fun." Eagle reached down and grabbed a handle sticking out of the top of the mass and pulled. Gears and chains caught, cranking away as it rose. The Rider slid one of the tubes from its slot and slapped it into a hole at an angle on the top thing's body. "It's called a crank-gun."

"What the fuck is a crank-gun?"

Beast laughed.

Eagle grinned. "Just watch."

He double-checked the long tube, pulled a pin on the body of the gun, and then started turning the crank sticking out of the other side. The crank caught with a *clak-clak* and bullets started spitting out at the dirt wall as fast as Eagle could turn it, kicking up mounds of dirt and shredding the hay target Grimluk had been practicing on. The tube went dry and the bullets ceased, the absence of the gun's firing blanketing Hunter's Hollow in a shrill silence.

Half the Hollow's residents wandered over to

see what was going on, crowding around the firing range. Grimluk looked at the Doom Riders and started laughing.

"What'd I tell ya, kid?" Eagle beamed proudly. "We did a job sometime last year for some big shot military guy up near Dragon Tongue. Dwarf's family was in trouble, offered a big reward. Turns out, he's a weapon designer. Said he could make us some kind of special weapon when we finished up. He made this."

Grimluk whistled.

Beast continued. "Thing's built out of dwarvish steel a lot like the stuff the Forgemothers use. It locks in the coffin for transport. This thing's almost as tough as us."

The crowd gave a few whistles of their own. One of the apprentices yelled for Eagle to shoot the crank-gun again. He obliged. It seemed to satisfy their curiosity about what they'd heard. The crowd started to slim as each headed back to what they'd been doing. Grimluk circled the crank-gun, looking the whole thing over with a grin on his face.

"Leave it to you two," he said, shaking his head. "Not that I don't appreciate it, but why bring it here?"

"Well, ya see," Beast began, "it uh, well, it was taking up space and we got no use for it travelin' like we do."

"Figure the leasts we can do with it is leave it here for Ythena and Flor to look at and maybe you'll find some use for it, too." Eagle patted the side of the gun's body.

"I'm sure I can think of somethin'. Another week and I think I'll be close to top shape again, and then we can start planning how we're gonna hit Fenton." Grimluk crossed his arms. "You two up for a scouting trip tomorrow?"

"We're always ready," Eagle said, punching his palm.

The three hunters left out at just before dawn the next morning, making a straight line towards Perfection. Grimluk, surprising everyone once again, opted to ride a horse instead of trying to crowd on the back of Eagle or Beast's nameless steeds. Time was precious, he'd said, and if they needed to escape, the fastest way was a horse. After everything that'd happened, he decided to trust the horse Jed Duncan had given them during their escape. They rode hard over the plains, the horses' hooves pounding up dirt.

The trio neared the town late in the afternoon, approaching from the backside of the courthouse, still far enough away they could dismount and walk in. From the top of a hill some ways back, they crouched to observe the town. As the Doom Riders had told Grimluk, the town seemed deserted save for the courthouse. Grimluk watched through Eagle's spyglass, making mental notes of what he saw. He saw the empty town for a moment before a rush of leather wings and hisses drew his attention away from the spyglass. Imps had spotted them and now rushed to the courthouse, already too far gone to draw a bead on and shoot. Parker Fenton would know they were there in moments.

"Ah, shit," Grimluk muttered.

Chapter 15

A flurry of wings rushed into the big building, the imps all squawking with malicious pleasure. They each found perches and let Fenton and Cholem know that they'd spotted three orcs behind the hill. Fenton smiled.

"Grimluk returns. How wonderful." Fenton stepped out of his chambers. "Stockburn. Time to stretch your new legs. Show him."

A wicked smile spread across the sheriff's face, sharp, yellow teeth punctuating the halfling's countenance. Stockburn let out a long, shrill whistle. A death hound appeared next to him, reined and saddled. Rider and steed took off, breaking right through one of the courthouse's big front doors.

"Idiot," Fenton muttered after him. "I hope this captain of yours was worth the trouble of summoning."

"Patience, Parker Fenton," Cholem replied.

Stockburn followed the imps to the hill, gun brandished and ready for murder. The trio of orcs had already fled and he saw they were riding back the way they'd come. He pulled the reins of the hound and commanded it to follow. The voice that came out was far deeper than it had ever been before. The death hound locked its burning red eyes on the horses and gave chase, snarling the whole way.

Grimluk looked back at their pursuer and growled. The huge black dog thing was barreling down on them like the embodiment of fury itself, a maw of razor-sharp teeth bared at the would-be interlopers. He pulled the reins with his left hand, pulling his revolver with his right, and turned the horse around to take aim. The Forgemothers had yet to build his new gun so he was still using the one he'd been practicing with. He pulled the hammer back and fired.

The bullet ripped out of the gun and slammed into the death hound's left cheek, driving it to the right. It tripped over its own feet, throwing Stockburn off. Grimluk spun the horse back around and drove it onward, rejoining the Doom Riders and renewing their pace.

As Perfection's newly-knighted sheriff sailed through the air, he tucked his body in a somersault and crashed to his feet, skidding across the grass hard enough to dig twin grooves into the ground behind him. Once stopped, he ripped off his hat and then his coat and shirt with a simple tug that tore the material apart, tossing it away like dirty rags. Stockburn's skin turned hard and red. Skin and muscle stretched as twin growths pushed out from his shoulder blades. He let out a shout and squeezed every muscle in his body. The growths exploded from his back, membranous wings spilling out in a shower of black gore.

"Go back!" he shouted at the death hound as it rejoined him, the hole in its cheek knitting closed. "I don't need you."

The demon-possessed halfling scaled the nearest tree and leaped from on high, wings spreading wide and filling with air as Stockburn took flight. New muscles pumped and twisted around new bones turning in new sockets, propelling the sheriff forward several dozen feet in the air.

Stockburn couldn't completely match the horse's speed but he could fly over the tree tops and avoid other such obstacles along the ground. And he still had his gun. He could feel his new power pouring into the weapon, changing it. When he pulled the trigger, it didn't fire lead at his targets.

It fired leeches.

The blood-suckers fired out in shrieking blasts. They slammed into the ground and into trees, hungry mouths clamping down on contact while their tails flailed around wildly. One whipped passed Grimluk's arm with a dull scream. Eagle and Beast pulled right, cutting through a rough traveled path usually reserved only for animals. Grimluk pulled left, hoping the split would slow Stockburn down or at least make himself the only target. He suddenly wished he rode more, wished he had greater control over the horse's movements.

Tiny mouths, sharp and eager rained down around him as he tried to direct his mount to avoid being bitten. He aimed the horse through a grove of trees for cover. The gesture proved futile as the leeches continued raining down at him. He pushed the horse harder, leaning low against its neck.

"I'm sorry, my friend!" he shouted to the horse.

Gunfire barked from ahead and the leeches stopped. Grimluk could see Eagle pointing a rifle from his horse, firing shots at the bat-winged halfling. Stockburn swooped and dodged awkwardly, clearly still unfamiliar with his new power of flight. He cut too hard, forgot to tuck his wings, and a bullet ripped through the membranous flesh like it was a sheet of tissue paper, sending him plummeting in a tight corkscrew. He slammed into the ground face first. His neck snapped loudly on impact.

Grimluk and the Doom Riders continued on at full speed, aimed straight for Hunter's Hollow once again. Eagle and Beast gave their horses each a pat on the neck as encouragement. Grimluk marveled at the beasts' courage. They'd need to reward the horses for their efforts if they escaped.

Stockburn climbed to his feet, wings tangled and broken along with his neck. His wounds began to shift and crack, resetting in an orchestra of snapping bones and meat. His head lolled uncontrollable while he waited for his neck and wings to right themselves.

"Ooooh, you'll pay for that, you gobby shitheads," Stockburn said, growling and spitting out dirt. He stood where he was for some time, his head and wings still bent unnaturally. He tapped his foot impatiently, like a bratty child before his head and wings snapped upright with a chorus of loud *pops*. Stockburn stretched his extremities and then took to the air again.

The hunters continued to ride hard, pushing for the safety of Hunter's Hollow as fast as the horses could get them there. Grimluk happened to look back and saw Stockburn's wings growing closer bit by bit. He wasn't sure whether the horses were slowing or whether the halfling was getting faster but he figured either way, they couldn't make it without some help. He gave a bellowing "Whoa!" that hit the ears of Eagle and Beast as well. They all came to a stop.

"That rifle isn't a demon-killer, is it?" Grimluk asked Eagle.

"No, just for hunting while we're on the road."

"Then we're gonna have to make this count." He dismounted quickly. "I'm pretty sure that thing chasing us is Stockburn. Looked like a halfling before all this. He's gaining fast. Find some cover and shoot that fucker's wings out again. Bring him down when he gets closer."

"Then what?" Beast asked.

"Then I do enough damage we can get back to safety. This shouldn't get too out of hand. I'd reckon he's probably drunk on the power right now. He didn't seem that bright to begin with, so he'll be extra sloppy."

Stockburn saw them all disappear behind some trees. He grinned a tight, malicious grin, flashing his sharp teeth once again. "They're trying to hide again. I'll have your blood, goblins! I'll rip you apart and chew on your bones!"

When he got close enough to start firing more repulsive leeches again, rifle shots punched his wings for the second time. Eagle worked the lever on his rifle in quick succession, each *clicka-click* ending with a bark from the muzzle. Stockburn tumbled and flipped, dropping out of the sky again. He seemed to have learned something from the first fall and managed to land on his back this time instead of his neck. His body bounced and skidded along the ground before slapping into a sapling tree that was thick enough to absorb some of his momentum. Stockburn and the tree came to a stop, face down in a tangled, dizzy mess of broken bones, splinters, and dirt.

Grimluk rushed out at him, planting one massive boot into Stockburn's spine, bringing a growl from the knight. Grimluk took a gnarled, busted wing in each hand, grabbing near the root, and pulled with a roar. Adrenaline pumped through him, lending him an extra bit of strength. He made good use of it. The wings, rough, leathery skin and tough muscle, cracked and popped before separating with a series of wet *snaps* that made Stockburn roar in pain and thrash impotently. Grimluk tossed the wings aside like kindling. Blood rushed from the stumps, nearly black, and rolled off in heavy waves.

That would take some time to heal. If he'd had the time, he would've locked Stockburn in a demon trap but that was generally something you tricked a demon into. Attempting to put one around a demon was folly even if the demon was busted up like this.

Instead, Grimluk fired two shots from the training revolver into Stockburn's red-faced skull and then drew a small demon trap in the dirt a few feet away where he kicked the sheriff's pulsing gun. The thing looked alive now, no longer steel but some grotesque hunk of flesh. Once inside the circle though, it erupted in flame and fell apart.

"I know you can still hear me, you little bastard. When you get back to your feet, give your bosses a message for me. Tell 'em we'll be coming. And tell Fenton I owe him." Grimluk sneered, growling as he looked at the broken body. Once back in the saddle, the hunters pushed on, leaving Stockburn in a bloody heap, ripped up wings twitching on the ground at his side.

It was well into the night, just past the Witching Hour before Grimluk and the Doom Riders made it back to Hunter's Hollow. Once they were sure Stockburn wasn't on their tail any longer, they'd slowed the horses to a more comfortable pace, stopping to feed and water them before heading on, and, once inside the outer limits of the Hollow's protection, they relaxed. All six, horses and riders alike, wandered back into the fort-town exhausted and sore. Grimluk wondered if he would sleep for days again or if he just needed the right push to really recover. The truth was probably somewhere in the middle.

They let the nighttime stable hands take care of the horses, trudging silently into the big house and collapsing onto the couches or chairs of the sitting area with heavy sighs. Grimluk kicked off his boots with a grunt.

"I think it's safe to say," Eagle started, "that

that was a successful scouting trip."

* * *

At some point after Grimluk had fled, Stockburn twitched, one ruined arm shoving the rest of his body over so he could look at the dimming sky. Yellow eyes blinked in pain while he growled in frustration. It'd be hours before he could heal enough to fly back to Perfection. He did his best to crawl away from the road and out of sight.

It was nearly dawn when Sheriff Stockburn landed with a lethargic thud in front of the Perfection courthouse. A frown cut across his blood-crusted face as he walked through the hole where a door once stood. He paced back and forth across the lobby in frustration, knowing that Fenton and Cholem would chastise him for such a gross failure. He could feel the slithering presence of the demon, Khastax, in his mind. It knew. Stockburn felt his other half talking about what had happened. For a moment, he cursed the devil, bemoaning his choice of accepting knighthood.

"Be calm, my good knight," Cholem said in his mind. "Come up and report to Fenton."

Stockburn swallowed hard and shifted his pudgy body back to its natural shape before stomping up to the second story of the courthouse. Thick, hairy feet slapped against the still warm wood, dampening against the carpet outside of Fenton's chambers. He reached up and knocked twice.

"Come."

The sheriff took a deep breath and entered the room, a shiver of insecurity passing through him as he remembered he was shirtless. Fuck it, he thought. He was already going to be in deep shit.

"What news, Sheriff?" Fenton asked from behind his desk.

"They got away." Stockburn held his head high but gulped when the judge's face changed.

"I'm sorry, Sheriff, could you repeat yourself? Cause it sounded like you said they got away! For the *second fucking time*."

"I chased them halfway to Eagle Point before they shot my wings out. Grimluk put two in my head and told me to give you a message."

"And what's that?"

"He's comin' for ya. And he owes you."

Fenton ground his teeth in rage and irritation. "You utter failure. Give me *one* good reason why I shouldn't rip that demon back out of you and feed you to Duncan! One!"

"Because, Parker Fenton, this is your fault," a voice said.

"What?" Fenton whirled and then realized who the speaker had been. "My lord?"

"Calm yourself, Fenton." The silver bulls-head bust spoke plainly in its metallic voice. "This happened because you keep underestimating the orc. You caught him off guard the first time. He has killed many of my kind. You would do well to *stop underestimating him*."

The words shook the walls, giving Fenton and Stockburn pause before the demon continued. "We still have time enough to right this. You have the womb and, soon, an army. Then it will not matter what Grimluk does. Begin the summonings."

Fenton stood still for a long moment, processing the demon's words, seemingly dazed. A rumbling growl snapped him back to attention. "At once, my lord."

Stockburn made a hasty exit while Fenton's back was turned. While the judge made his way to the dungeon, the sheriff wandered back to his mound to tend to his wounded ego. Next time, he would be ready. He resolved to grow closer to his demonic half. If need be, he would completely embrace becoming someone…some*thing* new altogether. The demon Khastax whispered inside him, declaring promises of vengeance against 'those gobby bastards.' He whispered back.

Parker Fenton slipped into the jail where Deputy Donal was pacing back and forth in front of the jail cells with a hungry look on his face. Like Stockburn, his features had been distorted during the transformation into a knight. Sharp teeth lined his mouth and thick hands ended in long, jagged, black nails. His head snapped towards Fenton with a smile.

"Time to feed our brothers again?" he asked.

"One more body and then we summon them," Fenton replied coldly. Hard focus had replaced the anger on his face. "Choose well and bring them to me."

The deputy nodded, grinning wide, all teeth, and moved to let Fenton pass into the dungeon. Beyond the heavy wood door, the room had been cleared of any other furniture. The only things adorning the dungeon now were the Abyssal womb and splashes of blood across the floor in front of it. The womb glowed a pulsing, eldritch purple that lit the room up brightly. Faint traces of dark flesh streaked out from the center like veins of mold. From outside, Fenton heard shouting as the deputy dragged someone out of a cell. The man's cellmates were screaming for the deputy to stop but it was no use. Donal dragged his charge, a strong young dwarf man from one of the farms with a shaggy head of obsidian hair, and short beard to match, into the pulsing light of the dungeon and slammed the door shut behind him.

* * *

Grimluk paced back and forth, waiting on Bakhor to return with the Forgemothers and the warg matriarch. Mint and Gwen were sitting with Eagle and Beast at the long dining table, lined up on either side. The Doom Riders were killing time with a simple card game while Mint chatted with Gwen about how she was feeling and how things were going with the Spirit and whether she'd picked a name for it yet. As always, he was friendly but clearly keeping to his duties as a healer.

Urgroz stood in the kitchen doorway, quietly watching his son pace. "You hungry, kiddo?"

"No, Dakka. Thank you."

"You keep pacing like that, you're gonna walk a hole through the floor *and* make yourself hungry. They'll be here in a moment."

"It's not that."

"I know. Just take a breath. Between those two, you, and Bakhor, you've got four of the best demon hunters in New Gilead. You'll be able to handle this."

Grimluk stopped and took a deep breath. "Thanks, Dakka."

Urgroz nodded and disappeared back into his kitchen just as the front door opened. Heavy boots thudded across the floor followed by the scruff of thick paws. Bakhor led the Forgemothers, Ythena and Flor, and the warg matriarch, Vu, toward the table. Vu looked like Fang, but bigger and grayer, with pale eyes. Each took a seat, with Bakhor sitting near the head of the table, near Grimluk.

"At this point, we're all aware of what Gwen and I went through and what Parker Fenton is doing." Grimluk leaned over on the back of the chair in front of him. "The Riders and I went to scout Perfection yesterday. It seems he has imps keeping watch around the town now. And at least one demon knight, which means Cholem is strong enough to be a lord." He filled everyone in quickly, recounting the whole ordeal.

Flor's tanned face scrunched up, her dark beard-braids wobbling as she shook her head. "Boy, that was a damn foolish thing to do. This judge of yours will be sittin' pretty, waitin' on you to roll in."

"I know," Grimluk replied, lifting back up off the chair and crossing his arms. "After everything in Greenreach Bluffs, I didn't want this spilling out any farther. And from what the Riders said coming in, it looks like they rounded up everyone in the area. I'm betting for sacrifices. And I really doubt Stockburn's the only knight. You don't just say an incantation and pull one of those fuckers up."

"Better to keep Fenton contained to his little base," Bakhor offered.

"Right. Fenton already wants to seize control of everything. At least if he knows I'm coming, he'll be focused on killing me and stay where he is. I've escaped him twice now. He won't be willing to lose me a third time. Reckon his master won't be too keen on that prospect either."

"So what's your plan, kid?" Eagle asked, not looking up from the card game with Beast.

"First things first, we prepare. Mint."

The old elf nodded in reply.

"We'll need some field bags, bandages, a few brews, some salve. One for myself, Cenka, and the Riders with enough supplies to take care of each of us several times over. If we do this right, hopefully we won't need them but things haven't really been going right lately."

"Consider it top priority, kid. I think we can have them ready whenever you are," Mint said with a nod of his head.

"Eagle and Beast were nice enough to bring us a gift, so I'll be taking that. Forgemothers, I need a new gun as fast as you can make it and replacement ammo for the, what's that thing, Eagle? A bullet tube?"

"Good enough," Eagle replied with a laugh.

"Take one of the other tubes and cast the

ammo from those."

Ythena smiled. "I'll make a little extra. I want to play with that beauty before you take it out for real battle."

"Ythena said she told you about the new runes I've been workin' on," Flor said.

"She did."

"Think I've got it figured out. And I think you'll need it for this."

"Do it."

"What about us?" Beast asked, pausing to look up at the younger hunter.

"I'm gettin' there. Vu, I hate to ask it but can you spare three of your pack for this?"

Vu looked up and growled.

"I want to send Cenka in with them from the east for support. I think the best plan of attack is to use myself to draw Fenton and whatever's in that building out. I can stall him some, buy some time, get him focused. Then Eagle and Beast can ride in the front of town and do what they do best."

Eagle let out a long, throaty growl. "What a rush!"

Grimluk grinned. "You two go in, bust the skulls of whatever tries to stop you. Cenka, if Vu agrees, I want you to come in from the east and flank them."

The warg seemed to consider the plan, growling low in her throat. Finally, she looked up and gave a soft "Woof."

"Thank you," Grimluk said with a nod. "We'll need your strongest."

"What about me?" Gwen asked from beside Mint. "How do I help?"

"You, little one, can help best by staying put and staying safe. I promise we'll talk about you training to be a hunter after this is over. Until then, I can't risk your safety again. You've already done enough."

"But I can still help! I can go with Leigh and we can—"

Grimluk held his hand up. "I know but little one…please, no. Please."

Gwen sank in her chair, looking away and sighing.

"Ythena, Flor, if you have any spare knives and hatchets, make sure they're demon-killers. And add runes to the crank-gun. We'll need to go in armed to our tusks and I'd wager I'll need to kill a lot of demons." He thought for a moment. "Mint, you got any spare war water?"

"Hmm, yeah, got a couple jugs somewhere. No one's used any in a while. Reckon it's pretty potent by now."

"That's good. I'll take both jugs. Anything else anyone can think of?" When no one offered anything else he continued. "We'll leave out the next day after everything's ready. And just so we're clear, everyone, I appreciate the backup."

"Ya know somethin', kid," Beast started, "this is just what we do."

"I tell ya, brother," Eagle continued, "this'll be one rip-snortin' rumble. Every loremaster on Ornesea's gonna want this story. Maybe even the whole of Arkod."

Bakhor smirked. "You two just wanna fight."

"Says the Troll Killer," Eagle said with a snort. The Riders grinned at each other, their tusks going a little lopsided. For a moment, they looked like kids again, all mischief and a desire to prove themselves. Grimluk wondered for a moment just how effective the pair would've been fifteen years earlier with all the knowledge and skill they had now. What a sight that would be.

The group dispersed, Mint and the Forge-mothers heading off to their respective buildings. Vu yipped at Bakhor and the towering orc followed her outside to further discuss sending three of the pack's strongest wargs off to battle. She was worried that if any travelers saw them, it might spark another spree of warg hunts through the region.

"I understand your worry," Bakhor began, "but Perfection's isolated, especially now. Besides that, I was planning to cut through the forest and stay off the roads."

The matriarch nodded and yipped again, asking if Grimluk could really handle things in Perfection.

Bakhor sighed. "I admit that I worry about my son's health of late but I believe he's still quite capable. He's mended quick and true. And this Parker Fenton weighs heavily on his mind. He weighs heavily on mine as well."

Vu agreed with a low growl, planting her butt on the grass to better look up at Bakhor. A short series of barks posed another question. Could ze truly keep the wargs safe.

"We both know the risks of a battle like this, Vu but I swear to you that I'll bring them home alive." She looked down at her own stump. "And as whole as I can manage."

Vu gave a sigh but seemed as satisfied as she was going to be. She let Bakhor know that they would be ready when Grimluk called. Bakhor bowed hir head and watched the matriarch head back to the warg pens. Anxiety coiled in hir gut. And, surprisingly, a hazy sense of excitement blossomed as well. One last hunt. Maybe this one wouldn't end with the loss of a limb and an escaped demon.

Chapter 16

The night was too quiet. The orcs that kept watch over the gates fidgeted uncomfortably on their guard stands, listening for some sign of night life but everything was as silent as the grave. No soft hoots from owls. No soft crunching of grass from deer and elk and the smaller creatures that wandered around near the town-fort hoping to find scraps. In the days since Grimluk's return from the ritual, they'd grown accustomed to the sight of Leigh Fenton's spirit moving back and forth in front of them. She and Gwen would join him for his daily tours around the Hollow sometimes. Tonight the ghost-child was nowhere to be seen.

A shriek ripped across the field outside Hunter's Hollow making the guards jump, rifles snapping to their shoulders as Leigh flickered back into sight, coming into view under the light of the big lanterns at the gates. Her true, hulking form was peeking through her more human visage as she came flying in towards them. Leigh slammed into the gate, rattling it hard, and screamed again.

"Gwen! Where's Gwen?"

Before the guards could respond, burning red eyes started blinking into existence at the edge of the lantern's light. Malicious cackling echoed across the field, sending chills down the guards' spines. Leigh renewed her cry, banging violently against the gates. One of the guards took off for the big house, bursting inside and shouting for Grimluk and Gwen. The hunter appeared at the top of the stairs, adopted sister padding out behind him, rubbing her eyes sleepily.

"What's going on? What is it?" he asked, running down the stairs.

"It's the ghost-girl. She's calling for—"

"Gwen!" Leigh shrieked again, easier to hear with the door open.

"Yeah," the guard said. "That. And somethin' followed her."

"Leigh!" Gwen almost squealed. "We have to go!"

Grimluk scooped Gwen up and rushed out into the dim, lantern-lit yard, making straight for the gates just in time for the other guard to finish opening them. Leigh flickered in surprise and pointed back towards the eyes shining bright in the darkness.

"I was wandering around, 'cause there's not much to do when you're dead, and the spirits you promised to help surrounded me. Chased me back here. Demanded for you to talk to them."

Gwen wiggled down out of Grimluk's arms and rushed over to Leigh, embracing her. The ghost's form seemed to settle, growing thinner and more human again. Gwen gulped and looked up at

Grimluk.

"Guess I did forget to talk to them again." She started to head out towards them but Grimluk grabbed her arm gently in protest.

"Little one, no."

"It's okay. I can control them. They're just gonna be mad I forgot but they won't hurt me. Then we can't help them."

Grimluk's fingers slid away, surprised at her confidence. Gwen continued on toward the edge of the light with Leigh and Grimluk following behind. Mint and some of the others had joined the guards, watching the commotion.

"Hi," Gwen offered the glowing eyes. "I'm sorry I forgot to talk to you again. Um, things have been busy." She could feel them bristling at her from the dark but remained steady. "You could've just asked politely. You didn't have to *chase* Leigh. She's a myling, she's been through enough. Please say you're sorry."

The spirits shifted and looked at each other, one eye winking out as it turned away to look at the one next to it.

"What sorry?" one of them asked in a voice like a chill, fall breeze. Or maybe it was all of them at once.

"You say you're sorry when you do something rude or mean, like chasing someone or scaring someone."

The spirits turned back and forth to one another again, eyes blinking in and out rapidly again. "Sorry?" The concept didn't seem to get much traction.

Gwen frowned at them but shrugged. "Good enough. Guess we need to talk about what you want help with, huh?"

"Help, yes, promise. Gwen promise!"

Grimluk reflected on their way of speaking. It reminded him of how imps and gremlins talked. Little spirits like these didn't seem far removed from those little demons.

"I know, but you have to say what you want."

"Want help. Gwen promise."

Grimluk sighed. "Little one, I don't think they understand what you mean. I'm not sure they know what they want until they want it. They're spirits. As far as I can tell, they were never mortal either."

"Oh." Gwen's mouth screwed up in thought as she looked at a dozen pairs of red eyes. "What do you like?"

The eyes twinkled in and out again. Now that Leigh was calm and the situation was under control, there was a certain beauty to the eerie light. A wind kicked up as the spirits discussed her question. Even with the heat of summer beginning its descent, the wind was cold. Too cold to be natural.

"Like scare. Like bones. Like Gwen."

"Me? Why do you like me?"

"Gwen not kill."

"You promised not to hurt Grimluk. Um, it's pretty late for me though. Past my bedtime. I don't guess spirits sleep but I do. Can you all think about what you want help with and tell me tomorrow?"

"Can stay?" The question was strangely pleasant given the source.

"No, I have to go back to bed."

"Us stay."

"Here?" Gwen asked. "Um, okay. Just don't get near the fence. And let Leigh walk around."

"No rude."

She nodded. Grimluk grumbled quietly, unsure of what to make of it all. He'd never heard of spirits behaving like this before. Or really at all. The spirits had a strange sincerity he never would've expected either. Like he'd told Gwen, hunters didn't ever talk to spirits. Gwen apologized to the nightwatch guards as they made their way back towards the house and promised the spirits would behave while they were there. The guards nodded dumbly.

Shortly after breakfast the next morning, Grimluk followed Gwen back outside. She hoped the spirits had figured out what they wanted. He just wondered *what* they'd want. In the morning light, they were faded and huddled together.

"Did you figure out what you want my help with?" she asked.

"What Gwen like?" one of them asked.

"Hummm. I like Urgroz's cookies," she said with a smile. "Do you know cookies?"

"What cookie? Like bone?" another spirit asked in an excited whisper.

"No, not like bone. It's um…well."

"It's like a tiny cake," Grimluk offered, surprising himself.

"Yeah! It's soft and made of dough and there's chocolate chips."

"What chocolate? Like blood?" a third spirit inquired.

"You really are like babies, aren't you?" she asked. She started pacing in front the spirits. Their eyes swiveled around, following her. She frowned but said nothing. She seemed to be focusing on an idea.

"Spirits," she began, "Can we make another deal?"

They bounced and chittered. "Deal. Yes. Gwen promise!"

"If you help me some more, I'll show you all sorts of things. Like cookies. How about that?"

"What Gwen want?" they asked in unison this time.

"I'm not sure yet. If I call you, will you hear me?"

"We hear. We watch."

Gwen nodded with a smile and headed back inside the Hollow. Grimluk blinked and scratched his chin, trailing behind the girl.

Trapped heat rolled out of the forge as Grimluk entered. Machinery clanked and slammed somewhere farther in. Ythena strode up to meet him, a grin on her face. She embraced him in another bear hug before leading him to a small room littered with workbenches and dozens of containers filled with small parts. Screws, springs, unfinished blocks of all sorts of woods that ended up as grips and stocks. Final pieces to the completion of firearms. Flor stood at one of the benches with a hammer and a small chisel. The chisel bit into the gun's barrel as it formed a series of runes.

"Flor and I worked non-stop to finish it. I did most of the building while she finished testing the new enchantment on a prototype," Ythena said. "It's some of our best work."

"I appreciate it," he replied. "What do these new runes do?"

Flor finished tapping away at the barrel and set her tools aside. "Punch a hole through a demon."

"I thought that's what the usual killing spell did?"

"It does. Usually." Flor frowned. "After everything that's happened, I wanted this right. These ain't just for general use. They don't work passively like the other. Those make sure that your bullets can *hurt* a demon. Period. They can still recover though."

"And this one?" he said, stepping closer to the bench. He was eager to see the new weapon.

"This is more like the guild talismans. It requires blood and it's only for emergencies. And I mean that. The trade-off for what these runes do is that once it's been activated, it'll leave you drained and weak. We had one of the shop hands test it, just a single shot. It works but she went pale. Any more and she'd probably be sleeping it off."

Grimluk's throat rumbled. "Is it ready then?"

"Almost," Ythena answered. "All that's left is binding the gun to you."

He nodded. "I don't mind telling you two that

I've had enough of giving blood for spells lately but this one saved my ass back in Perfection."

Flor laughed. "Asshole tried to shoot you, eh? Bet his eyes just about exploded when nothing happened."

Grimluk offered his arm. "Somethin' like that. Let's get this done."

Half an hour later, Grimluk exited the forge with a new gun belt around his waist. Fresh rounds filled each loop of the belt, brass glinting in the sun as he walked away. For the first time in what felt like a very long time, he felt like himself again. Now he just needed to get his hat and coat back. Mint met him as he made his way back to the house.

"Just wanted to let you know, all the bags are ready. Bandages, salve, few potions, and stitching."

"Good to hear. Thanks, Mint. What about the war water?"

"Everything's all piled up and waitin' for ya."

Grimluk nodded. "Reckon it's time to get everything packed up and ready. Tomorrow, we go to war."

"Maybe we should have one last hurrah in case this goes sour," Mint suggested.

"Maybe so. I'll mention it to Dakka."

"And I'll bring a bottle of my good stuff," Mint said with a smile. "Haven't had an occasion to bring out any of *my* whiskey in some time. Got a bottle that's older than you."

Grimluk smirked. He knew better than to drink with Mint.

Later that night, the hunters prepared for battle with a feast. Urgroz filled the long table with pies of all kinds, piles of roasted vegetables, flanks of goat, a ham, and several chickens. The kitchen hands rolled in two barrels of ale with a tap and easy access. Urgroz made sure to have a pitcher of lemonade for Gwen, too. The Doom Riders were as rowdy as ever, though less bawdy around Gwen than they normally would've been. In truth, it'd been a very long time since either of them had spent more than brief moments around a child, and they said as much. Grimluk couldn't help but be amused at the girl's impact.

The atmosphere was grim but defiant. They all reflected on what would be coming soon. Hunts could take weeks, sometimes months, and very rarely, years. This would be a battle though. There was no hunting. The quarry wasn't running or hiding. The demon and its lackeys would be waiting for them. Or at least for Grimluk. So they ate and laughed and smiled, crowded together at one end of the table for the long evening hours. Various inhabitants of Hunter's Hollow wandered in and out, taking food or joining the revelry for a time before fading away.

As the hour grew late, Grimluk quieted them down, his face shifting from a worried but sincere smile to hard-eyed determination. He looked at Eagle and Beast. At Bakhor. At Mint, Gwen, and Urgroz.

"I know the three of you have agreed to help me but I'm offering you an out. I'm dead set on returning after this is over but we all know that might not happen. Things could go badly in Perfection. If I need to, I'll do it myself. Pack some dynamite, whatever I need to finish this." He swallowed. He knew what they'd say but he didn't feel right not giving them the opportunity to back out.

"Grim," Bakhor said, "my wonderful child, light of my life, fruit of my loins, my good little hunter."

"Cenka," he replied, smiling flatly.

"I love you dearly but you are so full of shit right now. Already told ya once to stop trying to carry the whole of Arkod on your damn shoulders. We're helping."

"That's right," Beast chimed in, "you called us in, you asked for help, so ya know what we're gonna do?"

Grimluk smiled in spite of himself. "What?"

"Tell him, Eagle!" Beast thumped his partner's shoulder with a thick slap.

Eagle let out a long, throaty growl. "My friend, we're gonna plow through those demons. We're gonna break some clavicles. We're gonna snap some arms. We're gonna bust up every bone and spine and disgusting little protrusion those gods-forsaken abominations have. Tell him, big man!"

"You don't have to worry about *us*," Beast said confidently. "We got ya covered."

"All right, all right, I get it," Grimluk said between laughs. "And thanks."

"We should be thankin' you, kid," Eagle replied. "We don't get these kinds of fights very often."

Grimluk sighed, letting out a measure of relief. "Well, you two will be heading out first in the morning. I want you to set up a ways outside of Perfection, to the south. Cenka, I want you and the wargs to do the same but from the west. Stay out of sight until I throw up a flare. Start heading in when you see it and don't let up." He thought about things another moment. "And Fenton likes to run his mouth so I'll bet I can get him talkin' some, too."

"How long will you be?" Bakhor asked.

"I'll need a wagon to haul the crank-gun so I'll be farther behind. You'll have to set up camp for the night."

Between the four of them, they had decades of experience with hunting. There was no need to go over every little detail of the plan. They'd all do their parts. Satisfied, everyone settled down for the night. Gwen had fallen asleep in Bakhor's chair. Fang was at her feet, snoring loudly. Bakhor and Urgroz disappeared up to their room, low voices and quiet laughs making their plans clear. Eagle and Beast wandered outside after letting Grimluk know they were too excited about the battle to get any rest. They could sleep when it was over. Grimluk scooped up his sister and carried her off to her new bed before crawling off to his own. Sleep did not come easy that night.

The Doom Riders left out before dawn. Their pauldrons and bracers had been polished bright, waiting to shine in the sun. Bakhor and hir party of wargs left shortly after, heading southwest towards the road to Eagle Point before cutting due west and then back south again. Grimluk watched them leave, wargs running behind the horse in formation like a cavalry squad.

After that, he found the wagon the Riders had brought the heavy coffin in. Ythena and Flor carried the contraption to the wagon for him after showing him the demon-killing runes on each of the long barrels. They'd also made three extra tubes and filled them with rounds. He hooked the horse from Perfection up to the wagon, realizing as he did that he hadn't been given the creature's name. If they survived, he could name the poor thing and retire it to grazing as a hero. He pulled the wagon up near Mint's tent and loaded his own supplies, a medic bag and two clay jugs of war water, in the back. He started the wagon for the gates but a bark caught his attention, making him come to a stop once more. Fang and Gwen looked up at him.

"Please let me come and help," Gwen asked. She looked ready to go, decked out in her boots and coat, hat hanging by its drawstring from her neck.

He recognized the look on her face all too well. Grimluk was sure he'd made that face at her age as well. That look of determination, of the need to fight and do good and help. His brows furrowed deeply and his throat rumbled. Part of him wanted to pull her up next to him. Hadn't she proven herself already? But no, no, he had to keep her safe. He'd promised. She was safe here, behind the wards and the gates, with Kort and Archel and a few dozen apprentices and hunters and the Forgemothers.

"Fang, watch the little one until I get back."

Fang tilted her head at him before giving a low bark. Yellow eyes regarded him for a moment, and then the warg turned and tugged Gwen back. Grimluk drove the wagon out of Hunter's Hollow and began his trek towards the main road that would take him south towards Perfection.

He rode in silent contemplation, the only sound registering to his ears the *clip-clop* of the horse's hooves against the dirt. He played out different scenarios in his head, trying to plan his assault to the best of his ability. He was going in essentially blind. He knew there would a whole host of demons waiting on him but he had no idea what they would be. His plan would have to remain elastic, flexible. Though, he thought, at least he had a big gods-damned gun to start things off with.

The wagon was slow going. He made camp off the road, near dark. He locked the wagon's brake and made sure to pour a circle of war water around the camp in a wide berth for protection. He elected not to light a fire. A lamp hung from the wagon so he lit it instead and spent the night curled up next to his transportation, very much not sleeping. He was grateful he'd recovered enough that the lack of sleep wouldn't impede him. He didn't expect to do more than nod off at best. As his eyes began to droop, a bone-white moth flitted against the lantern. Sleepy eyes distorted the thing's size, making it seem huge. Grimluk ignored it and drifted off.

The horse snorted sometime around dawn, jarring him from a hazy dream about Gwen and Fang that slipped from memory immediately. The lantern had burned out in the night and the horse stamped a hoof and shook the wagon. Grimluk yawned and grunted. He hastily fed himself and the horse and got going again.

A few hours later, the wagon cut off from the road, heading for the hill where the imps had spotted them and Stockburn had given chase. He spun the wagon around and unhitched the horse from it.

"How 'bout it, Horse? You gonna stay and fight, too?"

The horse snorted and shook its head at him before trotting away into the trees to graze.

Grimluk pulled his bags free, slinging them over a shoulder and then pulled the coffin forward, barrel-end pointing out. He bent down under it, resting it on his shoulder, pulled it forward some more and lifted the colossal load. Orc and gun marched up the hill in a silent procession. As before, a flurry of imps flew past overhead. "Good," he thought. At the top, he pulled the flare gun from his belt and fired it into the sky.

"Parker Fenton!" he cried as a swarm of imps flew overhead. "I'm callin' you out, you demon-worshipin' sack of rancid troll guts!"

A chorus of howls erupted from down the hill, filling the air with malevolence. From his vantage point, Grimluk watched as five death hounds, dark as the deepest shadows, walked out from the side of the courthouse, each with a rider. Stockburn led his deputies out to meet him. More death hounds followed along with a slew of slow-moving ghouls caked in dry blood and torn flesh, groans of hunger mixing among the growling and snapping of the hounds. Behind them all lurched another familiar sight. Insect-like feet propelled fat, spiny bodies led by heads with too many black eyes. Mouths split open, pincer hands barreling forth and rubbing against themselves in eager anticipation.

The group held still, splitting down the center as something passed through them. Parker Fenton, the hanging judge himself, stepped forward all in white. White pants, white vest, white shirt, white coat, all of it a perfect, bleached white, save for his black shoes and belt.

"We've been expecting you, Grimluk." Fenton opened his arms wide and bowed lightly.

Grimluk tossed the flare gun away. He shrugged the coffin down off his shoulder, dropping it down to stand upright where it could plainly be seen. "I know. And I brought you a gift. I hope you remember the message I sent you. I owe you." He tapped the coffin with one hand, hoping Fenton understood the implication.

Fenton's face carved itself into a furious scowl. A less controlled man might have screamed, given voice to his sudden rage. The man known as the hanging judge remained quiet but fuming.

"What's the matter, Fenton? Orc got your tongue?"

"Sheriff," Fenton nearly hissed, "kindly kill that man and bring me his fucking head. The rest of you ready yourselves to help."

Stockburn climbed down off his mount. He was shirtless again. Red skin shifted over unnatural muscle as the halfling-demon walked toward the hill. Grimluk lowered the coffin to the ground, loosing the catch that held it shut, readying it for what was to come.

"You wanna talk debts? I owe *you*, ya gobby piece a shit. Fucking goblins crawling all over the world like they got a right to still be living. And what a fool you were, comin' all by your lonesome. No one to defend you now. Just me and you." Stockburn climbed the hill with ease, stopping a few feet from the coffin's edge.

Grimluk stared hard, measuring up the demon knight. Stockburn grinned his jagged, yellow smile and spread out his wings, no popping or tearing this time. The leathery appendages simply slipped out of his back and unfolded like the sails of a ship. He flexed his hands, stretching fingers that ended in vicious nails.

"I have a question before we do this," Grimluk said.

"Already gonna beg for mercy?"

"Is there anything left of the man you were or did you give yourself fully to the demon?"

Stockburn began to laugh from deep in his gut. "I *am* the demon. We are one. I'm better than I was before. Stronger. What say you, eh? You ready to die you gob—"

Grimluk slapped leather, cutting Stockburn off. The gun's dark, gleaming barrel rose up and spoke the hunter's reply, sending a bullet through the sheriff's mouth and out the other side. He sneered. "I think you talk too gods-damned much."

Chapter 17

The wagon pulled away steadily from the gates while Gwen watched, silently stewing in her frustration. Despite understanding what her newly adopted brother was saying, her desire to help and fight back wouldn't waver. Once he was far enough away, fading into the distance, she walked calmly out of the gates of Hunter's Hollow and into the field beyond them. Dim, red eyes blinked into existence.

"Watch Gwen. See Gwen," a voice like leaves in a storm said.

She took a deep breath. "Leigh, are you still around?"

The myling appeared next to her accompanied by a chill breeze. "Yes."

Gwen looked at the spirits surrounding her, her mind working out a plan. Translucent eyes stared back at her, eager and waiting. Leigh's eyes held a quiet fury as well, tempered only by Gwen's influence.

"Leigh, you said your father, um, killed more children, right?" An idea was budding in her mind.

"Yes. There were several towns between home and Perfection. Farms, too. He would use the demon's powers and use some sort of door to grab them. Always as he left the town."

Gwen nodded. "Spirits, do you still want to help me?"

The spirits seemed to perk up, swirling around each other in excitement. "Yessss. Help."

"Do you think you're strong enough to get the other mylings together? Could you get them and take them to Perfection?"

The spirits seemed to mull the prospect over.

"Help Gwen."

"Spirit?" she asked inwardly.

They have no real concept of their power, Gwen. They are, at best, mercurial, grabbing onto desires and whims with fleeting attention. They just act. That said, they should be able to herd the mylings. And as for whether the demon will attack the spirits if it senses them, it is doubtful. Demons attract spirits like these regularly. Cholem will no doubt be occupied by Grimluk as well, providing further stealth. It paused for a moment. *Though, there is the chance it will sense the mylings. Be cautious.*

Gwen set her jaw. "Spirits, I need you to go and find the other mylings who were sacrifices to a demon named Cholem. They'll be kids, like me and Leigh. Find them and then take them to Perfection. Can you do that?"

"Yessss. Help." Red eyes blinked. "What 'Perfection'?"

"Um, just find me once you have them."

They agreed enthusiastically and faded quickly, rushing away like a cold, stiff breeze.

"Leigh, you and me are gonna head to Perfection and say hi to your father."

The myling grinned wide. The grin was malformed, eager for action and bubbling with wrath. Gwen marched into the Hollow and made her way toward the house, where she found Urgroz, sitting at the dinner table with a frown and his breakfast.

"Urgroz?" she said, stopping next to him. Fang came padding up behind her.

"Mornin', kiddo."

"I need some food and a water thing, please."

The orc's brows creased in curiosity. "Oh? What for?"

"I'm gonna go help Grimluk," she replied, holding her head high, jaw tight, little fists clenched shut.

Urgroz looked at her for a long time. "I told him it wasn't his choice to make."

"What?" Confusion washed over Gwen's face.

"Your big brother. I told that boy that you'd already made the choice to be a hunter. Just like him." Urgroz stood up. "Fang."

The warg yipped in reply.

"Grim told you to watch Gwen, right?" Fang nodded once, a peculiar sight given the creature's fuzzy-skull head. "Then I'm gonna put together a bag of supplies for the two of you and you're gonna take her to Perfection."

A solid bark was her only reply. Urgroz smiled and disappeared into the kitchen, coming back some time later with a bag of jerky, a couple of big, red apples, and a loaf of bread. He held his hand out, directing Gwen back outside and followed after her. Fang darted out ahead of them, humming with excitement. Urgroz tied the bag to Fang's neck and knelt in front of Gwen.

"You sure you wanna do this?"

"I gotta."

Urgroz smiled and embraced his adopted daughter. "Then go on, kiddo. Kick some ass."

She squeezed him tight. "How am I gonna get there though?"

"You're gonna be a warg rider." He winked and set her on Fang's powerful back. "She's as fast as a small horse. You'll catch up in no time. Head out." A great sigh rushed out of Urgroz. "Just be careful. I was afraid any time Bakhor went on a hunt and I was afraid when Grim left. I'm afraid to send you off now, too. This family has a habit of jumpin' into trouble with both feet though. So be careful. And have fun stormin' the castle."

Fang strode back out into the field where Leigh Fenton was waiting silently. Gwen waved her over. "Follow us. Fang, follow Grimluk but don't catch up. He'll just try to send us back. We'll go around." She leaned forward and wrapped her arms around Fang's neck, taking two handfuls of her fur. The warg's legs pounded the grass with purpose.

* * *

Sheriff Stockburn shuddered as the bullet passed through his skull. He looked up at Grimluk with a dim rage, black gore spilling out of his mouth. He tried to speak, tried to curse the orc but all that came out was more blood, pouring from his nose and down his throat.

Grimluk held his gun out, pulling the hammer back and fired a second time. The top of the demon knight's head exploded, showering the hill with brains. One more shot exploded through Stockburn's heart, sending his already tipping body tumbling back down the hill. For a brief moment, the demon's body twitched violently and went still. Fenton and his army looked up in surprise.

The judge turned and bolted, shouting for the hunter's death as he fled. A variety of roars blanketed the area, all aimed at the hunter.

The great revolver slid back into its holster as Grimluk bent down and ripped the coffin open. One hand plucked an ammo tube from the inside of the lid and the other jerked the gun up with a grunt. The gears turned and locked as the body rose to its apex. The ammo tube slipped into its housing with a *click* as his other hand went to the crank, turning it as death hounds, snarling viciously, bounded towards him. Bullets screamed through the barrel, ripping through the huge beasts with extreme prejudice. He reached down and snagged another tube before the first went dry.

One of the death hounds roared ahead of him as he went to swap out the tubes, leaping off the body of its fallen brethren. Grimluk pulled the empty tube out with his right hand, jamming the fresh one down with his left, and hurled the empty tube at the hound's monstrous snout. The blow hit hard enough to rob the demonic dog of some of its momentum and it came crashing down ahead of its mark, slamming a slavering, rotten jaw into the crank-gun's barrels. Grimluk turned the crank for everything it was worth, filling the death hound's throat and body with magically-imbued lead until the tube ran dry.

Robbed of life and power, and a fair chunk of its torso, the body went slack and fell away, rolling down the hill into the pile of bodies below. The four remaining demon knights were preparing to attack, leading with a charge filled with more death hounds and the chitinous monstrosities behind them but sudden roars from the other end of town caught their attention. Two huge horses thundered down Perfection's main street with two orcs on their backs wearing a matching set of shining, spiked pauldrons and bracers. Two of the remaining knights turned and took some of the death hounds to meet the incoming riders.

Grimluk reloaded the crank-gun one more time and went to work taking down anything still headed his way. What seemed like a legion of ghouls started dropping like flies as the bullets ripped through them, tearing apart limbs and heads and ripping holes in bodies.

The two remaining knights, once again preparing to charge, were stopped by the sudden appearance of Bakhor and the wargs from behind, crossing in front of the courthouse as the other knights headed for Eagle and Beast. The trio of wargs slammed into the death hounds full force, throwing riders from mounts. The crank-gun stopped firing as the group plowed through a row of demons and ghouls.

Grimluk pulled his revolver out and reloaded

it, dropping the spent shells into the coffin below. He snagged a jug of war water and made his own charge down the hill. The war water jug flew into the air above the remaining demons. Grimluk fired and watched as the jug exploded, magical brew scattering over the heads and backs of everything under it. Smoke and screams filled the air as the rust-colored water ate through whatever it touched that was undead and demonic.

* * *

Eagle and Beast charged into Perfection, snarling and ready for battle. The demon knights, human and elf, and their death hounds raced to meet them, skin black and yellow, mouths split into vicious rows of jagged teeth with claws to match. Rage burned in their eyes at the death of their sheriff and they seemed to decide against wasting time talking as he had. The time for talk was over.

The Doom Riders launched themselves from their steeds at the knights, crashing down on top of their enemies with triumphant glee. Each orc pounded with a flurry of brutish fists that also burned the knights under their mystical power. The death hounds snapped at the horses but were rewarded with hooves to their jaws. Deterred, the hounds turned their focus to the Riders, ready to bite and pull them off the knights. Sharp back-hands answered as they closed in, the black spikes from Eagle and Beast's bracers biting into the sides of the hounds' snouts.

The orcs rolled away, getting clear of the

snapping teeth of the hound's jaws and sprang to their feet. Eagle threw a hard right into the eye of the death hound attacking him, followed with a left, and got underneath it while it was dazed. Every muscle in his body worked in tandem, trained and focused, scooping the demonic dog into the air. The death hound tilted up, ass dangling toward the sky, and then rolled and landed on the demonic elf with a sharp yelp that sounded more like a snarl.

Beast, true to his name, met the death hound attacking him with his own head, cracking the demon dog's nose. Black blood dribbled out, thick and hot. Green arms wrapped around the hound's shadowy neck and squeezed tight, directing the snapping jaws away with concentrated effort. The hound's rider started to get to his feet again only for Beast to boot the knight in the face, sending him rolling backward, feet flipping up over his head, kicking up a cloud of dust. Beast wrenched on the hound's throat, squeezing tighter. Behind him, Eagle continued his work on his own death hound, stomping the thing's ribs before it could rise back to its feet.

The demon knight underneath the death hound Eagle was beating on hooked her arm behind Eagle's grounded boot and yanked, sending the hunter toppling long enough to get to her feet. Eagle dropped one last boot into the death hound's skull from his back before rolling out of the way of a flurry of taloned stomps from the knight. The hunter let out a shrill whistle, summoning his horse. The steed charged out of its hiding place and trampled the knight.

Beast, death hound's head still firmly locked underneath his arm, grabbed for one of the hatchets he'd carried into battle on his belt and buried it deeply into the hound's skull. The demon went limp as the other knight rose back up and charged, claws ready for attack. Beast pulled the lifeless demon corpse towards the knight, using its body as a shield.

"Hey, brother, remember the doomsday cult?" Eagle called as he got to his feet and slammed his own hatchet into the other death hound's injured skull.

Beast grinned and shoved the death hound corpse into his attacker, bowling him over. The dazed knight yelped in surprise as Beast jerked him up. Suddenly, the knight was very high, sitting on the hunter's shoulders. Eagle ran full speed at them and used the death hound's corpse as a step, leaping off of its body and all but ripping through the confused knight with a huge, meaty arm that sent the knight flipping away to crash onto his neck. Eagle's second hatchet slammed home. The pair approached the tangled mess of the surviving demon knight. The once-elven woman twitched, desperately trying to will her body to heal so she could flee her executioners.

"Kill you," the knight choked out, "fuckin' kill you..."

Beast pulled out his remaining hatchet and did what he and Eagle had done for decades.

* * *

Bakhor and the wargs charged in from the east in time to see the two demon knights take off for Eagle and Beast, leaving the larger group still focused on Grimluk and the crank-gun. Two of the wargs leaped and smashed into the remaining two demon knights, Donal and another dwarf, before setting to work killing ghouls. The crank-gun ceased firing. Bakhor pulled out a hatchet and hurled it at the head of one of the insectoid demons. The blade bit deep, sliding into what might have been the demon's skull with a wet *shunk* sound.

Ze slid off of hir horse and sent it running in time for Grimluk's jug of war water to explode overhead, soaking everything below it in rust-colored water and bits of iron. Bakhor ignored the water and pulled out another hatchet from hir belt and began hacking away at whatever got near. Hir prosthetic steel fist slammed into the head of a ghoul that stumbled too close and the creature's skull split open. It crumpled to the grass in a rotting heap.

Bakhor, huge and graceful, danced and dodged in and out of the reach of jagged teeth, rotting hands, and razor-sharp pincers flailing about from mouths that were too small and too big, attack cries escaping hir mouth in sudden bursts. "Wah-tah! Ha!" Long limbs weaved a tapestry of gore across green grass as clouds filled the sky in a sudden rush of blackness. Bakhor twirled out of the way as sharp and very poisonous spines flew past hir. One of the spines struck a stray ghoul in the skull and it dropped, dead once more.

Gunfire barked and the pincers and head of the attacking demon vaporized into a mist of black ichor. The remaining insectoid demon screamed, the sound like a thousand cicadas all at once. The spines lining its body shifted, thickening and reaching out in curved points. The chitinous armor covering its body grew as well, its long neck receding into the safety of its shell. It screamed again and shook violently.

"Down!" Grimluk shouted.

Parent and child dropped to the blood soaked ground as spines exploded from the demon's body, rushing towards where they'd stood moments before. Bakhor rolled into a crouch and took three great steps before launching into the air and on top of the demon's back. Ze slammed down the hatchet into one of the chitin-armor's seams, pushing down on the hatchet's handle with a grunt. The chitin crackled in protest but held.

Ze growled and slammed hir metal fist down onto the flat back of the hatchet with a loud cry. The blade split through, hitting the soft body within. Ichor oozed around the hatchet blade, along with another cicada scream, and Bakhor swung again, breaking through more of the thing's armor. Bits of chitin scattered as ze chipped away with renewed determination.

As ze hacked away, Grimluk slammed his own hatchet into the eye of a snapping death hound, giving it severe pause. With a growl, the hunter struck the beast's snout with a headbutt and yanked the hatchet back out, dragging the hound's eye with it. Blood gushed from its nose and eye socket. A ragged shudder ran through it as it swung a weak claw at Grimluk in defense. He stepped in toward the hound's body and wrapped his arm around the attacking limb. Bone snapped in a direction it wasn't supposed to, even on a demon, and the hunter swung the hound to the side with all his might, bowling over several still-standing ghouls. The wargs piled on the flesh-eaters, stamping and biting their skulls.

Bakhor lifted hir hatchet again, ready to strike but something slammed into hir, sending her flying off the crumbling demon's back. The demon knight that was Deputy Donal landed on hir a moment later, sickly yellow hands wrapping around hir throat. Jagged teeth snapped at Bakhor's face. Translucent eyes, all blood vessels and jelly, glared at her with murderous rage.

Bakhor blasted the side of the knight's head with hir metal fist once, twice, a third time. Donal's face split open, the last blow sending him rolling away. Ze stood, rubbing hir throat with her good hand. The knight roared at hir again, flexing its fingers.

Ze leaped at the demon knight, throwing out a huge boot at his head, letting loose one of hir focusing cries. Donal ducked away and swung one of his yellow hands at hir. The nails had grown long and sharp, tearing Bakhor's shirt at the stomach. Four gashes opened up, welling with blood.

"Hope it was worth it, demon," Bakhor said with a growl. Ze lashed out with a speed the demon knight hadn't been prepared for, delivering a devastating palm to his nose, shattering the bone. Donal staggered back, growling and hissing. He hesitated.

Bakhor held up her flesh hand and motioned for him to attack.

Unfocused rage filled the demon knight, spurning him forward. Claws swung wildly, left, right, left, right, always just a moment too late or blocked outright. Each miss fueling the knight's anger. He swung both arms in a double-fisted clap and this time, Bakhor stepped in, throwing up hir arms to block and bringing hir knee into the knight's jaw, barely even lifting hir leg to do so. The demon stumbled away for a second time.

"Ya know the thing about being a demon knight," Bakhor began, bouncing in place, foot to foot, before taking a fighting stance again, "you have to take some time to really get to know the power. Until then, you're weak."

"I'll show you weak!" Donal said with a growl, spitting blood.

Bakhor danced in, feigning a kick. The knight grasped hir speed now and stepped away from the feint. And into the courthouse wall. The abrupt stop jarred Donal, robbing him of whatever focus he'd had. Bakhor's metal fist slammed into the demon knight's face a moment later, splintering the wood of the courthouse wall. Ze drove hir other hand into the knight's chest, where its heart would've been and then dug hir fingers in and twisted. The demon knight coughed up a sudden rush of black blood as Bakhor stepped away.

"You don't have long to live. Use your time wisely."

Deputy Donal pulled himself out of the cracked wood. "I'll fucking kill you, you goblin tra

—" His head and chest split open in a shower of gore. He slumped over with one final breath.

Behind them, Grimluk drew on the remaining knight, catching him by surprise and putting two bullets in the head and heart as he tried to flee.

* * *

Gwen and Fang ran east, trailing far behind Bakhor and the wargs, keeping to trees as best they could to keep out of sight. When Gwen asked to stop to eat, she also asked Leigh if she could direct them towards Perfection, to keep from following Bakhor farther than they needed to. The myling nodded, some of her monstrous form showing through the closer they got. Leigh led them at an angle, aiming straight for her father. The pull for vengeance guided her.

They stopped sometime in the dark so Gwen could sleep and Fang could rest. Leigh watched over them, growing ever more hulking. Ghostly footsteps left imprints as she circled warg and rider. Gwen was exhausted but she remained filled with determination. Just before dawn broke, the spirits found her, stirring her.

"Help Gwen."

"Oh," she yawned, "did you get the other mylings."

"Had to carry. Help." Three child-like shapes dumped out in front of her, pale and clear like Leigh, like Owen Duncan.

The mylings stood, or floated, upright, looking around before catching sight of Gwen. Their faces contorted, howls building in them. Gwen frowned and held up a finger.

"Shush, I'm trying to help you."

The mylings blinked, looking at each other and the other spirits, quite bemused. "Home?" one of them ventured.

"Soon. I need your help first. We have to help my brother stop the man who did this to you. Do you understand?"

The mylings shifted. Two girls about Gwen's age probably and a young boy who looked a few years older. One of the girls nodded. The other two followed her example. Gwen yawned and pulled out some jerky to eat, thinking about what to do when they got to Perfection. She remembered that Fenton's house was behind the courthouse. Maybe she could use that. Maybe she'd need to watch and see what happened with Grimluk first.

Leigh led the spirit caller and her newly-formed posse of spirits onward towards Perfection. They stayed out of sight at the edge of the forest some ways behind the courthouse, watching. The spirits shivered, sensing all the demons gathered in the big building. The mylings gathered near Gwen, huddled close at her behest, keeping calm with gentle reassurances from her. Leigh shook visibly, clearly trying to hold in her desire to fly out screaming and tear her father to shreds. Gwen took her cold hand, a hand larger than it should have been, and tried to reassure her as well.

"Spirit," she said inwardly.

Yes?

"Wait..."

Do you sense it now?

"Oh gods," she said out loud. "There's so many of them...so many more. I..." Tears welled in her eyes as she realized she could feel all the new mylings that had been sacrificed while they were in Hunter's Hollow. Their monstrous forms came into view, hazy but growing clearer by the second. Their anger and sadness threatened to overwhelm her for a moment but she pushed it down, fought it down, swallowing tears as well.

Call them.

She did. She pushed her mind out to them, a strange intuition telling her to do so. One by one, they appeared near her, calmer, some touch of humanity restored by the interaction. Twelve more mylings joined her all together. Gwen stood, hands at her hips, and surveyed her small army of spirits. A flare exploded above the town. Far to her left, Grimluk stood at the top of a hill with a coffin on his shoulder. The time had come.

* * *

Parker Fenton watched in shock as Stockburn collapsed, head and heart blown away, and rolled down the hill. His legs moved instinctively, turning around and carrying him away from the demon hunter while his mouth worked on its own accord, screaming for his army of demons to attack, to kill, to protect him. Death hounds surged forward but a strange sound met them. Gunfire like he'd never heard before. Too much, too fast. Fenton ducked around the corner of the courthouse and dashed along the wall towards the entrance. The judge rushed inside, making straight for his chambers.

"No! No!" Fenton shouted to himself. "This isn't fucking right! That wasn't supposed to happen!"

More yells caught his ears. Not demonic but terrifying in their own right. And horses. A horse and three wargs thundered passed the open doors of the courthouse, making his head whip back in fear. Panic began to set in, filling his mind with a rush of images, all of them ending with him very dead. He had to escape. Had to find somewhere new to settle, somewhere far away. Maybe head into the Wastelands. He could gather more sacrifices along the way and build an army of demons no one could stand against.

"Master! We have to run! He'll kill me!" Fenton snatched the silver bull's head from the wall. The head gleamed, polished and like new. Not a speck of the demon's essence remained on the bust. Before he could turn and flee, the windows in his chambers blew inward, spraying glass and bits of wood everywhere. Grinning skulls screamed through the windows straight for him. The skulls bounced away, however, crying out in pain.

"Foolish spirits. Begone from my sight," Cholem said from nowhere and everywhere.

Fenton ran, heading back out into the lobby of the courthouse, gripping the silver bust to his chest. More skulls came screaming towards him, driving him outside. Rocks pelted him from the side, pushing him around the corner, towards his house. He dove in and slammed the door. This was good. He needed supplies anyways or he wouldn't get far.

Parker Fenton turned around and saw the last thing he'd ever expected to see in his house again: Gwen Quinn, smiling pleasantly at him with half of his furniture spinning around her. Ectoplasm dripped in heavy gobs from each item.

"Hello, Mr. Judge."

Chapter 18

The wails of the dead filled the house with such volume that it shook on its foundation. Utensils whipped passed Parker Fenton's face, jamming into the door and the wall behind him. A chair flung forward, skidding across the floor and jamming into Fenton's stomach. The judge doubled over, breath exiting him in a dull grunt.

"What are you doing, Gwendolyn?" Fenton asked, hissing through clenched teeth.

"My *name* is Gwen," she said, her face suddenly serious. "And I'm helping the children you killed."

One by one, the mylings appeared around her, pale and grotesque and angry. Bits of debris passed through their heads and bodies, dragging ectoplasm with it. Each child's spirit glared ahead ominously, ready, waiting to strike, taking their cues from Gwen's plan. She had an army of ghosts ready to fight. The red eyes of the mischievous spirits never appeared though. A sliver of worry slipped through her.

"Cute," Fenton said, regaining composure.

"Such a shame though. My friends are stronger."

Everything swirling around Gwen stopped, floating in the air for a long, still moment before dropping to a heap in a loud clatter that made her jump. A haunting laugh echoed through the house while the mylings went rigid. The specters flickered and then disappeared in soundless puffs. Fenton stepped around another chair and stood over Gwen, glaring down. Gwen stared back, utterly defiant while her heart pounded in her throat and her legs screamed to run. Her hand slipped into her coat pocket, wrapping around the handle of her knife.

"It's such a shame I couldn't make better use of you, child. You remind me so much of Leigh." Fenton shifted the bull's head under his left arm, holding his right up in show. "But my master doesn't need your blood any longer."

The back of Fenton's hand slammed into Gwen's cheek, sending her stumbling. She hit the overturned table and used it to steady herself, tears of pain pouring out of her eyes. A lone sob slipped from her throat but she held back any others and looked at the judge again.

"I see you got some sand in your craw these days. Not the sad little thing with the dead parents, eh?" He laughed once, cold and mocking. "Did your *brother* send you in here alone? That's an orc for you. Can't be trusted to do the right thing."

From outside, gunfire and howling death cries filled the momentary silence. Fenton growled. The hunter would be coming.

"Grimluk doesn't know I'm here," Gwen

replied.

"How fortunate for me then. I need an insurance policy. Time to come with me." Fenton lunged at her with his free hand, trying to grab her by the throat.

Gwen ducked under his arm and ran for the door. She ripped it open with a grunt only to shriek. Jed Duncan, gray-skinned and sunken-eyed, stood at the door. There was no mistaking what he was. A low moan slipped through the ghoul's mouth, its faintly green-glowing eyes looking her over, and then to Fenton.

"Mr. Duncan," she murmured. From behind, a hand clamped down on her shoulder. "No!" The hand spun her around.

"You're lucky I need you or I'd feed you to this miserable sack of shit."

Gwen flicked the knife open inside her pocket and, in a rush of adrenaline and panic, she ripped it out and jammed the blade into the judge's forearm from underneath. The tight grip on her shoulder loosened with a snarl of rage. The silver bull's head fell to the floor in a clatter as Fenton grabbed a hold of the knife.

"Take her!"

The ghoul stood still, shuddering for a moment. The green glow disappeared, showing the faded eyes of a corpse. Its jaw worked slowly as it looked at Gwen.

"Guh…go…" The voice was like rotten leather grinding on rocks.

"What?" Fenton shouted, confusion filling his voice as blood dripped down his arm and off his fingers to puddle on the floor.

Gwen slipped past, leaving the ghoul and the judge behind, and ran for the other end of the courthouse, shouting for her brother.

* * *

Someone was shouting his name. Grimluk went running when he realized whose voice it was. Heavy boots thudded across the ground in front of the courthouse. A trail of demonic corpses lay scattered behind him but now panic finally touched his heart. She shouldn't have been here. He turned the corner and she slammed into him. The mylings began to return slowly. The mylings cried out, anger and sadness wrenching their ghostly voices in a warbling tremor that filled the air. The red eyes of the mischievous spirits flickered around them.

Gwen clung to his shirt. "It's Mr. Duncan… he's a ghoul but he told me to go."

"What are you talking about? Why…how… what are you doing here?" He looked up and saw Jed Duncan standing in the doorway of Fenton's house while the judge shouted at him. Leigh appeared behind Gwen, looking at her father and the dead deputy.

"I need…vengeance," she said in a shivering whisper, her form huge and disgusting.

The other mylings echoed the word *vengeance*. The spirits of those sixteen children all flickered, turning horrible and monstrous. Leigh repeated herself, taking a step forward, the others once again echoing her in voice and action. Jerky, arrhythmic steps pushed them towards the ghoul and the judge. Bakhor and the Doom Riders joined Grimluk and Gwen, the whole group staring at the mylings, transfixed at the sight. The little spirits disappeared again, a chilly breeze signaling their presumed retreat.

Fenton watched in surprise as the ghoul stood still and the mylings inched closer. He looked down at the silver bull's head. "Master?"

It remained silent as Leigh stopped just behind Jed.

"Vengeance has come, Fenton," the ghoul said in its torn-leather voice.

Grimluk waded forward, moving through the crowd of spirits. He took in the sight of each of the mylings as he passed them. They'd been child-like moments before and the knowledge had grabbed hold of him, deep in his guts, and twisted. So many children. He stepped up beside Leigh.

"How many?" he asked, breaking the death drenched silence.

Parker Fenton's eyes were wide and full of fear, his breathing sharp and quick. He took a step back, batting the bull's head with his shoe.

"He asked…how many…" Jed said, some of the flesh in his throat tearing as he spoke.

Grimluk pushed past Jed. "How fucking many, Fenton?" One huge hand shot out and took the judge by the throat. "How many kids did you feed to that thing?" In all his time recovering, it hadn't occurred to him what this man had been doing, at least not fully. That comprehension sank in his guts like an anvil.

Fenton tried to speak, barely choking out the words. “Not enough.”

Grimluk roared and hurled the man backwards, sending him sprawling into the pile of debris. Ragged breaths came in and out as the fires of Grimluk’s fury burned through him. Some part of him had understood though. He’d seen Leigh Fenton. Spoken to what was left of the child’s spirit. Seeing all of Fenton’s victims in one place though, ghouls and mylings alike, pushed him near to breaking. Tears streamed down his cheeks.

“Give me one reason I shouldn’t end you right now. One reason I shouldn’t call every spirit outside this house in here with us.” The request was half-sincere. The part of him that had finally seen what Parker Fenton had done warred with the part of him that refused to kill another mortal.

The ground shook. Softly at first but it quickly grew more insistent, more intense. “Because, Grimluk, his life belongs to me.”

The blood from Fenton’s knife wound swirled into the air from the floorboards. More poured out of the wound itself, hurling the knife out of the man’s arm and away, drawing more and more out, drawing shouts of pain from the judge. His skin paled as the blood flowed out and he sank to the floor unmoving, drained of his strength.

“Why?” Fenton cried out as the blood flowed out of him. “I gave you what you wanted! I gave you children!”

“You gave me what *you* wanted, Parker Fenton. Did I ever tell you I wanted children? All I told you was to feed me." A huge sphere of blood spun in the space between Grimluk and Parker Fenton, crimson and wet and filled with a dim light. "Did you think you really had any power here? Did you think you were in control? At the first whiff of power, you fed me your only child. Gleefully."

The blood twisted in on itself, shifting and pulsing. The light grew stronger, suddenly glaring and hot. The blood ball sucked into itself in a sudden burst and everything went silent. Moments later, the top of the house exploded away, a wave of mystical energy slamming into Grimluk, throwing him into Jed Duncan.

"And you did it with a lie. That you knew how to bring back her mother." The demon gave a mirthful laugh. "The mother you murdered. Oh, Parker Fenton, you were such a good little toy. The time for games has ended though."

A towering form stepped forward, knocking away any remnants of the house that touched it. Blood pulsed along its huge body, at once solid and viscous, pumping with eldritch life. Huge, cloven feet held up powerful legs that supported an immensely thick body. Muscle and sinew slithered underneath the bloody body as it flexed its three-fingered hand, sharp nails adorning the ends of each digit. Two pairs of long and twisted horns pushed out from the grotesque head of a bull, the lower of which wrapped in and then out in sharp points under the thing's jaw, while the upper horns curled back and then forward. Hateful, yellow eyes gazed at everything in front of it.

"I am Cholem. Despair and perish."

Grimluk regained his feet, staring up at the demon. The thing made him look like a halfling in comparison. He scrambled away, pushing everyone away from it, to take wide positions and wait.

"Foolish orcs! You continue to defy my will, Grimluk. Death comes for you. I will feast on your souls!"

The demon stepped forward, kicking through the shattered doorframe and hurled away the mylings with a wave of its hand. The specters disappeared with shrieks and wails. It focused on Grimluk and let out a long, grinding laugh.

The hunter did what his instincts knew best. His gun whipped out and barked shots as he fanned the hammer, true and steady. Six bullets ripped into Cholem's body, punching into the crimson form with wet splashes that splattered blood everywhere. Ripples rolled down its torso and legs with grunts of what Grimluk hoped was pain.

"That was not very nice, dear Grimluk."

A hatchet and two big knives slammed into the thing's body. The weapons stuck into the blood-flesh, burning the blood that touched them. Grimluk went to work reloading his revolver as fast as he could while Cholem swatted aside the bladed weapons, mere inconveniences at most. The charred blood immediately went smooth and red again.

"Shit, fall back," Grimluk yelled.

Before Grimluk could fire his gun again, bloody tendrils whipped out from the demon's hand and slammed into him, sending him rolling into the dirt. Bakhor scooped Gwen up and took off towards the other side of the courthouse. Eagle and Beast let out shrill whistles for their horses who returned to their riders dutifully. The Doom Riders circled around and charged at the demon while Grimluk got to his feet again. Eagle reached the demon first and leaped off his horse.

Cholem tried to grab Eagle with one hand but the hunter batted it away and slammed his fist into the demon's jaw. Blood turned black and sizzled. Eagle grabbed one of the thing's horns with his other hand and prepared for a second strike, feet planted on demon's chest. More tendrils pushed out of Cholem's body, hurling Eagle away. It snatched the hunter out of the air, holding him out for all to see. The loud crunch of bone followed and Eagle's body fell away, tossed aside without a second thought. Beast screamed and rushed to his fallen partner. Bakhor sent two of the wargs to help Beast drag Eagle away. Powerful jaws took the man by his arms and pulled. Cholem watched, a satisfied smile across its face.

"Hey! You want *me*," Grimluk yelled.

"Do I? I gave you every opportunity."

"Well I reckon we got business to settle then, you and me."

The demon snorted, dropping to all fours, kicking up grass and dirt clods as it stamped around, preparing to charge Grimluk. Instead of a thunderous charge, it just stamped forward, shooting several tendrils of blood-flesh out at the hunter. Grimluk's gun fired, splitting each tendril down the center. Two more shots barked, slamming into Cholem's eyes. The bloody bull roared but its hate-filled, yellow eyes reformed moments later. Grimluk stared into those eyes, his own charcoal eyes holding hard. The demon's eyes flashed.

"Fool, mortal. To gaze into my eyes again so willingly."

"What can I say, I like to take the measure of the beasts I'm about to kill." Fresh brass slid into emptied chambers and the cylinder locked back into place, ready to fire again.

"What? How? You are mortal. Your mind should be lost!"

"I came prepared this time, you gods-damned sack of troll shit." Grimluk fired again, hitting the demon square between those yellow, madness inducing eyes. The demon roared with malignant fury and charged. Grimluk spun away and took off towards the courthouse front. Cholem followed, clipping the corner of the building, leaving a gaping hole.

Grimluk turned and fired again, catching the demon in the shoulder but it kept barreling forward, undeterred. He leaped to the side, attempting to roll away but a slick tendril caught his foot and whipped him up into the courthouse and through a second-story window where he crashed through an army of wooden chairs, sliding across the floor and into the judge's bench. Cholem roared as it climbed inside after him. The hunter roared back and started flinging chairs at the demon's face, catching it off guard for a moment. He chased after the last chair, jumping and firing two more shots into the beast's skull, rocking the demon's head back. Grimluk slid out his knife as he flew over Cholem's head, twisting in mid-air and jamming it into the demon's back. His weight pulled the knife down with him, slicing through the blood-flesh and creating a long, dark gash that sizzled and oozed black ichor. A tendril of blood lashed out from the wound as he landed, ripping open Grimluk's chest.

* * *

As hunter and demon began their fight, Jed Duncan's corpse stirred, a repeating whisper on his lips. "Vengeance." Rotten hands dug into the earth and pulled. Broken, useless legs dangled behind as it crawled forward, toward the ruined house of Parker Fenton. Leigh Fenton flickered behind it, ectoplasm splashing across the grass noiselessly in thick puddles. The same word echoed from her dead lips and she descended into the ghoul's body. Jed's oath for revenge merged with the dimming spirit's hunger for vengeance.

New power surged into the ghoul's arms, propelling it forward and into the rubble. Fenton lay underneath part of the roof, protected in part by a fortuitous collapse next to his former dining table. Ghoul, or myling, or spirit of vengeance made flesh, scraped towards the man. Labored breath shook from the judge's pale body, chest rising and falling unsteadily. The ghoul reached out, grabbing Fenton's shirt and pulled with its other hand, climbing up onto the prone body of Parker Fenton.

Weak eyes fluttered open, rolling around groggily before locking on to the ruined visage hovering above him. He tried to whisper, tried to move and protest but the ghoul held him down. Fenton lifted a hand, pushing against the ghoul's shoulder, shaking the whole time.

"Hello, father," the ghoul said in the voice of Leigh and Duncan. "I'm so hungry. I need to feed. I need vengeance." It leaned in close to Fenton's ear. "I need to see my son again. So hungry."

Parker Fenton screamed in a hoarse whisper of pure agony as his ear tore away, caught in the teeth of his murdered deputy…of his daughter. His eyes rolled back in terror as the rotten corpse of Jed Duncan, filled with the last shred of his daughter's soul, devoured him piece by bloody piece, ripping away chunks of flesh in savage, gluttonous bites.

* * *

Grimluk backed away, ignoring the blood flowing from his chest. Cholem let out a scream of pain, ripping away at the courthouse wall. It turned around, glaring at Grimluk and charged again. The hunter charged as well, firing his last two shots at the demon's face before sliding underneath and slashing away with his knife. A huge hoof came down for his head but he rolled away, instead taking a glancing but heavy blow to his left shoulder. A cry of pain erupted as the joint dislocated.

Bakhor pulled him to his feet, the third of her wargs growling at the demon more in terror than a desire to attack. Gwen sat on Fang's back, delicate little fingers white-knuckling the warg's fur.

Grimluk flipped open the cylinder with one hand and grunted, holding his left arm tight against his stomach. "Help me reload," he said, dumping out the spent shells. "Make it fast."

Gwen and Bakhor both reached over and plucked at the brass shells from the loops on his belt. Bakhor managed to get three of the shells into empty chambers before Grimluk darted off as the demon circled back and charged at them. Bakhor hopped away as well while Fang surged forward after Grimluk. Gwen gripped the three shells she'd grabbed, squeezing her legs around Fang's body as tightly as she could. He fired one shot at Cholem, catching it in the neck. This time, the wound didn't disappear. Thick blood flowed freely, prompting a rumbling growl.

"I will swallow your souls," Cholem spat, blood running down its chest. The wound slowed its attack, a touch of caution showing in the demon's movements.

Grimluk flipped open the cylinder once more. "Hurry," he urged. Gwen did her best to slide the brass in as fast as she could. A thought sprang to Grimluk's mind as she slipped the last shell into the chamber and he locked the cylinder back into place. Bakhor, riding hir horse once more, came circling around hurling a hatchet at the demon as ze passed. Tendrils lashed out, ripping into the horse's side and tearing through Bakhor's leg as well. Horse and rider tumbled down with the wounded animal trapping its rider underneath. Grimluk dragged the top of his revolver's barrel across his bloody chest. The runes lit up with a pale light, filling the gun with a power that shook its frame for a moment. Bakhor tried to push the horse away, but hir leg was bleeding too badly. Cholem stalked forward.

"You! You gave birth to Grimluk. I will make you regret that act."

The gun barked. Instead of a black wound opening up where it hit the beast's shoulder, the blood-flesh disappeared outright. The hole passed completely through the demon's flesh. Cholem let out a bellowing roar, its arm hanging limply against its side. The demon whimpered as the wound refused to close or even bleed. Cholem fell away from Bakhor at once, trying to shield itself.

"No! Where did you find such pow—?" The gun fired again and this time, the blood-magic infused bullet ripped through Cholem's jaw, obliterating teeth and muscle. Ichor spilled out of its nose and eyes and ears while garbled words dripped from its ruined mouth.

The hunter squeezed the trigger again. The hammer slammed down and sent another bullet out that ripped through Cholem's chest. Grimluk let out a ragged breath. The Forgemothers' warning rang in his mind as the shots took their toll on him. His hand shook as he thumbed the hammer back. He could feel the mystical energies draining him, bringing him down to one knee. Demon and hunter looked at each other, both bleeding and wounded.

He squeezed again just as a tremor hit his hand. The shot went low, striking the demon's thigh, eating away at the blood-flesh and dropping it down to one knee as well. Cholem shook with fury and pain, yellow eyes trying to burn holes in Grimluk in kind. Tendrils slithered out of its body, slowly and with effort. Grimluk wheezed as he breathed and his vision blurred. The revolver slid back into its holster. He'd have to pin this all on one last quick draw, one last burst of energy.

He willed himself back to his feet as bloody tendrils, ends likes spears, launched out at him, a silent roar filling the street. Grimluk slapped leather. His left arm screamed as he willed it to slam down onto the hammer and the gun fired. One of the tendrils drilled into his shoulder while the others went slack and dropped at his feet. Grimluk's blood spilled out, running down his arm. He pulled the tendril out and threw it away.

Cholem's head had all but vanished with Grimluk's last shot. Black and bloody chunks held up the demon's horns but their weight brought them down a moment later, snapping the ruined flesh forward. The massive and terrible body went forward as well, slamming down into the dust with a wet thud. Obsidian gore poured out of the stump where the demon's head had been, soaking into the ground, blackening the soil with a faint sizzle.

Beast wandered over, carrying Eagle in his arms. Gwen climbed off Fang and rushed over, slamming into Grimluk, squeezing him as hard as she could in her little arms. He grunted and winced.

"Easy, little one." He gave her a weak pat on the back and sighed, not sure how he was still sitting up.

Beast laid Eagle's body down next to them

and went to help Bakhor get out from under hir horse. The horse whinnied and snorted in pain as Beast lifted it up. Ze slithered out and hobbled up, limping around to look at the horse's wound. It was bad but not fatal. A pained grunt slipped out of Grimluk's throat as he wobbled to his feet, sliding his revolver home.

"Can one of you put my shoulder back where it belongs?" he asked raggedly, wobbling and nearly falling over.

Beast walked silently over and readied Grimluk's shoulder, looking to him for the okay. Grimluk could see the hurt in the big man's eyes. He nodded after a deep breath and the Rider reset the joint to its proper place. Grimluk let out a sharp hiss but made no other signs of pain.

"Thanks." He rubbed his shoulder absently, starring down at Eagle. He squatted and placed a hand on the hunter's chest. It was still. "I'm sorry, my friend. Beast?"

"Yeah, kid?" The rider was quiet. Quieter than Grimluk had ever heard.

"We're gonna need the horns. Feel free to hack that sack of pus to pieces in the meantime."

Beast snorted and called his horse over. Eagle's came as well, standing near its master, waiting silently. Beast snatched a hatchet from his saddle and turned to release his anger on the demon's corpse, silently hacking away, grunts of effort his only outcry. Grimluk took a step towards the courthouse, wobbling for a moment before steadying himself.

Bakhor looked up as ze applied salve and bandages to hirself and hir horse. "Where you goin'?" ze asked.

"To find my gods-damned hat and my coat. I liked that hat. And it's got my first thirteen demon teeth." He wandered in through the busted double doors, surveying the lobby, Gwen trailing behind him. The courtroom floor was a pile of rubble on the other side where Cholem had smashed it in a rage. He tried several doors, trying to remember which room Jed had gotten his bag out of. One door led to a small storage closet. The next was locked. Grimluk steadied himself and kicked the door in.

The room was filled with large, very plain, wooden cabinets. He tried each one. The first had a few old muzzleloader rifles. Several others were empty. The last one had a crumpled coat in the bottom of it. He plucked the coat up. His hat lay underneath, mushed under the weight of the coat but safe and whole.

"Hold this, little one," he said, handing Gwen the hat. He slipped his coat back on, sighing contentedly at its familiar weight. "I missed this." Gwen held up the hat with a grin. Grimluk took it, pushing the crown back out methodically before setting it on his head. He felt whole again and gave Gwen a smile before leading her out of the little room.

Chapter 19

As Grimluk and Gwen left the little storage room, red eyes flickered into being ahead of them as the spirits returned.

"Help Gwen," the spirits said in unison. "Demon stop."

She nodded. "I figured. Thank you."

"I thought they already helped you by not hurting me?" Grimluk asked.

"Well," her face screwed up. "I asked them what they wanted for that but they didn't know. They decided they liked me."

"Is that how you got here?" Grimluk's brows creased.

"No, that was Fang. Urgroz told me I'd be a warg rider and gave us food."

Grimluk's throat rumbled. He gave her shoulder a little pat. "I'm just happy you're safe. Besides, I can't entirely be mad at you for following. I did the same thing when I was your age."

Gwen giggled, giving him a big smile while she twirled absently.

"Still help Gwen," the spirits said in the quiet. "People down. Abyss down."

"There's still survivors?" Grimluk asked urgently.

"Suuuuur...vive...ors...down."

"Beast! Get in here! There are survivors!" Grimluk rushed over to the jail door and flung it open, pushing away a pile of cracked chairs. Voices cried out at the noise, shouting for help. He dove into the darkness, plucking a lantern off the wall and opening it, saying the spark-spell. Nothing happened. He handed it over to Gwen, who ably lit the wick within. Beast came thumping down the stairs a moment later. They found no key ring, no hook. Stockburn must have kept them. Grimluk doubted he had it in him to tear the bars off the hinges.

"I think you're gonna have to rip the doors off," he informed Beast.

The Rider marched forward, still silent, and proceeded to tear each cell door off its hinges with a savage roar. The remaining survivors huddled away from the terrifying orc. Grimluk's presence further encouraged them to shout for mercy. He sighed.

"We're here to help. The demons are dead. Head on outside."

A halfling and human, farmers from the looks of them, and a lone elf, wandered out, running away once Grimluk turned his back to address the next group. A dwarf couple, shaking and sickly looking, wandered out of their cell, too disturbed and worn out to show much fear any longer. The other cells were noticeably empty. Grimluk looked to the dungeon door, afraid of the carnage he would find within. When he finally opened the door, what he found was even worse than he'd expected.

The room stank of brimstone, almost gagging everyone who smelled it. In the back, the Abyssal womb pulsed with corrupted flesh and sinister energy. Tendrils of flesh arced along the edges where dark energy crackled weakly. The thing was grotesque and sphincter-like, dripping ectoplasm. Growls and shrieks and angry chittering floated out of it.

"Ah, shit." Grimluk's hands went to work, flicking his revolver out and open, brass shells tinkling into his hand. He shoved the shells into his pocket before being replaced them. "Beast, there's a jug of war water up on the hill by the crank-gun. Get it. I'll make sure nothing pokes any heads out."

The Rider disappeared up the stairs and out to the hill, kicking away the bodies of fallen ghouls and death hounds alike. The jug sat next to Grimluk's supply bag where he'd said it was. Beast snatched it up and sped back down to the dungeon where Grimluk took the jug in his free hand and walked cautiously into the room.

Disgusting appendages covered in tiny mouths reached out, slapping the wall, giving the hunter pause. The appendages slipped back into the dark maw of the portal, a long, low growl trailing after it like thunder after lightning. He stepped closer. Talons slipped out, reaching in vain for him, scraping the air. Grimluk popped the cork from the jug and ventured closer, slipping the gun back in its holster.

"Feeeeeeeeeeeeeeeed," a thousand voices rumbled from far inside the portal.

"How 'bout somethin' to drink," he said and splashed the war water into the portal. Howls shook the dungeon. He swung the jar from left to right, sending more of the water out in sloshing waves that splashed the portal and the wall. The war water ate away at the pulsing flesh to the sigils underneath that supported the womb, burning and smoking as a dozen hands and limbs reached out for their attacker. Each one was terrible and deadly. He slung more water and it sizzled as it hit the demon's blood that had been the foundation of the portal.

The womb twisted, sucking the outstretched appendages back through one at a time and then all at once. The eldritch light flickered in and out before the portal closed for good with a violent flash and dizzying pop. Light from the lantern cast his shadow against the back wall as the remains of the summoning circle burned away, war water dribbling down to the floor. When he was finally sure it was closed for good, he let out a long sigh.

When the trio emerged from the courthouse, Perfection's last survivors were pressed together behind Bakhor, whimpering at the sight of all the silent and staring mylings that filled the yard. Gwen rushed over to the group.

"It's okay, they won't hurt you," she assured the survivors. The mylings all looked as mortal as they could, ghostly visages aside. The faces of toddlers and older children stared on, a vague peace settling over their wavering bodies. Gwen looked around among the spirits. “Where’s Leigh?”

In unison, the mylings pointed toward Parker Fenton’s house. Gwen took Grimluk’s hand, leading him towards the ruined building. Grimluk held her back at the door, recognizing the sight of a ghoul over its victim.

“Stop, little one. Let me.” Blood and bits of viscera lay strewn about the two bodies. Fenton was all but a bloody smear on the floor. The ghoul rolled over as Grimluk approached, gore covering its face in a crimson mask speckled with meat.

“I avenged myself…my son…” the dual-voice of Jed and Leigh said in a wet wheeze. “Stuck in this shell now.”

A frown worked its way across Grimluk’s face. “It’s over then. The demon’s dead as well. I never got to thank you properly for helping us escape, Jed.”

“Least I could do…for both of you… Gwen?”

She peeked inside. “I’m here, Mr. Duncan.”

“So am I…I mean we…” Leigh’s voice seemed to dominate the words. “Don’t come in… made a mess…”

“Leigh,” Grimluk said, kneeling down, “what did you do with the amulet Gwen gave you?”

The corpse wheezed. “Deep down the well… under a rock…a big one.”

Grimluk sighed. “Reckon that’s the safest it can get right now then. The two of you should rest now. Thank you.”

“Soon…I’m…we’re…fading… Thank you… both of you.”

Grimluk nodded, touching the brim of his hat. "Rest easy, friends. May your next lives come to a happier end."

The ghoul shook, convulsing for a moment, and then went slack. Bone cracked and split, its forehead opening and loosing a hazy cloud of mist that dispersed a few feet above the body. Drops of ectoplasm rained down as it faded away. Grimluk turned and joined Gwen, holding his hand out for hers. As they walked back towards the living once more, tears rolled down Gwen's cheeks.

"Is Leigh free now?" Gwen asked.

"Reckon so."

When they turned the corner of the courthouse, all the mylings had vanished as well. Beast sat next to Eagle's body while Bakhor hobbled around the survivors, tending to their wounds if they had any. Ze'd sent the wargs away to hide after Grimluk had yelled about survivors.

A hushed silence settled over the group. The survivors had flinched away from Bakhor at first but when ze showed them the bandages and food, they collapsed, a couple of them snatching at the jerky and bread offered. Grimluk wandered over towards Cholem's corpse before a sudden thought hit his mind. He laughed to himself before he realized what he was doing. Bakhor looked at him in confusion.

"What's so funny?" ze asked.

"No, it's nothing…just," he made his way back towards Beast, a stupid smile spreading across his face for just a moment. "Ghost towns."

Bakhor sighed. "I'm going to punch your

father when we get back."

Beast let out one, loud laugh.

"Yeah, I know. It was bad," Grimluk said, shaking his head and sighing at himself. "Let's get everyone patched up and fed and we can start heading back later. I'll take you folks to Eagle Point."

The elf, a slim, tall woman with pale hair and icy blue eyes, spoke up. "How do you expect us to start over?" The question wasn't angry, wasn't even accusatory.

"Reckon a couple of gluts for each of you ought to take care of that."

His response caught her off guard. The mention of the coinage piqued the others' attention as well. "Why would you offer so much?"

"Because it's just money," he said, idly stepping closer to the huddled survivors. "And you need it more than I do." Grimluk made his way back towards Beast. "You injured?"

Beast shook his head. There were a few scrapes and cuts peppering his arms and bare stomach but nothing serious. Even under the tattoos etched on his face, the hurt he felt over Eagle was plain.

"Twenty years, kid," Beast muttered. "We rode together for twenty years but we were brothers even longer. Grew up together, fought together, trained together. My brother's gone."

Grimluk looked at the empty buildings, the afternoon sun shining around the clouds overhead, casting huge shadows and long beams of light. "Gone but never forgotten." He held out his hand to the Rider. "Come on, let's get him wrapped up." Beast took Grimluk's hand and the hunter pulled the Rider to his feet before leading him into the abandoned hotel to find sheets for Eagle's body.

An hour or so later, the survivors and hunters set out for Eagle Point, the wagon Grimluk rode in on packed down with the coffin-gun, Cholem's horns, and several other passengers. Gwen sat up front with Grimluk. The crimson horns were lashed to one side of the wagon, while the coffin was strapped down against the same wall on one of its sides to make room for the sickly-looking dwarf couple and the halfling farmer. The human and elf rode together on Eagle's horse. Beast rode with Eagle's body over his saddle, wrapped in mismatched linen sheets.

Bakhor hobbled along next to hir own horse, who limped from the gash in its side, now covered in a long row of salved bandages. All were silent with exhaustion and a lack of anything meaningful to say. Perfection's survivors sat in quiet disbelief at what had happened. Nightmares would no doubt haunt them for some time, possibly to the grave.

The wargs traveled far behind, sticking to trees and tall grass. When night fell and the group made camp, the four beasts used the darkness to slip past and back to Hunter's Hollow. Gwen shooed the spirits away after they startled the survivors, putting on a bit of a show in hopes of making them feel safer.

A few leagues out from Eagle Point, the group split up. The elf woman and the farmer slid off

Eagle's horse and Beast took the reins, leading the steed and making for the Hollow with Bakhor. The farmer slid onto the back of the wagon, letting his feet dangle off as they made their way toward the town. The elf woman walked alongside the wagon. Gwen watched her for a moment before the woman met her eyes.

"Hi," Gwen said with a warm smile.

"Hello, child." She returned the smile briefly, politely.

"If you wanna talk about what happened, I'll listen."

The woman's eyes narrowed for a moment, slight confusion showing in them. "I mean no offense, child, but I doubt you could understand."

"My father was killed by a dragon and my brother killed our mother for a demon," Gwen replied flatly.

The woman blinked rapidly in bewilderment, turning away to look at her feet. She finally looked up ahead and apologized. "Are you going to become a demon hunter then?"

"Yeah. They're bad. But I got a new family now. You could get a new family, too."

The elf gave a half grunt and went silent again.

When the wagon finally pulled into Eagle Point, Grimluk helped the dwarves and the halfling down out of the wagon and then did as he promised. Two gold gluts, stamped and official if they decided to leave New Gilead, slid into each of their hands. The old dwarf man fussed, saying that the two coins would be enough for them but Grimluk gave his wife two anyways and walked them to the local hotel, the Eagle's Eyrie.

Once settled, he wandered over to the peacekeepers' offices and found the sheriff. She was a small woman but still taller than a dwarf, with straw-colored hair, and sharp, green eyes. Grimluk's messenger had sent word on to the capital before letting the sheriff know that Grimluk should be arriving and what had happened. The sheriff, naturally, wanted proof of the demon. So Grimluk led the woman out to the wagon and showed her the massive curved horns strapped to the side of it. The sight of them provoked a whistle as she cautiously reached out and touched them with two fingers. The blood was still wet somehow, but her finger came away clean. A shudder ran through her and she wiped her whole hand against her pants, plainly eager to be rid of the feeling.

"Reckon the governor will send some Rangers down to check it out," Grimluk offered. "I'll leave the big horns with you."

The sheriff looked at him dubiously. "It's totally dead?"

"Totally dead. Makes ya feel any safer, I'll put it in a demon trap."

The sheriff was reasonably familiar with the hunters. They passed in and out of the town on business and had helped it out on occasion as well. She nodded at the mention of the trap. "Better safe than sorry."

Grimluk unstrapped the horns and carried them off to the sheriff's jail. One demon's trap later and the door locked tight on the horns. "If you need me for anything, I'll come back in a week or so. Figure the Rangers might want to have a chat. Whole towns don't usually disappear this far from the Borderlands and the Wastes."

"Suits me," the sheriff replied, extending her hand to the hunter.

"Oh," he said as he took her hand, "might be some folks that come in from the Wastelands at some point. Probably led by a half-orc named Tril-gor. If they come in, put them on my tab."

"Understood." She nodded to him as they parted.

The wagon rocked as Grimluk climbed back in. He clucked his tongue and turned the horse around, circling back the way they'd come. He looked down at Gwen, who beamed at him with a smile, her hat hanging from her neck.

"Let's go home, little one."

The next few days passed slowly as Mint made preparations for Eagle's body and his funeral pyre. Every person and warg living in Hunter's Hollow attended the procession, forming a long tunnel leading out into the field passed the gates, guns or blades held high. Gwen stood across from Urgroz, who held up his favorite kitchen knife while she held up her folding knife.

Grimluk, Beast, Kort, and Bakhor carried the fallen hunter out on a wooden palette, each one holding a corner and moving in somber steps. Straight on from the gates, in the middle of the field, was a group of tables covered with a massive feast. The orcs carried their fallen comrade beyond the last pair of raised guns and turned left.

The pyre sat on a fresh mound of dirt a foot high. The denizens of the Hollow folded out pair by pair after the palette passed and followed behind, stopping a ways out from the mound. The quartet laid Eagle's palette on top of the pyre and stepped away. Grimluk and Beast were given torches by Mint, who lit them with his own spark spell, snapping his fingers and a simple uttering of the word, "Flame."

Bakhor stepped in front of the crowd, hir clothes fresh and clean like everyone else's, boots polished bright, metal fist absent. "I'm not an elegant speaker," ze began, "but Eagle was not an elegant man."

Beast smiled as a few chuckles filtered through the crowd.

"Eagle died in our efforts to fight Parker Fenton and his demon master, a death that will only truly be remembered by those here now. He died a hero. And though he bore no blood relation to any of us, I think I can safely say that he was family all the same." Bakhor sighed. "May he find such love in his next life. And may it be filled with as much purpose as he made for this one."

Beast and Grimluk turned to face each other.

Grimluk frowned. "Before we do this, I'd like to take one of his bracers in remembrance, if that's all right."

"Sure, kid."

The torch flame shook as Grimluk held it out for Beast while he climbed the pyre mound.

Eagle's body had been stripped and wrapped in a shroud before being redressed. His arms rested at his side, spiked bracers polished once more, the matching pauldrons likewise gleaming black in the noonday sun. Grimluk gently turned Eagle's right wrist over and unbuckled the straps holding the bracer in place, and then slipped it away. Cool leather brushed his own wrist as he strapped it on, deft fingers catching the buckles with his free hand.

Beast handed his torch back and the two moved to stand at the head and foot of the pyre. The lone Rider nodded solemnly to Grimluk, taking a deep breath as the pair plunged torches into the pyre, spreading the flames into the kindling. Together, they stepped to their right, moving to their respective sides of the pyre and repeated the act. The pyre lit up as the flames caught and began to burn away at the rest of the kindling and cloth of the shroud. Grimluk and Beast stepped away, dropping the torches into a waiting bucket and joined the crowd to see the fallen hunter off.

The fire raged, licking the sky, heat spilling away in great waves. After a time, Beast turned and made his way back towards the tables. One by one, the crowd followed, all taking seats. All the wargs, save for Fang, returned quietly to their den in the back of the Hollow, led by their matriarch. Once everyone was comfortable, Urgroz stood and waited for their attention.

"We'd hoped to do this under better circumstances but life moves like the wind. We lost one member of our family but we also gained a member. Most of you have met Gwen Quinn by now.

Grimluk adopted her into our family as a sister. Bakhor and I wanted to make that notion public, to share the honor with all of you."

He held up a tankard of ale in one thick hand, the metal dully glinting in the sun. Bakhor joined him with hir own. "First," he said, "we salute you, Eagle of the Doom Riders. As my ever lovely partner said, may you find love and purpose in your next life. Hail!"

"Hail!" the crowd echoed.

"Second," he continued, "to my new daughter, Gwen, wounded and changed so early in her life. We embrace you as our own. May your life be filled with long days and pleasant nights. Cheers to you, kiddo." He gave her a wink. "Hail!" The crowd echoed the sentiment once more. Bakhor and Urgroz downed their tankards, prompting everyone else to follow suit as well, while Gwen giggled and smiled so hard Urgroz asked if her face might pop. Plates filled with food as everyone began their celebration of the honored dead and new family. Beast smiled as somewhere around the table, he heard someone begin a story about the first time they ever met the Doom Riders.

Gwen, finally able to honor her promise to the spirits, gathered up a plate of Urgroz's massive cookies and walked them over next to a tree. She sat the plate down in the grass and called them.

"These are cookies," she said with a nod. "I'll bring you more later if you want. Try to behave while we have our party."

The spirits agreed and inspected the cookies with curious prods, poking them with faded claws.

Finally, one of the spirits snatched half a cookie up and gobbled it down, forming a dripping mouth to do so. "Good!" it proclaimed, sending the others into a frenzy for cookies that ultimately ended with crumbs all over the grass.

Gwen rejoined Grimluk and the others just in time for Urgroz to set down a pan in front of her that housed a strawberry cake. She squealed with delight and clung to Grimluk with a mighty hug.

"So, little one, you still sure you want to be a hunter?" Grimluk asked when she finally let go.

"I am. Helping Leigh and the others makes me feel better. I don't miss Momma and Daddy so much." A sliver of hurt washed over her face for a moment only to fade away.

Grimluk nodded, throat rumbling in thought. "We'll get you properly set up as an apprentice then. For now, enjoy your cake. Try not to make yourself sick though." He smiled and gave her tiny back a light pat.

"I won't get sick," she replied. She looked at the cake absently for a moment before looking up at him again. "I think I know what I want to call the Spirit."

"I see. And?"

"Mint gave me the idea. He said maybe I should call it something special, to sym…sym…bolz—"

"Symbolize," Grimluk suggested, cutting her a slice of cake.

"Yeah! To symbolize us working together. Daddy's name was Peter and Momma was Cassie. So I was thinking, I could name it Peca," she finished, enunciating it carefully as "pee-kuh."

Grimluk nodded. "And what does the Spirit think?"

Gwen seemed to listen for a moment. "Peca says it's honored and thank you. And that it'll do its best to be worthy of my choice. It feels happy." She smiled and, with the naming of the Spirit finally settled, she tore into her cake with glee.

After the feast, as dusk rolled in and everyone began the return back to their routines, Grimluk sat quietly out in the yard in front of the house with Gwen leaning against him in his lap, watching the stars appear slowly as the sun sank.

"Been a long time since I've taken some time off for myself," he said. "Was thinkin', maybe I could take you fishin'. There's a nice pond a little ways off. Lots of fish last time I was there."

She yawned as she replied, "Okay." Then she blinked and sat up. "What's a fish?"

Grimluk's jaw fell agape at the question. He couldn't help but laugh. "It's a little scaly critter that lives in water. I guess you could think of it like an underwater bird. Kind of. Maybe. If you squint real hard. You catch and eat them."

"Oh," she said, pausing for a moment. "They don't look like rabbits, do they?"

He laughed again, "No, nothing like rabbits."

"Okay, good. Are you gonna go back out helping people again?"

"I will soon, but not yet. Sometimes, you have to take care of yourself before you can help others. And there's always someone to help."

She nodded and reclined again. The two sat

quietly, watching the velvety darkness of the night sky grow deeper, fading out in deep blues and purples before settling into blackness. The stars twinkled in the sky. Grimluk sighed deeply and closed his eyes. A dim sense of peace settled in his mind for the first time in a good long while.

With everything settled, they took a trip to the pond and then spent the next few days getting Gwen enrolled as an official apprentice demon hunter. Kort and Archel inducted her and Vatris wrote her name in his big book of records. The Forgemothers gifted her with a new knife, stamped with the Elder Sign, and a leather sheath to go with it.

Once Gwen was official and at her lessons, Grimluk waited a week before beginning preparations to set out into the world once more. Mint had cleansed and recharged his guild talisman. Anything left from the supplies from the battle in Perfection, mostly a few extra bottles of salve and bandages, went into the elk-skin bag. He'd also gotten a small skin of war water. Grimluk looked at the talisman before putting it away, thinking about Selbie's amulet, sitting under a rock. He wondered if he should find some way to retrieve it, though he doubted anyone would find it at the bottom of the well for a long time. Especially now. He slipped into his coat, buckled his gun belt, adjusted Eagle's bracer, and headed for the gates, hat in hand.

Gwen was waiting for him.

"Peca said you were gonna leave without saying bye," she said.

"Reckon so, little one. But I'll be back. Someone's gotta take you on your field lessons after all." He pulled one of the gates open and a glint caught his eye. Selbie's amulet hung there, swinging gently on a nail.

"Peca told me it'd probably be a good idea to have one of my new friends bring this back, too. So I did it this morning while you were still asleep."

He looked at the amulet in surprise. And colossal relief. One less thing to worry about. He pulled it off and held it out to her. "Thank you, little one. Take it to Mint. Vatris would just want to study it first and it'll need to be disenchanted. Or just locked away. And tell Peca thank you as well."

Gwen held up a leather-corded bracelet lined with purplish stones, trading it for the amulet. "I made this for you. Mint helped me. I found the rocks when we went fishing. He says they're lucky but I just thought they were pretty."

Grimluk took the bracelet and slipped it onto his left wrist, smiling at her. He gave her shoulder a soft squeeze with one meaty, green hand, and then passed through the gates of Hunter's Hollow. Grimluk lifted his hat to his head and let his feet carry him to the road. Once he dealt with the Rangers and left Eagle Point, he'd go wherever the road took him. Maybe southeast. As he walked on, a breeze flowed over him. Autumn had begun to roll in, pushing away the summer's heat. It was time for change. It was time to hunt again.

INDIEGOGO BACKERS

Stephanie Lehenbauer
Samantha Tohtz
Rachel Sharp
Steven Ott
Evan Bassett
James Jakins
Rachel Nowlin
Kibret Ledoux
Lisa Richardson
Erica Lindquist
Eileen McNulty
Goran Joksimovic
Alex Haigh
Melissa Shumake
Tim Feely

Thank you all!

RECOMMENDED AUTHORS

You've read my book now (and thank you for that!), and I'd imagine you'll be hungry for something new so here are a few recommendations for folks I know and enjoyed.

James Jakins, Author of *Jack Bloodfist: Fixer*
K.S. Villoso, Author of the *Agartes Epilogues*
M.Todd Gallowglas, Storyteller & Author of the *Dead Weight*, *Tears of Rage*, & *Halloween Jack* series.
Amalia Dillin, Author of the *Orcs Saga*
Edward M. Erdelac, Author of the *Merkabah Rider* series.
Krista D. Ball, Author of the *Tales of Tranquility* and *Spirit Caller* series.

Happy reading, everyone!

ABOUT THE AUTHOR

Ashe grew up watching and reading about adventures and having horrible nightmares. He spent most of his young life wanting to know more about what scared him but also doing so from between fingers and from under the covers. Eventually, the realm of nightmares became home. Heroes and villains and the struggle of Good against Evil, combined with Horror, helped mold him into the weirdo lover–of–the–strange that he is. Ashe lives in Tulsa, OK with his partner.

Where you can find Ashe on the web

ashearmstrong.com
ashearmstrong.tumblr.com
twitter.com/ashearmstrong
facebook.com/ashearmstrong
goodreads.com/ashearmstrong

www.ingramcontent.com/pod-product-compliance
Lightning Source LLC
La Vergne TN
LVHW041111080826
845145LV00007B/1774

* 9 7 8 0 9 9 6 3 4 0 9 3 9 *